All Gomorrahs Are The Same

Thenjiwe Mswane

Legend Press Ltd, 51 Gower Street, London, WC1E 6HJ
info@legendtimesgroup.co.uk | www.legendpress.co.uk

Contents © Thenjiwe Mswane 2021
The right of the above author to be identified as the author of this work has been asserted in accordance with the Copyright, Designs and Patents Act 1988. British Library Cataloguing in Publication Data available.

First published in South Africa in 2021 by Blackbird Books
www.blackbirdbooks.africa

Print ISBN 9781915643087
Ebook ISBN 9781915643094
Set in Times.
Cover design by Gudrun Jobst | www.yotedesign.com

All characters, other than those clearly in the public domain, and place names, other than those well-established such as towns and cities, are fictitious and any resemblance is purely coincidental.

All rights reserved. No part of this publication may be reproduced, stored in or introduced into a retrieval system, or transmitted, in any form, or by any means electronic, mechanical, photocopying, recording or otherwise, without the prior permission of the publisher. Any person who commits any unauthorised act in relation to this publication may be liable to criminal prosecution and civil claims for damages.

Thenjiwe Mswane is the author of the Sunday Times Literary Awards shortlisted novel *All Gomorrahs Are the Same*. She has also written for numerous publications including HOLAafrica! the GALA Queer Archives Queer Realness. Although writing is a large aspect of her career, Thenjiwe is also a full-time public servant in Higher Education and a PhD candidate.

To
Abafowethu : Ntobeko Mpumelelo Mswane, Nkululeko Cyril Zondi and Nhlakanipho Mswane.

I am missing without you. I hope this work makes you eternal.

To
Dingeni Mswane, and Fana Mswane

You did well by us.

To
Asanda Mswane. I am deeply sorry.

We're the last ones left, no pressure.

*I feel most coloured when I am thrown
against a sharp white background*
– Zora Neale Hurston.

PART ONE

1

Thulani

We did not bury my daughter.

My mother does not remember how old she was when she buried the first of her children.

I have not yet buried a child. I have waited on that door every day from the day she left.
    She left a long time ago. Perhaps it was the day we forced her to grow too fast. The day of her first day at crèche. She was too young to start crèche.
    Then she was too young to go to Class 1, but she did. Her mother applauded. She received it. Worked harder. My daughter was learning how to leave from her first day in school.
    By the time her body left – disappeared – from all our lives, she had been missing to herself for a long time. I watched my daughter leave.

2
Makhosazane

My siblings and I spend every holiday eMpofana, Mooi River, KwaZulu-Natal. Right in the middle of the Midlands Meander.

There is me, Makhosazane, and my two brothers, Mpumelelo and Nkosana. My brothers are older than me and have started to show signs of growing less and less interested in this place.

Mpumelelo only started packing an hour before we were due to leave. uBaba became his angry self, which is speaking words under his breath. I always imagine the swear words, because why doesn't he say them out loud, properly? Mpumelelo has taken to responding under his breath too. It is like watching a whisper fight.

Mpumelelo was looking for the wardrobe key under the bed. The space between the wardrobe and the bed was too small for him to bend down properly and look. He tried anyway, turning half his body against the wardrobe, his arm not getting far enough under the bed. I knelt at the bottom of the bed; moving the shoes, lost socks and balls of 'bhoning socks' around.

Mpumelelo was still whisper fighting with uBaba.

'Angazi nje ngiyokwenzani mina laphayana,' he whispered.

I looked back and saw uBaba still impatiently standing by the door, peeking over at Mpumelelo, who was barely trying.

'Found it!' I screamed, jumping up and giving Mpumelelo the key.

He opened the wardrobe and started throwing clothes into his school bag. Nowhere close to enough clothes; but I didn't care. All I wanted was for him to be packed, and ready. I knew both him and Nkosana wanted to stay behind to play iTV game; which I thought ridiculous because they play that thing too much. It was not helpful that uGogo didn't allow them to play it at her house. Complained it broke her TV.

There are more than twenty of us here during school holidays. There is no way of regulating who plays Sonic the Hedgehog, or when. Still, they tried to play, stealing the TV game from where they hid it, under the heaps of unfolded clothes that were still in their bags a few days after we arrived. Ikamera labafana is always dirtier; uGogo doesn't go in there as often to shout at them about packing and unpacking. I have to share the bed with her, so I can't escape unpacking. I unpacked on my first day. The only thing hidden under my heaps of neatly folded shirts and shorts is shoes. My favourite shoes, which I will wear on the day I leave so no one can borrow them. I don't want everyone to know I have them. That way there is never any fight.

Gogo was away that day, it was the day of impesheni, and she would be back late. The TV game playing ended in some fight I didn't care for. Which was one of the reasons uGogo hated that thing. They always ended up fighting.

Me, I prefer sitting at the top of the hills and mountains. Looking down on iMpofana. They are endless, the hills and mountains. From up there you can see streams, rivers, stagnant waters, and the footpaths in between the hills and mountains.

There is a not so big road in the middle of the valley. You can see it clearly, sitting at the top of a hill. The road comes down from a hill too; you cannot see the other side of the road because of how steep it is. The road has slight turns and bends before it disappears again at the far end, behind more mountains and hills. Most of amakhumbi and cars stop only on the main road. Estopini.

uMkhulu's house is on an old farm, although we call it kwaGogo. I only knew it was uMkhulu's house because he told us often – 'this was the same farm where my father, and his father before him lived.' Iplazi. Although the fence that once showed it was iplazi had been taken down. So it was less iplazi and more amakhaya. Even though everyone eWembezi says we are going emaplazini when we go there. So maybe it was both, because it had been iplazi.

'Wazimoshela yena umfana kaGraham, kwakungonakele lutho.'

My grandfather would recite the story of how his grandfather had lived there and there was no fence. The son of Graham then built a fence. They had bought the land, Graham said. Which made no sense, because he couldn't buy the land. Land belonged to everyone and was fairly distributed by izinduna.

Yes, some people had started working for the Makhulu Graham, but not everyone wanted to work for Graham after Makhulu Graham died. The young Graham was known to be a cruel young boy, 'unlike his father,' uMkhulu said.

So many people were angry when Graham said he had bought everything, and that it was his farm. No one was forced to work for him, but if you did not, you had to give him a cow every year as intela. Even then people did not understand and many did not give him their cows. Eventually Graham and the other men from Mooi River came to make isimemezelo. They even had a person to tolika, that uhulumeni was going to come and make sure everyone paid intela. Five cows, because many people were behind and still owed uGraham. uMkhulu said the people laughed at Graham's friends and uhulumeni. Then one day, Graham's friends came again. This time they said all their cows had diseases and needed to be killed. This made the community angry so, that very night, they tore down Graham's fence and put it outside his house.

No one went to the meetings at Graham's house after that. There was no longer iplazi without the fence. 'What even are fences?' uMkhulu would laugh.

Graham's friends tried coming to each household to find out who had taken down the fence. Sabakhathaza, uMkhulu would say. Told them every structure was its own household. Giving them more work to do. The tolika tried to argue with them, but he was from kwaNongoma. So they remained firm, izinkolo azifani. Nongoma had its own izinduna, amakhosi and even amasiko, which was true.

In every second 'house', there would be no man – because it was either the kitchen or a bedroom. In those 'houses', the women listened and listened to the tolika. Asked many questions. Asked for more and more clarity, only to say later, 'Well, we hear what you are saying. We do not understand. But it is not ours to understand, anyway. The head of the house is not here, as you can see. You are speaking about our house. And our house is headed by him. Come back another day to tell him.'

Mkhulu said the friends tried coming back again and again. Bringing Graham with them this time. Then they went into the house of inyanga, who cursed Graham.

Graham died, and his wife was left alone. Mkhulu said they sang outside her house every night for a month, claiming they were helping her mourn. She got scared and left. That was the end of it being a farm, iplazi. After Graham died, the village banned fences.

Fences make people think they can own not only things, but lands and people too, the village decided. So there was no clear separation of a 'yard'.

But you can still see the different yards, especially from up here on my hilltop. Our yard looks like many other yards on the old farm. There is a main house, ilawu, which is where abakhwenyana sleep when they are here. Only for the week before Christmas. Each mkhwenyana arrives with a car boot filled with food, and they shower us with money and sweets.

Big meals are made for them. After Christmas, on Boxing Day they leave. The end of Christmas, almost the new year. No more showers of money. Almost school time.

Our yard also has a few rondavels, and a cemetery just near the apple trees. Sacred land. We seldom play there. The only time we enter there is when trying to pick apples. The dark green sour-tasting ones grow there mostly. No one told us not to play there. Just sacred land, we all seemed to know.

There are thirteen graves in the cemetery. Most of my cousins' parents now lay on that ground. I wonder what it feels like to grow up knowing your parents are in the same yard but can't ever come to your rescue. Christmas must be the worst, when someone has stolen your money, which my older boy cousins do. A lot. Those of us who can, run to our fathers, who will shower us with money again. My cousins run to my grandmother, who turns to uMa to give her money. They tried hiding this exchange when we were younger, but the older we grew, we knew things. Saw things. The one time, my other cousin Njabulo teased uEnhle, saying it was still his money because his mother gave uGogo the money, and his mother's money was his money. Mamncane Thandaza, Njabulo's mother, was the first to land a slap across Njabulo's face. She later hugged Njabulo, after he had performed a dramatic cry. Nobody hugged Enhle.

uMalume omncane uMgedeza, one of my uncles, is not buried here. He requested to be buried in the local cemetery in town. The sign from the main road says 'Mooi River' 37 km, Giant's Castle 15 km. uMkhulu was not happy with this. I remember Ma convincing him that this was what uMalume wanted. That it was his wishes, and they needed to be respected. It was still far. uMkhulu insisted, but uMa gathered her mother and sisters to rally behind her and uMkhulu was outnumbered. Although I always thought he was right. It was far on the day of the funeral, and it was far after the funeral, when we had to go fetch him from many places and bring him back home with ihlahla. I don't know why no one ever listened to uMkhulu, even my cousins sometimes didn't listen to him; or they talked back, which I would never do. He was old, and wise, and had many children. Of the thirteen graves in our yard, six of the graves were his children and he still had more. The adults always insisted there were other children. Five more.

It is just after lunch, and from the top of my favourite hill I can see my cousins playing in our yard. Which I also don't care for. Boys play with boys, and girls with girls, except when playing umasgcezu, which is a very stupid game of playing grown up. Older children find weird things fun. Like getting up very early to get clean, and then try stay clean the whole day, even during holidays. Blasphemy! My cousins tease me often for not liking amanzi. 'Schools are closed, not the water, Makhosi,' one of them will say. Which is also a stupid thing to say. I drink water every day, do I not? I know water is not closed. And anyway, you close taps, not water.

If they were trying to sound smart, they seldom succeed. So, I prefer not playing with them. They play and play until uMkhulu disturbs them with whatever next chore they have to endure. He prides himself in his annual ukuvuna, although I have never seen him on the fields with us.

The chores start very early. uGogo wakes up the girls a little after the boys have finished milking the cows and they make umdoko. I fight about not having been woken up earlier to milk the cows too. I prefer milking over making umdoko. But I don't mind eating umdoko. My tantrum calms down as soon as the food is dished out. We eat and then head to the fields, emasimini. I didn't mind the fields when I was younger, but now I like herding cows.

Depending on the day and my mood, and if I have put up a great enough performance about being forced to do things I don't want to do, I disappear. Which is more my cousins letting me disappear for their day's sake. I disappear to the top of this hill and watch everyone busy in the fields. It's not that I'm lazy. I like the view; it is quieter up here as well. From my far distance I make up what I think people down below are saying. uGogo watches me less the older I grow. Not that she has a choice. She knows I always find a way to disappear. Sometimes it is a headache, other times a stomach ache. Other days I hold my chest and use asthma as my escape. Or annoy everyone with my complaining.

The afternoon is the best time to sit on my hill. A lorry from Baas van Vuuren arrives every day before the sun sets. People jump out from the back. Baas van Vuuren, I learn from watching him, is not a very patient man. Some days he drives off while people are still trying to jump out. There are women with ibovu all over their faces. I asked uGogo about this once. She told me it protected them from the sun and stopped them from getting too dark from working the fields all day.

'What do they do on the farms?' I asked her.

'The same thing you do emasimini. It's just when unamasimi amaningi like Baas van Vuuren it is bigger and needs many people to work there,' Gogo said.

Baas van Vuuren has two little children, who never work emasimini like us. We sometimes see them driving down the main road towards Mooi River. I have never seen Baas van Vuuren with his mother, or grandmother, or grandfather. I wonder what he does with so much food.

'When those people are working on Baas van Vuuren's big nsimi, who is working on their nsimi here, Gogo?' I asked.

'Children do well for little farm workers,' Gogo said, laughing. I did not know what was funny, working ensimini wasn't funny. Maybe Gogo was laughing because she knew I hadn't been working that day.

Soon after the lorry leaves, you'd begin to see taxis, many carrying men who are coming from town. They are dressed differently from the people who jump out of Baas van Vuuren's lorry. The khumbis are also loud, but not like Baas van Vuuren's lorry loud. The lorry is big, and the people make a lot of noise when they jump out or scream for Baas van Vuuren to not drive away while they are jumping out. The khumbis are loud from music. And they have very bright lights, which hurt my eyes as they come down the hill. Out of them fall well-dressed men, who stumble home, screaming apologies to the angry driver who tells them not to bang his door. Their apologies are as delayed as their walking; by the time they scream, the taxi has left. They wave it away as if the taxi needs to be waved away by their falling hands. These men, dressed well, stumbling as they walk home, are a sign that it is already becoming dark. uGogo will probably shout at me for also bunking cooking duty.

Overall, though, a productive day. It is time to go home. By the time I get to my grandmother's yard, some of the taxi men are stumbling into their yards. Shouting goodbyes at people who probably left five minutes ago. Shouting at children to come open the locked doors. Sometimes the door isn't even locked, they are just drunk. Month end and '4th night' are always the best days to see drunk men (and sometimes drunk women) stumbling to their houses. There are rumours, which I believe to be true, that women who drink also have many children of whom no one knows the fathers, which is why they are not married. People don't seem to like unmarried women who drink. Except the men, many of them married, who stumble with them in the dark of night when they are all drunk.

No one ever told me whether the men also had lots of children from different women. No one seemed too concerned about that. There were once rumours about uMkhulu wakwaShabalala, that when he died half the church hall was apparently his children. People gossiped about it for a week or two. But you don't speak ill of the dead.

On warm days, you can hear children singing 'ungangiceli, angifune kucelwa bengihlatshwa ngedwa' as they walk down from the forest above the mountains. They have been picking wild berries. I try picking them too, but I always get pricked by thorns so I stopped.

One thing I enjoy is swimming at the dam, which is almost towards the end of the curving road. Except uGogo tells us we aren't allowed. I tried 'stealing' swimming once, even stole the tub of Vaseline to hide that I had been swimming, but I forgot to lotion my legs. I got my most memorable hiding that day.

'You will drown!' my grandmother said as she beat me with the vadoek I'd had the honour of washing earlier. I can swim though, I thought. Although swimming in the pool at school was easier, because you can see underwater. The dam is too brown for me to see when I am underneath. I wasn't going to drown though.

'U-ZE UQEDA NO-VASELINA WA-MI!' my grandmother shouted. I might have missed swimming today, I think, as I go into the kitchen where I hope the food is ready, but at least I had my day on the hill.

It is getting closer to Christmas. We know this because every house is getting painted and there are more people drinking alcohol. Even the teenagers suddenly have access to alcohol. Or did they always? Everyone is happy. Brenda Fassie's 'Nomakanjani' can be heard throughout all the dusty streets of amakhaya ami.

3

Nkosana is my oldest brother. He is older than my other brother, uMpumelelo, who is also my older brother.

They both go to school eWembezi. Their school is not too far from where we live, but far enough for uMa to wake them up early every morning. Their school is close to where Ma works, in another section of Wembezi. I am still too young to walk that far, and I do not have friends who live there to visit.

In the mornings, uMa goes into their room and wakes them up. uBaba comes many minutes later, after uMa, who they often seem to ignore, has tried waking them up; uBaba goes in to repeat what uMa has said. They repeat this pattern every school day. uBaba is harsher with his voice. Ma is softer, yet in a hurry. She is more concerned about time. Every day she says, 'We are late.' For the boys to get to school, for her to get to work, for uBaba to get to his work.

He is less concerned about time though, uBaba. He is often the last one left in the house after they have left. He makes himself a cup of tea. Glen Tea. Leaves the tea bag in the hot water for too long. Puts too much sugar. The smell of the strong tea and the sugar travels through the house. I get out of bed and go to him. He is often watching the TV, with the sound off.

'Ngikuvusile, sisi?' he asks.

'Cha, Baba,' I say.

The question and answer are always the same. I do not

mind that he asks me the same question every day. It's a pattern. The same way it is part of the pattern for him to go into the boys' room to wake them up after uMa has woken them up.

uBaba waits for usisi osizayo to come look after me. We watch the morning news. I do not know how to read well and fast yet.

'Kuthiwani laphayana, Baba?' I ask, pointing at the words moving across the screen as the woman with the straight face and straight clothes moves her mouth. Does she know there are words moving under her on our screens every morning? I wonder. The words stop, an advertisement comes on. It is the early morning and the adverts are of the sun rising and families sitting at tables eating and smiling for milk. Or bread for children's lunch boxes. Or the Melrose cheese adverts. I like Melrose cheese. Sometimes Ma buys it for the boys' lunches. She doesn't laugh as she makes her skaftin, or Baba's skaftin. The boys make their own skaftins now, although Nkosana says he is too old to carry a skaftin. He tried asking our parents for money instead of iskaftin.

'The day ulambile is the day you will know you can't leave food at home to buy food because you are old,' uBaba said.

Nkosana didn't ask again. Nor did he ever make a skaftin. I guess he didn't get hungry. The families on the screens move fast through their day, laughing a lot as they prepare. They must move fast, I think. They don't have enough time to show us everything. The adverts are shorter than the news, or whatever other show is playing when the adverts come off. The adverts change a lot during the day. The faces and families change. The shows change too. After the news, puppets and children's shows with oPopeye come on.

uSisi who takes care of me has arrived and uBaba says his goodbyes. The sound on the TV is on now.

'Ukhule,' he says to me.

I don't understand what he means.

In the evenings, he comes back and asks me how much I

have grown. I don't control growing. I don't even feel or see it as it happens. When I do not know how to answer, he holds his two picking fingers apart, leaving a tiny space through which only an ant could pass through. 'Kangaka', he says. That is how much I have grown that day. I do not see myself. He does. He leaves me the whole day and thinks about me as he goes on with his day. This is why he can tell how much I have grown.

When everyone is away, I spend the day watching the TV, as uSisi cleans the house. I move my feet up onto the sofa to allow her to sweep and mop under them. When she has finished cleaning, uSisi spends time on the phone. Or doing her hair. Or a neighbour's hair. Sometimes, her friends visit.

The TV plays on and on. At 11am, 3pm and 6pm, uSisi and whoever else is there turn off the sound to listen to istory on the radio. Ukhozi FM. uGogo also does this.

'Akeve engakuhluphi yazi uMakhosi,' some of Sisi's friends will say. 'Hawu, mawuvele nje wamubeka phambi kwe TV. Akahluphi qobo,' Sisi responds.

During the day, a lot of the stories are repeated. Bold, Days. And others I don't know. I sit in front of the TV, watching the white faces on my screen, imagining the black voices on the radio. I know the people on the radio are black, and not white like the people on the TV, because they speak isiZulu a lot on Ukhozi FM.

At first, imagining the bodies with different voices makes me laugh and giggle. Then I start to wonder why the voices I hear on the radio I don't see on my screen. The voices and faces on the TV are different from the voices and faces I see at home. The men on the TV wear nice suits, go to work very early. On weekends. TV weekends. Which aren't real-life weekends. They wear shorts and go play sports with their children.

uBaba has a yellow leather jacket he likes to wear. He wears it with his brown polo neck, a black belt, brown pants with a sharp pleat in front and black shoes. Shiny shoes. The boys shine his shoes every evening when he comes back from work. They sit on the veranda with a newspaper on the floor, 'to not get the floor dirty with polish,' Nkosana says. A black brush and a brown brush. The boys and uMa wear black shoes and uBaba wears brown shoes to work.

He shines his shoes again in the morning when he waits with me, or waits to go. I don't know which one it is. He doesn't seem as excited to go to work as the men on TV do.

The stories on the radio start to bore me. They sound the same. The TV also bores me. It doesn't look like real people. So I start creating my own stories for the faces. During our mornings together, I start telling uBaba the stories I made up the day before. I don't see Ma's face in the morning. I also don't see her a lot at night.

Then uBaba tells uMa I must go to school now, socialise with more children my age; and something about saving money on uSisi; and sending me to the crèche where he works. A lot of his friends send their children there.

Does he not like my stories? I wonder. I never tell him my stories again, after I hear him say I must play with children my age. Are the stories I tell him boring to him, so boring that he wants me to play with children my age?

It is cold when I start school. The mornings are the coldest. uBaba still drinks his tea in the mornings, after everyone has left. I am still the last person he wakes up. While he is making the ties for the boys, he stands in my room and summons me to wake up or I will be left alone in the house. By the time he is drinking his tea, I am putting on whatever clothes have been left out for me on the top of the sofa. uBaba sometimes reapplies Vaseline on me. Especially on the sides of my face, my back and tummy. I didn't know why I need lotion on my tummy and back; no one sees me there.

Ma always leaves a hat and gloves with my clothes. Brown, navy or black gloves. The other girls at my crèche also have hats and gloves, but theirs are red and pink, with hearts and flowers. uBaba bought my gloves at the store where he buys the boys' school uniforms. They look like my brothers' uniforms, and the wool hat on my head makes me look a little like a boy. I look like Nkosana and uBaba, people tell me. The girls in my class make fun of me.

I don't like waking up in the mornings, and the other children don't want to tell me the stories they think of in their heads. I don't like going to school. All the other children in my class, and the school, were already there before I started. They like painting and drawing with the crayons in class. My favourite time is sleeping time. Close your eyes, Makhosi, I tell myself, begging for a fun dream to visit me. Colours. I dream a lot in colours. Blue, green, red and black are the colours most of the people in my dreams wear. Familiar faces, doing unfamiliar things. Sometimes I hear the voices. Sometimes I don't. It doesn't matter. I make up the words when I can't hear the voices. They all look a lot like us, like my family. I don't try telling the other children my dreams, or ask them about theirs after a while. I don't know why uBaba wanted me to spend my days with them instead of at home.

I don't like crèche. I want to sleep through all of it. Maybe I do. My teacher quickly tells my father that I am a fast learner and easily bored. uMa thinks I am smart; uBaba thinks the teachers are lazy.

'These teachers do not want to be challenged. They push challenging children through. Children need to stay children for longer,' he says as we are driving home after a meeting at the school.

I am not challenging anyone; I want to tell them. I just like sleeping. I finish everything early in hope to start sleeping early. I prefer sleeping earlier so I can miss the giggles as I'm trying hard to sleep. The other children are able to laugh a lot, then fall asleep soon after. They run around the grounds a lot too, but I don't like falling. uMa has a lot of clothes to wash when she comes back from work, and I don't want to make my clothes dirty. Even though she washes them anyway.

Children are not even supposed to listen to adults when they speak, unless they are speaking to them. I learned this while visiting uMkhulu eMpofana once, when I commented about the cow he was selling.

'It gives a lot of milk,' uMkhulu said to another mkhulu who was coming there to buy.

'Not lately, it doesn't make a lot of milk lately. And it should be making a lot of milk because it has little babies. I think it's sick,' I said.

The other mkhulu did not take the cow and my mkhulu was angry at me. He told me to never, ever comment on adults' conversations unless they asked me.

The teachers tell my parents that I should start Class 1 next year. They want me to be in class with the older children.

'She is already learning to read, and is very creative,' my teacher tells my parents in a meeting they have on my birthday.

'She must have been learning to read and write at home. You both have a very exceptional child here. Harness it,' the teacher says. 'Her imagination is encouraged.' She smiles.

This woman is not the class teacher. We call her the principal. I wonder where she found out all these things from; she doesn't even talk to me. The few times she walks into our class, we all stand up and scream 'GOOD MORNING, PRINCIPAL,' the way we do when other teachers walk in. But with her we shout principal instead of teacher.

'Schools are lazy,' uBaba says on the way home.

I think I agree because this woman had never even tried to speak to me and here she is, not wanting me to be taught for a year. She wants me to leave the school. I will have to do Class 1 in another school. I don't mind leaving crèche and going to school with the boys eWembezi and not here at the crèche in Estcourt where my father works.

'Makhosi, uyafuna ukuya ka Class 1?' Ma asks me in the car after the meeting.

'Yebo,' I say. I don't know what else to say. I don't think I can say no. The one time adults ask me a question, they ask me something I don't know the answer to. I don't know what they do in Class 1; I have never been to Class 1.

I graduate with the older children that December. Nkosana tells me I will not sleep in Class 1. I know now why I should have said no. No one asks me again.

4

Dudu

'Ma, yini amaqentsu ngesingisi?' Makhosazane asks, as she buries her head in something. A novel, a drawing book. Or both. She draws in her library books, cuts them out and sticks the cut-outs in her drawing books like she is just cutting magazines. I don't know the answer, but she never listens, this one, anyway. Which is good when I do not know the answer, like now. Other times, it leaves me with a problem.

Makhosi has a listening problem. She will ask the same question more than once. I don't know why she asks if she is not interested in answers. Or maybe the bigger problem is she cannot solely concentrate on one thing, umtanami. Her school has banned her from taking out any more books, or bringing her bag into the library in case she has crayons or pens to draw in the books with. They sent us an invoice for all the books she has damaged. Her father cackled and said, 'Abelungu bacabanga ukuthi nginemali yokudlala yazi Angithumanga uMakhosazane ukuthi abhale emabhukwini mina. Uyoyikhokha mhla wasebenza.'

I've asked her why she does this, explained she is making me use money I do not have. She just looked at me. Like I spoke a language she did not understand, as if I was asking her for something that couldn't be done. She didn't answer, nor did she stop. I think she wasn't listening again. Except, I know she isn't listening when she is doing too many tasks at once. It is when she stares right back at you, then continues to do the exact opposite of everything you said that it is the most frustrating.

'Ufana nawe you also did whatever you wanted, and listened to no one,' uMaDlamini, my mother, once said when I grew frustrated with Makhosi in her presence.

But Ma said that about Nkosana too, when I complained about how he secluded himself to his corners. Or waited for an empty room.

My mother had all these theories about parts of me.

I didn't do whatever I wanted. No, kude nakho.

I did the things which needed to be done.

Took the only choices available to me.

I listened too. I listened to her when she said in passing that Mkhize's child had gone to learn to be a doctor, and what good was it? Many years at school to be a doctor, or a lawyer, when his family was struggling now.

'Hawu, Ma, mhlampe into ayithandayo,' I tried arguing in his favour.

'Uthando olumosha isikhathi alondli,' Ma said.

I remember how poor people didn't have the privilege of 'loving' things which take too much time, instead of putting food on the table.

And no, unlike Nkosana, there was never a room or a corner for me to be alone in the house. Not with ukutheza, ukusenga, ukusinda, ukupheka, ukulusa, neskole. There were too many of us, and too many joint chores for me to have ever been alone.

Thulani was not helpful to Makhosi's failure to listen either. As he kept reminding me, 'Our daughter should not have gone to school so young. She just wants to cut and paste things. We should have let her spend another year, even two more years, in crèche', he said.

He seemed to have forgotten it was he who said Makhosi should start crèche.

'Children should spend time at home, play at home. This thing of sending children to school too soon like we don't like them. Ingane must be ingane,' he preached now from intaba yakhe yokulunga.

It was he, though, who said Makhosi should suddenly start crèche halfway through the year. We had not budgeted for school fees that year. He said we could swap the budget kaSisi osizayo for the school budget. It wasn't the same. She needed clothes for school that weren't the clothes she used at home; and although there was no uniform in crèche, she needed new clothes. Warm clothes. It was a cold winter that year.

In the service, we didn't know what was going to happen with our jobs. We had been trained in the South African Police before it became the South African Police Services. The government was changing. During the transition and joint government, it seemed easier in other places, perhaps the places which dealt with just the ANC and NP politicking.

It was harder in KwaZulu-Natal. The strong hold of the IFP would not be overlooked. Could not be overlooked. The IFP was the most present here – or at least the most visible in acts and actions. My colleagues in Richmond complained about the violence of the UDM. It was harder Kwa-Zulu.

For months, we did not know if we were keeping our jobs. The payslips stopped coming. We didn't know who the government was. Everything was going to change in 1994, though, they had all said. The negotiations and talks were coming to an end, or something. It would be a democratic election. Whoever would win fairly would rule where they win. We did training after training about how the new policing system may work, how the new constitution would affect how we worked. So much was changing, with very little known about the security of the future. It didn't matter who won anymore. Anyone at all could win.

Everything had gone up, fewer shops were open and a new market was starting. A market of those brave enough to be a part of this new South Africa, which had certainty only for a few. The rest of us were hanging by threads. Watched and listened to the news until the days when there was no news to report except: a New South Africa was upon us. It was here! Freedom! Democracy!

But it felt cold. Everything felt cold. We had voted. Did we not remember? We went out and filled schools, halls and churches. Voting stations. We waited and waited to vote. Waited for the results. And it was here. It had arrived. This was what people fought for.

It was not easy at Thulani's job either. He worked in the local prison; a prison warder. Some of the people still arrested had been arrested fighting, in whichever way they had thought fit, so that we could get this freedom. For these elections to happen. There had been havoc in the prisons about whether political prisoners, or any other prisoners, were voting. There was havoc about the many who were returning from exile, with what looked like hopes of ministerial positions, while others were still in prison.

Thulani had been slightly involved in politics when he was younger.

'They left us here, they left us, the younger ones, saying we must be foot soldiers. Siqhube umzabalazo on the ground, while they went to nice countries to get degrees, so they can come back and be ministers. Hypocrites, the whole of them,' Thulani would say. Especially when the issue of money came up. Which was coming up a lot with three children at school and Makhosi's school having started sooner than we had budgeted. Not that we hadn't budgeted; we had intended budgeting for it but it came months earlier. During an uncertain period. We were unprepared, and we needed to be honest about money.

'Some people went to guerrilla exile kodwa Thulani, it wasn't jelly and custard for those people either,' I tried speaking logic into him. I had fast learned this would be the course of the conversations. I would have to entertain the conversation as rationally as I could so as to not get him riled up, send him storming out the house. Thulani liked not dealing with the imminent issue, getting himself upset about every topic but the topic at hand.

'And what is guerrilla exile going to help? Who are we killing? Did they not negotiate? You think the foot soldiers in camps across this Africa are going to get positions? Bazobuya bezodla izinkobe nathi la. Just you watch. It will be the ones sent out to your overseas, I tell you.' This was how he would vent. An old vent.

The transition was hitting him hard. Friends, politically arrested and otherwise, were under his watch in the prison. Many people had started getting released but many more had died. Or there were rumours of their deaths. He didn't trust that much was going to change with these elections.

'Not emajele,' he said. 'It will take long for those people to see freedom.'

He wasn't lying. The lists of those eligible for release had stopped reaching them. Many were due to be released on 'parole', while others had awaited trial, and had never been tried. They too were awaiting their releases. The last list received by their prison was in October 1993. Something about preparation for the upcoming elections meant the prisoners would be left in limbo, awaiting the transition.

'Children don't need izinto ezibizayo,' Thulani said.

When we eventually reached the issue at hand – that we did not have enough money for another child in school – Thulani promised he would be the one who bought Makhosi's clothes for crèche. Month by month. Neither of us could overspend. There was too much uncertainty about everything. He was inconsistent with his buying, but I didn't like shopping. Least of all for girl children's clothes.

I always knew I didn't want a daughter, which I felt all the more when shopping. There were so many options to choose from. Most of them exceptionally bright, or simply uncomfortable for a child. Life was mostly uncomfortable for a girl child. I didn't care to spend time shopping for hair-tying things and earrings either; those, too, seem uncomfortable for little children.

After my sons, I told myself I was done with children. Thulani wanted a daughter though, and so we tried again, and he got his daughter. Of the three of them, she is more his than the other two. His first daughter, umafungwase. Even if it's two days a week where he fetches her or goes to town with her. He doesn't do the same with the boys. Maybe it's because she is the spitting image of him. He calls her his bodyguard. She laughs, he laughs. They look like they have known each other all their lives. But only for two days a week. The rest of the week, well, he says he works for his children and I am grateful he works, at least.

I hope the two of them grow closer to each other. Nothing in me has the energy to raise another girl child. It's just, they can fall pregnant. Boys can impregnate too, but I don't have to raise those children. Traditionally, if Makhosazane gets pregnant, that child is mine.

5

uMa had eleven children, three boys, and eight girls. Two of her children did not make it past the first day, so we did not count them, especially in conversation. I was the eldest. I became a teacher's assistant, then a police officer, because it was the easiest way to put my siblings through school. Those were uMa's words.

School stopped being available less and less eMpofana the higher you went. I stopped school in Standard 8, Junior Certificate; JC, we called it then. I was able to practise as a teaching assistant in school with a JC. Which meant often in the schools around eMpofana, and Umtshezi. I was less a teacher's assistant than I was a teacher. Some of the students in high school were my age, others older. Many of them had started and stopped school as they went. It was not uncommon. Sometimes, a student would wait until their family found a school in another area because the school in their area only stopped at Form 2, or even Form 1. If you didn't have a family, you would have to rent. If your parents didn't have money to rent, you started working and came back, if you could. If you wanted. Many would stop simply because there was no money for uniform.

All the way till my JC year, school had been close to free. The last two years were expensive, and the closest senior secondary school was in a town called Howick. I had no relatives in Howick and had already studied further than most girls.

My friends and I prepared to do bridging courses at UNISA. It would take us four years to study part-time, and it was expensive. So, work and save.

The British had grown invasive with marking their 'territories', setting rules and borders. My father and I seem to remember the time differently.

'Ah, Graham. We defeated Graham by being clever,' was what he told the children.

Oh, memory. He knew, like everyone else, it wasn't like he claimed it was, nor was it as easy. Especially in the houses which only had women, and worse still, when girls tried going to school. Simply passing Graham's gate was a gruesome task. It was a few older girls who started using the hole in the fence, towards the end of the farm. It led to just above the Van Reenen farm, which was a farm with old white people who only had the cleaning staff moving in and out of there. No one young lived there, and so there was seldom movement inside or security there. The older girls told a few of us, and so the fence became our new gate. Eventually, the sheriffs, who were higher than the security guards and only came to check the 'numbers', realised the girls were no longer passing by the gate, but were still being seen in uniform on the other side. Heading to school. That was when they banned girls from going to school throughout Nottingham Road and iMpofana. They came to the schools to drag us out if we were found. Those of us who were younger could get away with looking like boys in class.

Philisiwe was caught by the sheriff using the hole in the fence once. She was beaten to near death. It was then that the fence was taken down. When they took Philisiwe away, izintombi went to see her in hospital. The rumour was she told them one thing; a thing we were never meant to know. A secret for izintombi ezindala, noMama. There were rumours about what the secret was too. Yes, they were demanding cow tax, but it was izintombi zendawo who tore the fence down in anger.

When izintombi came back from the hospital that day, they looked possessed. Even the men could not stop them, so they joined, and eventually took over. Graham's fence was left outside his house. The Van Reenens disappeared in the middle of the night in fear.

The sheriffs would not let us rest for months after. Basking in the moments when they would find women and girls alone in a rondavel.

Everyone endaweni knew to show no sign of weakness. We rejoiced when we heard uMaGcina had made Graham eat ushevu. She was known as a witch and remained feared as a witch; but she was the witch who freed us.

Then they introduced compulsory school fees in higher secondary school, and immediately the number of girls in school decreased. Even the girls we had walked to school with disappeared. After everything, after having taken down Graham's fence, here they were, at the mercy of school fees. They couldn't destroy school fees like they had destroyed the fence.

I started noticing the walk to school when there were fewer of us. At a distance you could see izintaba zokhahlamba, in winter. The mountain would gather a white blanket covering the earth. There were many more buildings and structures blocking what had been a clear view.

Now there was a factory by the new road which was being built. They said the road would be long, and there would be ilokishi at the end of the long dusty road to make for the new people who would come work in the factory. People come from far, every morning to fesa outside this new factory. More and more was happening in the small town of Nottingham Road. A convenience store too. And some of the women who came into the town in the morning from around Howick, they did not come to fesa. They came to sell boiled eggs, umbila and umgxabiso.

By the time I came back from school, there were fewer women, fewer people standing outside the factory, speaking to another security man who probably didn't even know what decisions were made, and when. Securities are interesting people. They protect the people who are the safest, from the least safe people in the world. Poor people who come to beg for work in factories. My father called them poor people and told me I was going to school so I would never be them. I must be better than the white man. Smarter than the white man. I must beg the white man for nothing. He must come to me and ask my expert opinion about the land of my ancestors.

But I couldn't be an expert on anything without a Standard 10 qualification. I wanted to go to school further, but I needed to work first, save first. Help my parents with my sisters, who seemed less interested in school than I was.

Most of my siblings never saw the entrance of a university, except uNombu, who was much younger. My brothers all impregnated some girl.

I held one of my younger brothers, uBheka, in my arms after they had stabbed him to death. But it was easier being a boy. Boys could find ways to make money. uMakehla found a way to become a teacher, having only finished Standard 6. Bought papers, they said. He did well for himself, as well as he could have until he died, with three quarters of the women in the neighbourhood dying soon after him. My brother, the home wrecker. He was proud of himself too. 'Ngiyisoka,' he would say.

Bheka. It was easy to let go of uBheka. He was never going to survive. Was most likely going to end up behind bars. He didn't work well with authority, of any sort, got himself involved in every kind of fight. That was how he died. Said the wrong thing to the wrong person, on the wrong day. Then they stabbed him. None of us was surprised. I don't think he was either.

My sisters, well, they all married young, having left school and had children young. Five of them babuya emendweni. Abusive husbands. Addicts. Cheating abusive alcoholics being the full package. They fell into the same trap they saw Ma live through. Husbands who want many children, and even when you give them those many children, that won't stop them from impregnating five other women.

Five children who are not yours, who you must love regardless.

'Ingane ayinacala,' uMa would say when we asked her why she loved them, my father's love children. 'How do you begin to not love a child who also comes to you and, like your children, cries to you when the man you all call father does not provide for any of you?'

'Ingane ayinacala' was our mother's motto. About all children. Even neighbours' children who we could not deny food if they happened to be at our house during meal times. It didn't seem to matter to my mother that food ran out, or would run out eventually. 'Ungaka umhlaba, nemvuno yawo,' she would say.

'You need to have itayitela to use umhlaba,' Nombu tried telling her.

My mother didn't care what itayitela was, or what it meant; umhlaba okaNkulunkulu and that was all, above all else. 'Sibusisiwe isandla esiphayo,' she reminded all of us.

My mother's hand never stopped ukupha, even though it seemed the blessings were not flowing as easily as her hand was giving. Still, my mother gave.

When Bheka died, his girlfriend was pregnant with his child. uMa took the child, Bongeka, saying that Nombu would understand what she meant.

'Okwenziwa kuwena, nawe kumele ukwenze kwabanye,' uMa would try guilt Nombu into thinking of raising uBongeka. Ma was old and Nombu was the only one without children and was young enough to raise a child. I knew with everything inside of me Nombu was never going to take uBongeka. I think uMa did too, but she still tried.

Nombu wiggled herself out of that though. While saying nothing at all. She managed to never have to directly say no.

When Nombu was at a nursing college in Estcourt, she lived with me and my Thulani, who by then was my husband.

I met Thulani teaching eMtshezi High, in my fourth year of being a teacher's assistant. He knew a colleague of mine. Some of us had gone to get amagwinya at the local tearoom by the main road. It was exam time for our learners and we were waiting for exams to mark, or busy marking already. There were fewer learners to send to go buy for us; normally we could temporarily remove them from class to go buy something, but we couldn't remove them from an exam. We didn't particularly like walking, especially during the day when anyone could just shout your name from across the street, outside the school. Sometimes even the learners, especially the older ones, didn't care about our professional roles and would also shout our names on the street. We were uMiss only at school, and occasionally when we were needed to help with the enforcing of discipline and fear in misbehaving children in the village.

The roads were dusty, and the dust would stick to our exceptionally shiny shoes. Vaseline shoes, our learners called them.

Thulani was a quiet man who drove a Toyota Corolla. A white one with an Orlando Pirates sticker at the back. His hair was combed, and slightly parted. He had a stick in his mouth, or something. He looked like something out of a bioscope film. He looked at himself a lot in the mirror as he drove. Wiped his shoes as he stepped out of the car, before coming into the tearoom to sit with us and share amagwinya ethu. Although he didn't offer to take us to go buy, even though he could clearly see the road was dusty.

'What use was his car if not giving lifts', a colleague of mine joked.

He was on a break, leave or something. He worked for Correctional Services. He told me he knew people in the police academy who could help me get hired. He asked to take down my address – he was not the first one to do that – and the tearoom phone number, so he could call me with an update. I didn't think he would really call – he seemed to only be concerned about looking good, like men on films – so I was way more excited than I expected myself to be when the woman at the store told me someone had called, a Thulani.

'Something about telegramming your JC certificate, uthe call him back on this number: 033139886635'. And she passed me a note on a piece of paper which looked like she'd picked it up from under the counter after it had stayed there for too long in a room not swept often enough.

'Ngicela ukumfonela,' I asked, passing her a R1 coin.

'Wee ifoni isafile,' she said, nonchalantly. As a person does when they do not know what is on the line for you.

I loved my students and enjoyed teaching but I didn't have ten years to give to experience, and only then to be considered for the promotion to teacher. Even then, the system worked only for those who knew people who knew the white people in the offices in Pietermaritzburg. Mostly, the children of men and women who had gone to missionary schools. I was just the child of an uneducated man and woman who seldom interacted with white people. And even if they did, it would never be to negotiate a way for me to get into a better position.

My father hated anything that made him have to interact with white people. Even umholo. At the livestock sales, where he would sell his cows, there he had power. He had the livestock they wanted, and if they didn't agree to his price, he would simply take his livestock back home with him. He was a man of intense pride; he would rather come back home with no money for school fees than be undermined by a white boy. He despised that the white older men didn't even come to these things anymore. Sending their sons who reeked of superiority; calling people as old as their grandfathers 'boy'.

Because I had acquired English, and Afrikaans, from school, uBaba would sometimes ask me to join him at the sales, especially the ones he was unfamiliar with. Where the boys refused to speak isiFanakalo, which he hated as much as he hated English; but the isiZulu-English conversations he was having with the younger boys were even more frustrating for him. So, he asked me to come with. Once we left a sale because a white boy, and what I assumed was his wife, laughed.

'What are they laughing at?' he asked me.

'Angazi, Baba,' I said. They spoke a language I did not understand.

So uBaba and I left in a fit of anger, uBaba also angry at me for not knowing a white people language after all the years I had spent in school.

'Bangahleki ungakahleki,' he said. That is when you know white people are really undermining you, when they laugh before you have laughed.

The new white boy was a young Jewish man, Lissak, who had started donating to all the local schools. Green boards, chalk and board rulers. Making sure everyone knew he was, and differentiating himself from the 'others'. He quickly set himself apart from the 'other whites'. No one donated teaching equipment to our schools.

Unfortunately for uBaba, Lissak had recently bought the auctioneer and sales halls. So uBaba spent months boycotting auctioning and selling his cattle. Every few weeks I would try to soften uBaba's heart by telling him all the things Lissak said he was going to do for our communities and schools. But uBaba never did trust him.

So, the girl behind the tearoom till will never know – or even care about – why that phone call was so important to me that day.

It had been raining, the summer rains, early January. Lightning had hit the telephone pole, so the line was down.

They were waiting for the telephone people to come, all the way from Pietermaritzburg.

'But what if it's an emergency?' I asked, not really caring for the answer; the words slipped out of my mouth.

'Go to Estcourt,' she said, shrugging as she walked back towards the darkness of the shop way too small for all they were trying to sell. Plug heads, wires, car chargers, bread, nappies, soups. It didn't help that the aisles were narrow, makeshift aisles, where the shelves looked like they would fall if a big enough person tried passing through them. But this woman in the shop didn't seem to care. She moved swiftly through the aisles and disappeared.

'Sisazothenga!' a girl screamed from behind me. Before I could properly turn to see the girl, the woman reappeared as quickly as she had disappeared, paying no attention to my disappointed self still being there.

I couldn't try the phone at school either. I was back just a few days before schools reopened for teachers to settle in and prepare for the new intake of students. The only friend I had who had a phone at her house was still on holiday. Eventually I went to Estcourt, and there I called Thulani.

'Uyazitshela,' all my sisters said when they met him. He takes care of himself too much for a man.

'Umfana wasethawini,' my mother joked.

Nombu and Thulani got along as soon as they met. Nombu outgrew home earlier than most of us. She wanted to live closer to town. Estcourt was no city, but it was enough for Nombu then, and it was closer to her college. It was also convenient for her to assist me with the children. It helped that she and my husband got along. Even if it was over a fascination with clothes and looking good.

'It's not that my husband is a good husband,' I once told Nombu when she asked how all our sisters had not found themselves a husband like my Thulani. 'I think every man has that, I just... Thulani is a coward,' I said. 'He is scared of failure. If he even attempts to treat me like his brothers treat their wives, I will leave. No Zulu man wants to be left. He is too proud to deal with such shame. He knows it. So, to avoid feeling like a failure, he tries a little harder. Which isn't much harder, because my sisters' husbands don't try at all. They make my sisters know that they are privileged for having been married. That is the gift that men in my village give women, the gift of thinking you suitable to be a wife. Whatever happens after, remember it is you who had been chosen from all these other girls.'

Nombu loved Thulani. She seldom saw what I meant when I said these things. She didn't believe them either.

'Hayi angeke nje sis, ulungile phela uThulani. You don't count your blessings right.'

I laughed. Perhaps, Nombu. Perhaps.

By the time I enrolled at the police academy I was already over twenty-five, which was the average age of most of the black 'cadets'. Thulani drove me to UNISA to fetch my Standard 10 equivalent, and then to Hammanskraal to help me move in. Turned out his car could actually be for lifts. I asked him often why he was helping me.

'A farm Julia like yourself will not survive starting up in Gauteng, Hammanskraal. Life is faster there. One mistake is a move for chancers,' he said, performing being a chancer trying to grab my bags.

'You play a lot,' I said to him. Shocked that the quiet man I had first met danced as he walked and talked in this thawini. Bigger cities really show people's colours, I thought. I knew that too from all the people who had disappeared to ithawini, iTheku, and iGoli.

'Playing is the only thing we are here to do. All of it, it's a game. You're a pawn in a game of chess bigger than yourself. If you don't want to play, you get taken out of the game. And the rest of us, we move,' he said, as he half-slid in front of me and struck up a pose. 'So, wena, do you want to play this game of life with me, ntombi kaMageba?'

'My life is not a game,' I said, 'and besides, I am here for police school. Not to play around. I am old now. There is no time for me to play around.'

'Well, I will marry you. Like old people should be. Married. As soon as you finish at that academy I will marry you,' he said, taking my arm and twirling under it.

'You've got time to play konje wena,' I said.

For the next twelve months of training Thulani would drive from Pietermaritzburg to Hammanskraal to visit me, and give me cut-outs of women in wedding dresses, asking, 'Which one do you like?' Giving me too many options. 'And this one?'

We started speaking about marriage before we even started ukujola, okwangempela. Which came easier when I accepted to myself that he was a better man than the men I was in the academy with. And many men I had known before him. Marriage had not been a priority in my life. If it was going to happen, it would happen; but I needed to become someone. That was the most important thing in my life. To become someone, work hard, help my mother; and, if I did have children, to be able to provide better for them. With very little concept of what better could look like. The stories of big cities scared me. I didn't want to go too far; but I didn't want to be close either.

We were not a small village, but everyone seemed to know everything about everyone. Even about the people who had left. Many people were having children with neighbours; marrying neighbours, and people they had known their whole lives. I knew very young that I did not want that, although when I eventually left home I would learn that all communities recreate a version of that.

In both eMtshezi and eMpofana somehow the news of me being with Thulani – and being in the police academy – spread fast. Possibly through friends and family, who would in return somehow find a way to let me know what a person in a conversation had said.

I was not young. Even at the academy, I was amongst the few who were not izingoduso or inkosikazi. Which was useful, because I didn't have as much an obligation to go home, if any. So I was able to save money and send it home instead. To uMa. I had seen what it looked like; her wanting to buy things instead of being presented with simple things like they were luxuries.

This was what uBaba did. Often just basic things, but expect the biggest praise for it.

At Christmas he would buy paint and Christmas delicacies. He would not just drive to town with isigadla that he used to go everywhere. No. On this occasion he would dress in a three-piece suit, a silver Swiss watch on his wrist and shine his shoes after we had already shined them. He would walk slowly towards the stop on the main road, probably high from all the benzine fumes on the way. Then, as soon as he was off the gravel, he would take out a cloth and wipe his shoes. uMa had started a ritual of gathering all of us to behold this show before us.

'Bukani phela,' she'd say as uBaba pranced around like a peacock waiting for ikhumbi.

Coming back, uBaba would not take plastics from shops, which were free. No. He would somehow manage to get a back seat full of groceries into the back seat. He would sit next to the food. And as soon as ikhumbi stopped at our stop he would send someone, anyone at all, sometimes the frustrated driver, to come call for us. Often, whoever had been sent wouldn't even go all the way to our yard. They would stop just before halfway and bellow out one of our names. It was time. Hurriedly we would get wheelbarrows and run to the stop, while uBaba shouted, 'Sheshani! Sheshani! Time is money!'

It was the only day when my father would speak a full English sentence without being forced. He seemed to not care that we were trying to run with wheelbarrows on gravel roads which had residues of muddiness from the summer rains.

Two of us needed to run first. Bheka and I were the fastest team for this activity. I would push the empty wheelbarrow out of our yard, trying to dodge small animals, and their shit. Out the gate, down a slope. Normally, we enjoyed sliding down this slope but it was tricky with a fast wheelbarrow. If you lost control, uBaba would shout even more.

'Nginithengela ukudla, bese nibulala izinto zam. Ningibona ngeplate lamasimba.'

Which was also reserved for this performance day. uBaba seldom swore, even at his angriest, and he was often angry. Inhlamba was beneath him. We'd also learned that although he was not a drinker, the Christmas period was an exception. And when he drank swearing was not beneath him.

He would stand there, straightening his suit, watching us almost fall over ourselves getting to the khumbi, and then sweating through our clothes trying to get the groceries out of the window. While not breaking anything. Bheka's job was to take the groceries out; mine was to place them on the wheelbarrow properly. The braver khumbi drivers sometimes tried to help us, in their hurry to rush back for many more trips with pompous old men.

'Yeyi, mageza empopmini beka kahle,' uBaba would scream at the drivers.

After I'd packed the wheelbarrow, Bheka would push the full wheelbarrow back; and I would quickly unpack at the other end. On good days, if we had managed to get a wheelbarrow from a neighbour and we had two, Bheka and I did not need to do another run.

We would start unpacking while uBaba slowly walked back home with his chest saluting the sky. As soon as he stepped foot into our yard, uMa had to begin her ululations and appreciations of her husband, of whom she was grateful and undeserving.

When we got older, we realised that uBaba knew that the

praises were performed with very little truth to them, but he did not care. uBaba would get into his car and leave soon after. Often we would see him only when he came back to sleep. Which, I would later learn, was how Ma liked it.

For whatever reason, Nombu carelessly asked uBaba one December why he didn't take the car to do shopping. She also asked him where he went. uBaba hated being exposed. That Nombu had asked these questions in front of his in-laws was what annoyed uBaba the most. They never did fix their relationship, him and Nombu. He didn't do his performance that December and stayed at home throughout. By the time I arrived, the day before Christmas, all uMa wanted was for uBaba to leave, go somewhere. Anywhere.

So, it was refreshing, Thulani's performances. They were about both of us; and that mattered, that I existed in the relationship.

In the force as women, we didn't really exist. Although we were told the trainings were not constructed for the male cadet, they truly were. The trainers were all men. Sometimes they would comment on our fat bums while we were trying to run or compete a physical test. If you complained, it was you who was disqualified.

Thulani expressed sympathy towards this old thinking.

'Arch-a-i-c,' he would say, lifting his neck unnecessarily to show the movement of his Adam's apple.

A clown. I enjoyed that he made me laugh. At everything. Nothing was exempt from being turned into a joke for Thulani. He seemed to have opinions different from the men I had known.

It was a purposeful dating from the start. The purpose was marriage. Even his sense of dedication made him seem different to the men I had known. The men in my life. We got married a month after I graduated from the police academy. He had been saving since our first month together. With a child on the way, I didn't have a reason to keep postponing marriage anymore.

The wedding was two days and had to happen at both family homes. Buses from Estcourt to Pietermaritzburg would cost us most of the budget for the wedding. There needed to be enough space in the buses for whoever in our villages wanted to come. Everyone was invited, although no invites were sent except to our workplaces, for me my final year colleagues and to both our churches. Thulani was raised Methodist, and I Catholic. It meant I was converting to Methodist, by marriage, but Thulani never attended church and didn't much care about where I went to church anyway. Not that I cared to go then either.

I mostly remember our wedding through pictures. There were too many people, and too many things going wrong; and too much travelling and too much changing. I had wanted a simple wedding, but neither of our families allowed that. Umshado wephoyisa, noJele. We were what entry-level middle class would look like in the future. Our families wanted to show us off. On the last night of the ceremony, after I had been officially handed over to Thulani's family, and everyone was still enjoying festivities outside, in a room filled with blankets and other presents Thulani and I both fell asleep while praying for everyone to disappear. We had changed out of our traditional clothes. The clock said it was already after 9 pm. 'I'm sure sebezohamba' is the last thing I remember Thulani saying.

Around 3 am I was woken up by a burning need to urinate. I could still smell the festivities as the final coals burned down. I really needed to go to the toilet, which was outside. So I squatted behind our rondavel. I suppose wives shouldn't urinate behind their rooms; I remember thinking and laughing.

6

Makhosazane

'Mama, what colour does pink and brown make?'

I am lying on the cold kitchen floor, putting together an old puzzle while she is preparing a meal. Ujeqe nobhontshisi, I think. It is a Sunday afternoon. Mama loves making ujeqe nobhontshisi for Sunday suppers. The smell of the Rajah flavoured beans carries out the window, to the garage next door where the old men drink umqombothi and smoke insangu.

Wembezi, my parents' house is a five-roomed house, amongst many four-roomed houses. The fifth room, a bedroom, was added at the back of the house instead of an outside room. It looks out of place, like a misplaced building block, in a street and township with houses that look like they can all fit into each other. Minus the outbuildings and imikhukhu at the back. Our parents decided against a back room and instead created this third bedroom which doesn't fit into anything. Every time I look at our house, I wonder what factories must do when they make mistakes making building blocks. Throw them away?

The yards all almost look the same, but our yard is the greenest. uMama asks uMzala to come 'help' with our yard. The grass is a bright sharp green, with a big round-looking tree in the middle, the stop nonsense breaking the grass at the end of the yard and the start of the neighbour's yard. On the side of the house in the front, the stop nonsense separates the inside of the yard from the outside. The grass outside has water bottles all over it. Everything is always so straight, except for the heaps of water bottles on the grass. They look out of place, even though there are many houses with water bottles on their front grass.

The grass is pretty. Like the tiles on my mother's kitchen floor. I like lying on the tiles and imagining the taste of ubhontshisi later as it will melt in my mouth. The tiles remind me of the grass. They are cold like the grass, but I cannot lie on the grass for too long or I will start itching. Besides, no one lies on grass except in the park in town. When I was smaller, I would wear long clothes and lie on the grass. I'd ask uBaba to take me to the park in Estcourt where I could lie on the grass and not look at our place. It was my favourite place. Eventually he said I was too old to do that anymore.

My mother's tiles are my new favourite place to ask uMama questions, when she is stuck in her kitchen. Other times she is busy coming in and out of the house, speaking to our neighbour uMaMntungwa on the other side as she does laundry. The back side of our yard doesn't have ustop nonsense. Just a fence. A green fence. Mama often organises for another mzala to come paint the fence, even painting on MaMntungwa's side. Sundays are laundry days. Our uniforms, her uniforms, izingubo zokuhlala ekhaya. All our socks, although we are supposed to wash them after school ourselves, which I don't always do because I knew that on Sundays all the socks will be soaked. The white socks with the white shirts. The grey socks with the grey pants.

The washing lines between the two houses are not far from each other. Nothing is far from each other, really. uMama noMaMtungwa both stand arching over izindishi, both doing their laundry. On a Sunday morning after church – church for most people; not always for them – they discuss the sermons, if either of them has gone to church. Then they discuss their children, often sending us off to do something else when it looks like we might disturb these 'catch up' sessions. That is all of Sunday morning gone already. After laundry, before lunch, is when uMa is alone in the kitchen. Silent. Although I can hear the church people singing from isonto labasindisiwe in the tent on the field a street above ours; amasonto abantu abasindisiwe goes on for way longer than the older churches elokishini. The other churches have big structures built a little way away from people's houses. These new ones pitch a tent anywhere and everywhere where there is open space; and the noise travels to the rest of us faster through those tents.

The radio in our sitting room is playing jazz music, which I am never sure if anyone really likes. I don't think anyone really listens to the radio in our house, even though it is always on. Sometimes it will be on in my parents' room to shut out the sound on the other side of the door. On Sundays, I think it is to shut out the sound from the church people; and our neighbour, who plays the same old-sounding sad break- up songs very loudly on a Sunday.

uMa is silent, taking time only to respond to my questions, distracted by opening and closing drawers.

'Angazi,' she responds, pulling and pushing at drawers.

'Purple. Pink and brown make purple. Do you know an isosceles triangle?'

'Yebo, Makhosi!'

'Do you really? Were algebra and trigonometry around when you were at school? Candice said we will do algebra and trigonometry when we are older. That's where we learn about isosceles triangles, but Candice and I read ahead. Do you know it?'

'Yes, futhi please go play ngalena,' she says.

'So, why are you a policewoman if you know algebra and trigonometry?'

'A police officer. Instead of what, Makhosi?' Ma's voice always rises when she wants me to stop doing something, as if I can't hear her when she speaks normally. Like teachers.

'A lawyer, a doctor, a scientist, an engineer,' I say. Naming all the jobs Ma could possibly have had.

'Different times.' She moves over me.

'But you can be all those things. And... and if you had studied all those things, you could've been like Candice's mom. Remember Candice? Her parents own a farm outside Colenso, and Candice was home-schooled till she was ten because her mother was so smart. Her mother is an engineer, and her father is a doctor.'

'Candice, lo mngani wakho owumlungu?'

'Just my friend, Ma. I don't introduce her as my white friend.'

'Does she introduce her parents as doctor and engineer?'

'No, but everyone knows that's what her parents are.'

'Because that's what Candice says?'

'Yes. And, and when Candice, Melanie and Tyler speak, I never know what to say. Have you ever been to Joburg, Ma?'

'Yes!'

'Well, Candice's mom has been to Joburg, and London, and New York and England.'

'England and London are the same place, sisi,' Ma says in an almost sigh.

'Have you been?' I ask with my eyes wide open. Maybe my mother is also well travelled, maybe my mother has a story after all.

'No,' she responds.

'Then how do you know?' I ask, unable to hide my disappointment as my voice drops.

'I just know, Khosi.'

The more questions I ask, the more irritated Ma seems. I wish she was more like Candice's mom. Candice's mom is always smiling and laughing. Ma, on the other hand, is always busy. She wakes up early to go to work, comes back late and cooks (sometimes). Ma is a bad cook, except for her Sunday supper meals. Then she helps the boys with their homework. I do my own homework though. I tell her I can. I came second in a class of 30 children. Second after Candice, but Candice gets extra lessons. So, actually, I am smarter.

My teacher says if I asked for help more, I would do better. I don't need the help though. I know why the sun is yellow, and where a rainbow comes from. I know there are no pots of gold beyond the rainbow, that that is a myth, although I don't know who started the myth.

MYTH (NOUN)
1. A traditional story, especially one concerning the early history of a people or explaining a natural or social phenomenon, and typically involving supernatural beings or events. 'ancient Celtic myths' mass noun 'the heroes of Greek myth'
2. A widely held but false belief or idea. 'the belief that evening primrose oil helps to cure eczema is a myth according to dermatologists'

I learned that word last week. MYTH.

Ma doesn't use big English words. Ma responds ngesiZulu even when I speak to her in English.

I think they taught her in isiZulu in school instead of English. You can hear it when she speaks English words. They sound like isiZulu. She doesn't even try hard to pronounce the words better. She pronounces the b at the end of bomb.

'It's a silent b,' I once said. She just looked at me and continued with what she was doing.

I really wish Ma was like Candice's mom. Ma nudges at me with her foot. I am blocking the way to the cupboard with oil. I roll a little, move out the way. Ma looks like she is away in her motherly thoughts.

Are my thoughts children's thoughts? No, my thoughts are smart thoughts, I quickly tell myself. I stare at the tiles. I wonder if she thinks about these things, about not just being a policewoman. Sometimes, I think I annoy her with my questions, by being in the kitchen. I like the cold of the tiles, I like the smell of this meal. I like lying here, on a Sunday. Stealing moments with her.

Everything will be busy again after supper. We will be polishing our shoes and cleaning our school bags. Ma will be busy ironing our uniforms for the week. Then we'll be busy again all week, rushing to catch imoto ek'seni. uMalume doesn't have time to wait. He only hoots once, twice at best. He is fetching other children who also need to be at school on time, we are not all in the same school. He's busy. uBaba doesn't take me to school anymore. The new school is not where my old school was, which was at his workplace. Which was where he had wanted me to go to school for longer, at his workplace. It was easier for him that way. Now, they also have to make more money to pay uMalume wetransport. I don't know what uBaba sits and does now since we all leave the house early; before him. Maybe he still drinks his tea and watches silent news. While uMa is busy. She is working even harder to make transport money.

uMa is busy. Everything is busy.

I lie on the floor. It's not busy here.

7
Dudu

I never wanted a daughter. It was something I had said through our years of marriage. Not with all the stories we heard, and the things we had seen. I never wanted to bring a child into this world and not be able to protect it. It's worse now without Nombu here to help with Makhosi and Thulani.

He tried harder when she was here. Performed his good responsible husband role more. Now, he just shouts about me spoiling the children. 'Ma, mina masengimdala ngifuna ukuba imbali,' Nkhosazane says.

'Imbali, sisi?'

'Eh he.'

'Ngobani?' I ask, amused at my daughter's softness. It constantly catches me by surprise. How does she even think of being a flower?

'Ngoba ngimuhle njengembali,' she says. Almost floating away, like flower petals in a river. She packs her books. Again, she has cut out pieces of books. The remnants of the cut paper fly up as she stands up. The paper is unable to float with her, and falls back on the ground.

I should probably call her back to clean up after herself and remind her she cannot cut school books. There are magazines all over the house that I have collected from friends at work for her.

'I don't like the pictures, and the pages are busy. I don't like them,' she said when I asked why she hadn't used the magazines. She threw them back at the table.

I had been planning to surprise her for weeks. Asking and gathering. Awkwardly finding myself staring at every person reading a magazine. A person waiting for someone at the station, a colleague reading during tea break, the magazines at the doctor's office, free old magazines at libraries. If it was a magazine that had served its purpose, I gathered it for Makhosi. And in one sentence, she didn't care. It didn't matter.

Everything is on the stove and the countertops are clean. All that is left now is the floor which Makhosi has added to. I look behind at the door, and from the way it leans against the wall, I knew the broom is outside.

Thulani barges in, like he has no balance or concept of gravity. The door hits the wall as it bangs next to him.

'Haw' manje, kwangcola nje esitting room khona la ekuhlala khona abantu.' he says. A bang does not bother him. A dirty house does.

Mxm, amadoda. Walking past the kitchen to the sitting room, where he is somewhat struggling to get himself landing safely on the sofa.

'Your daughter was cutting books again. As usual. And since you won't pay the cost of the books, or speak to her, you can help clean up after her.'

He mumbles some words about how tired he is. When I am back in the kitchen, only then do I hear his body thump against the sofa. He is fast asleep soon after.

I may as well start sweeping around him. It is almost 7 pm on a hot Sunday evening, after heaps and heaps of chores. Next, finish the week's laundry. My husband has become the person who spends his Sundays drunk.

Nombu still had some Decembers to herself during her nursing college days. This meant I could send her with the children to visit my mother, uMaDlamini, during the December period. My sisters usually went on leave after the 15th and they would all go down to visit uMaDlamini, spending a week at home, often longer.

December was always busy for me. Real, and 'imagined' busy-ness. The force demanded more from us in December. Blocking the roads coming from the freeway, and the roads inside the city. Estcourt was a small town, and between us and the traffic police our roles were becoming redundant. Out of sheer boredom my colleagues would start raiding taverns, shebeens and other drinking places, asking to see permits to sell alcohol. This was the fastest way of making money while also getting drunk. I would go there to look out for young girls too drunk to go home, who might find themselves in vulnerable positions. December is dangerous for girls who drink.

The strong smell of insangu in the shebeens and beer halls welcomed us as we walked in. A group of police officers in uniform made the patrons and the owners equally uncomfortable. Laughing with us, in hope we would leave soon. Which was the case if I was joining my team; cutting down the 'random' searches to make sure my colleagues would not find themselves drunk on beer hall tables. There was seldom anything happening at beer halls that really needed us. Often when we were needed, people would laugh less with us. Co-operate less. Did not want to be seen with us.

'Angazi lutho mina,' people would say at just a greeting from one of the people in uniform.

There was no need for us to be there, the smallest thing. A child running away from home and no police available to assist would land us in quick trouble. It was hard, trying to get my colleagues to stay sober. Many of them were young, coming into a police force in a rural township in a dead town. In a police station which, although claimed to be run by us, was run by the white police station in the town of Estcourt. In December the Estcourt police station's vans were out looking for imagined danger on the freeway while the few Wembezi station vans were juggling. A child burned at home because there was still no electricity and something caught alight. A boiling pot tipped over from the stove. A stabbing in a tavern. A rape on an open field. A domestic assault and blocking roads.

We had tried begging for more cars, but we got into trouble for that too. We were demanding too much. 'Outside of our jurisdiction,' they said when we asked them to at the very least redirect some of their vans on the freeway to eWembezi. Again, we were demanding too much. I never did understand how they understood 'demand', because from where I was standing we were begging, not demanding. Spending weeks, months, trying to figure how to best structure this request. Gathering instances as evidence of our need. A need which should have been as clear to them as it was to us.

My older colleagues had given up trying with Estcourt police station, which also meant they were not scared of being too drunk and getting in trouble. How do they expect us to work without enough vans, anyway? So, I had to guilt trip them with their duty to their children. If you lose your job, what will your children eat?

It was the young boys coming into the service who were the hardest to guilt into anything. It was worse when they had formed relationships with the older colleagues and were not from around Estcourt. Shame works with a sense of community, of belonging. The boys from eThekwini though, they walked straight into ideas of what it means to have come from the bigger amalokishi. With youth, it also meant they spent their salaries frivolously.

'You cannot be seen passed out drunk in a beer hall in uniform,' I tried telling Ngwenya.

Ngwenya had just turned twenty. He joined the academy straight after Standard 10. They were coming in younger and younger. Spending less time at the academy, and more time in the field; at the stations. There was suddenly a call for more black police officers.

Ngwenya was from KwaMashu, just outside Durban, He had trained eXopo for only three months before being placed 'in the field' for what was meant to be six months eWembezi. There was a delay in getting the cadets back to the academy. The security was being brought up for the upcoming elections. After the elections, they would return to the academy, we heard. But there was going to be no peaceful 'after the elections' eWembezi.

It didn't take long for Ngwenya to find the service boring but profitable. He spent days on end complaining about the slow pace of Estcourt, how boring Wembezi was, and how there was nothing else to do but drink. We couldn't instill the fear of his parents in him either. None of us knew his parents; none of us even knew where exactly KwaMashu he was from. A stranger on familiar ground. There was another Ngwenya who worked in the police station in Weenen, just a few kilometres out of Estcourt. He was the only person we knew who could help us tame the young boy, for no other reason than ukufana kwezibongo. There was a shared respect.

Ngwenya was my partner one December. The captain thought I could do something to sober up the young man's habits and, to an extent, he was right. Every December after that I was the only person Ngwenya feared enough to not be dropping on the floor drunk working next to. I didn't want to be a babysitter, and I told the captain that. He said something about my maternal abilities and Ngwenya being ingane yomuntu who needed guidance, my guidance. It was a useless battle to try fight.

I was happy that Nombu could still go home, and be a familiar face for my children when they visited their grandmother, especially when I was babysitting Ngwenya.

MaDlamini always put my children before anyone else's children. Maybe because they were younger than most of my siblings' children. Or the money perhaps; maybe she thought if she didn't give my children the extra attention, I would stop sending as much money in December.

Makhosi hates being 'faffed over' by her grandmother.

'She makes the others want to bully us,' my daughter complains.

MaDlamini won't let their cousins borrow their clothes. She doesn't allow my children to play on the main road in case an accident happens.

'uGogo nje, usenza amaqanda, Mama, and it draws attention to us.'

Unlike my sisters' children, who spent almost every weekend and holiday ekhaya, and my brothers' children, who were already being raised by uGogo wabo, my children came in and out as visitors. Maybe it was because MaDlamini didn't want them to be picked on that she was so careful with them.

When Nombu was there she'd laugh, saying, 'Wee, uMa wakho. She thinks the day any of your children come back with even a scratch you will think her house dangerous for your soft lokishi children.'

Ma had grown old. Nombu and I laughed. Scratches and scars had been a part of both our growing ups. uMa once worked ekhishini to one of the white people on a nearby farm. She came back late in the evenings, and during the day something would scratch you – a thorn as you were walking the cows, a fence as you were trying to create a shortcut from one house to another, a teacher who hit you too hard. A fight that ended badly. We were constantly scratched, and scratching, there was nothing worth telling. My nieces and nephews who lived with her also had the pleasure of running to her and telling on the other children from around. MaDlamini would stand in the middle of her yard, hands on her hips, screaming at children she couldn't even see. Hidden behind bushes, or who had run away. 'Yeyi nina! Yeyi!' she would scream, telling other children to leave her grandchildren.

The older they grew, they must have learned this was not effective and they stopped telling uMaDlamini to fight their battles. We heard the stories of her running after children in bushes less and less now. Even so, other children were allowed scratches; mine were not. Which didn't work with Makhosi, who was constantly stuck between people's fences. She didn't quite know how to hold her dress while holding the fence such that it doesn't scratch you, not yet having the hand-eye co-ordination to get under one wire over another and onto the other side. There was only a fence around isibaya to keep the cows safe.

Nombu loved the stories of rescuing Makhosi from the jails of barbed wire. Makhosi did not like the joke.

'They do it so fast, Ma, bavele badlule nje. Every time I try to jump over, my dress gets caught up in the sticky things,' she'd say.

Makhosi only wore dresses in her grandfather's house, although my father eventually let her wear pants as she grew older. When we were younger, he believed girl children should only wear skirts. With Makhosi, who was constantly getting stuck between fences, up trees and on roofs, he was more embarrassed by the many boys who would laugh, watching her hanging at the top of something with her underwear showing. He couldn't stop her from climbing things, and she was really helpful with the cows, which they both loved.

Nkosana, my eldest, hated physical activity. More so if the physical activity involved group work. So he seldom did anything. Mpumelelo just told jokes and entertained everyone instead of working. A comedian, and lazy like his father. Makhosi, though, she loved cows and, eventually, she was allowed to wear her shorts, which made jumping fences easier for her.

Nombu reminded me about the time I'd told her I wanted children who wouldn't know how to jump fences. Nombu had jumped a fence and gone to a boy in the middle of the night. I'd shouted at her, and said, 'uJesu angisize and give me children who will not know how to jump fences.' We laughed, remembering that. I had arrived the day before Christmas.

Makhosi had been stuck in a fence again and her brothers had avoided saving her. Nombu and I were still laughing about the memory of me shouting at her that day when uMa walked in.

'The two of you are doing lento yenu of sitting as just the two of you, when the house is full of your sisters,' our mother reprimanded us. An old reprimand. Nombu and I were always being teased by our sisters for being the 'professionals'. We sat in rooms 'having conferences', one of our sisters said once. 'Abaphathi', they nicknamed us. It was meant to hurt and humble us; it didn't.

They often discussed their horrible husbands when we were together. My husband was with me on every trip. It wouldn't have felt right to sit there and dissect him when he was in the same yard, so I stopped joining in on those conversations. Nombu, well, Nombu said it was old and tiring. They complained about these men, and new men, every time we were all together. Every time.

Ngwenya finally left the police force. They never were called back to the academy; instead they were absorbed into the force. Ngwenya said he wanted to go back to school.

'You have all the time in the world, usemncane,' I said to him. It was my first December in over three years at home.

8

The thing about people who come after you, sibling or child, is you watch them have no conception of life before them.

Yes, they know. You lived, breathed and existed before they existed. Of course, as they grow older, they come to understand the cycle of life. Birth–School–Work–Pension–Death. All of them, eventually they understand. That it is the same for the ones before, as it is for them, as it will be for the ones who will come after.

You sit and watch as a few try to break away, but there is always another system awaiting them. Different systems. Different lessons. Different pains. Different traumas. All living is traumatic. From the start. No one asks you if you want to be here. How you want to be here. No one asks you how the rest of it should go for you. It's just this path before you. With little option to deviate. Unless you have extraordinary talent supported by severe ambition, and then maybe you can try it eGoli. Even then, it is work. But maybe eGoli you can do nicer work, which also comes with its nicer problems. All living is work, for yourself and others. No living is isolated.

You are here, doing what you need to do. Some of us do it better than others.

I have listened to boys in the back of vans, in holding cells, in court corridors, inside courts. I have heard girls, too. In life-threatening situations in trucks and cars near the N3, on the way to Harrismith or Durban, the ones we pick up in taverns, somewhere between a fight and being beaten. Often they are outnumbered by the men, who want them there to project onto them all their insecurities. One mistake is a goal for the men; they gang up on the woman, sometimes physically. Best is if we arrive before it has escalated there. 'It is her fault', they say in unison. Many of the taverns are run by women, it is in their eyes where I often see the truth. But men are their customers. Their livelihoods. They are not completely safe either. Shebeen queens get abused, regularly. When the men who came pretending to have money eventually don't have the money to pay. Or, if you're really unlucky, the wives of these men start calling you names. There have been 'witch hunts' over the simple accusation of a shebeen queen being isifebe, then a witch. The men do not protect her. They do not care. There will be another shebeen soon, if there aren't a few options already.

We hear the stories. The pains. They are everywhere.

Eventually they, too, learn. The ones who come after you.

My first 'incident' in a suburb, was behind the Spar at the top of Estcourt.

It was a quiet area, near the local high school opposite a church.

The road leading up to the house was gravel, but from ukugudluzela of the van I knew their gravel was 'managed' often.

We passed a few houses with many ornaments at the front, the houses all painted in one colour, no pattern. Just plain walls or plain fences, fences that lacked even the character of being a broken fence. Trees and flowers. And those creepy men with water coming out their eyes and noses. Little men creatures with little man-made fountains, and those trees that creep all over walls. Their gardens were immaculately kept. Everything in place. Even the house that looked like the garden was not being kept was kept.

We would frequent number 46 Weenen Street, Estcourt often. The police at Estcourt station passed the case onto us, calling it an 'incident', as if crime did not happen here. The family was black, Nigerian, with a teenage boy acting out. They had not been in South Africa for more than two years when their son started stealing from the neighbours and from school. At first the parents were fighting about disappearing valuables, the wife screaming at the husband, accusing him of cheating. The first time we were called in was not because of that. We were called in because of the strong smell of insangu from the back of the house. A black family fighting, and smoking drugs, in a town caught in Anglo-Boer history. They did not speak isiZulu, and drove big Mercedes Benzes which meant they must be important; but I couldn't place why.

That they were Nigerian, with a thirteen-year-old, Eli, who smoked insangu was what sent our station up in fury.

'Bazodayisa amadrugs la,' Dladla said as we were driving out of the house. Without the thirteen-year-old. We would need to process this via child court. Get social workers involved. Which also did not impress uDladla. It could not be a simple case. We couldn't take a thirteen-year-old boy who seemed to have little grasp of isiZulu into holding cells, then to the magistrate and 'off our hands' except for the monthly court cases. We had to pay regular visits with a social worker instead. Too much work for uDladla.

If children elokishini smoke insangu with all the soccer on the streets, and the walking together to school in groups, and the communal nature of everyone at the very least asking how you are and knowing way more about you than you would like them to, then why couldn't Eli? Township boys at least have a community.

Yes, peer pressure, but that little boy must be lonely living here. Worst of all, with his father as the new principal, a professor in education was what a certificate (or was it an award?) hanging on his study wall said. That was the only thing in this 'study' that told us anything about what he did. Just a local principal? Why would a professor be a principal in Estcourt, we wondered.

This didn't help Dladla's conspiracy theories.

He stormed into the office, saying, 'Drug problem, I tell you. We are about to grow a drug problem. That Nigerian boy is going to start a brothel here. Our country is being sold, ngiyanitshela. Estcourt iyamosheka nje.'

'Ngensangu? How is a thirteen-year-old boy who has had to move countries to this here bewitched town of bloodshed a drug problem? Ngensangu? How many boys smoke insangu right here, eWembezi? Is that a drug problem?' I asked uDlala. Insangu was everywhere, and he knew it.

As men do, he argued.

We saw more of Eli, although he seldom said anything. I just... I saw it. The thing I saw in shebeen queens, and those women on the N3, and boys trying to escape systems.

Sometimes I wanted to tell them they were not the only ones who thought the way they thought. Slow down your minds, the system is driving you insane. Sometimes literally. That was what I wanted to tell them. Insanity itself is a trap into another system. Mental asylums are their own system. Each system with its own hierarchies, its own irrational rules, its own frustrations. Trying to escape systems is like trying to run away from the wind.

Others of us learn to love the breeze of the wind.

Because it's better to feel the wind than be trapped inside systems of isolation; or your head.

It is dangerous to be trapped in heads.

The only way out is the one we know. The safest way out is the one we know, the one that has been tried and tested, and can be navigated with fewer physical scars. The path of chains and cells and restraining, that is the least safe path.

I imagine it is exhilarating, but still. A few months later, we went to the house but Eli was gone. Boarding school. Now the neighbours could not ignore the screams we first heard when they called to report 'a drug boy'.

Eli had not done better with the social workers. The man from the pawn shop in town, De Villiers, lived a few streets away from them. Unfortunately, as good as Eli was at stealing, Estcourt was small; a friend of the store owner saw their watch at the shop. De Villiers and Smith spied on Eli for a few more months.

We were called.

Both the store owner and his friend, Smith, were standing right outside Eli's gate with a list of all the things Eli had sold to him. The list included the family valuables. We took Eli around for a 'drive'. The closest Boys Town was in Pietermaritzburg and Dladla was not willing to drive to Maritzburg on a Saturday morning. He had an umsebenzi at a family friend and he planned to attend. Work was not going to distract him. The social worker on call was also at the head office, in Pietermaritzburg.

Dladla wanted to throw Eli in a cell. I begged him to take him home, that we rather fetch him on Monday. In a cell there would be drunk men and boys who did real crimes. Violent crimes are popular on Saturday afternoon. Boys high on things that are not insangu. And he was a foreign child, the child of a professor, I reminded him. If anything happened to his son, there was no way that man would let us go. We did not know the extent of his 'powers', but we had learned he had some.

Dladla agreed, but he also wanted to scare the boy. So we took him to the police station and started processing his 'crimes', and Eli was shouted at and called names. I called his parents. If they fetched him at the station in the early evening, the neighbours wouldn't see him come back 'on the same day', even if they tried. It was getting dark, and all those trees would surely block their vision.

Eli's mother arrived three hours after I called, apologising for being late and promising she would make sure no such thing would ever happen again. Thanking me without end for letting her child come back to sleep at home that night.

'Thank you, my sister,' she said, over and over again.

Eli had recently turned fourteen. I tried explaining to her that it was his right to not be in a cell with older men. There were the two incidents of insangu, for which he was already going to court-ordered SANCA meetings, which he had been consistent with. His urine tests had also been clean for a few months. But now this stealing.

'He is a good boy, he is adjusting,' I said. 'And it must be hard for him in that school. There aren't even many kids who look like him. Those who do live eWembezi not in town, on Weenen road. A stone's throw away from the school. He will be fine. Boys here smoke insangu all the time, and many outgrow it.'

She shook her head, and said it was me. My mercy. Her son had done abominable things. He deserved to sleep in jail, but because I am a woman like her, because I knew the pains of childbirth, I had shown mercy.

'I know God is not a woman, because only men can give away children as sacrifices,' she said.

If only she knew, I thought.

Then Dladla brought Eli out, whose lesson had left him with physical scars.

Mrs Oko fell on the ground. Eli did not flinch as Dladla took off ozankosi. Headed straight to his mother. And without looking down picked her up with the strength of one arm, as if he had done this one too many times for a boy his age. Walked straight to their car, and didn't look back.

On Monday, I went to fetch Eli, but he wasn't there. His mother told me he had gone back to Nigeria, to a boarding school.

'It will mean he can't come back to visit. He has fled,' I told Mrs Oko.

'It is fine, my sister. There is nothing for young boys in this country. My husband thinks it is because they cannot hit them at schools. All the students in his school call him names during assembly. The first day he came back, sister, I think my husband was drunk from the shock of white boys. The teachers did not help him. In fact, the deputy principal, who had thought he was going to get the post, also joined in with the children. What can a man do in this god-forsaken country as a foreigner? We didn't first come to Estcourt, I tell you, sister.'

My feet would not move. I guess my feet also knew how often I had wondered about how this family came to be here, in 1996 South Africa.

As if reading my mind, she continued. 'We were at the university there in Pietermaritzburg. My husband was headhunted by the incoming government even before they came in. He had been a friend to many. Ensuring others got scholarships to study, on the continent and across European universities. He, too, had studied in Germany for a few years. The Europeans love the African who comes to study; they hate the African who stays. This helped, because I prayed day and night for my husband to not want to leave Nigeria forever. Eli was conceived during one of his visits back when he was doing his post-doc. I wanted to raise my child close to home, sister.

'So that decision was easy. He came back.

'But there had been student protests at the university. Not only in Nigeria; in Ghana and Uganda too. South Africa, on the other hand, was opening up to black academics. A few of my husband's friends were at universities here. Fort Hare was the most popular. We fell in love with Fort Hare when we went to visit our friends there. But his faculty did not exist at Fort Hare. So, University of Natal it was. But no one prepared us, sister. Not for the hatred we would receive, from everyone, sister. White, black and brown.

'Eventually there were accusations made against my husband. So we were moved here, by our friends in government. A year, they promised him. Ha. Friends in government.

Politicians. It's our fault for thinking the ones in South Africa would be different. They, too, have forgotten us. One year, they said, and how many years is it now? We are approaching our fourth year, and we have lost our child as a result.

'Eli's problem, my child's problem, is he thinks he is the first one to encounter the things he has. Well, him and those loud rap artists he likes. I'll miss those,' she said. Her face brightened for less than a minute, then she said, 'And he, too, thinks he can free himself. He thinks all these things he is doing will free him, but they will not. The cycle of life is Birth–School–Work–Pension–Death. If you try to deviate, you'll be in jail, or in a mental institution. But Eli…'

Dladla started hooting outside.

'Mrs Oko, I must go,' I said.

She said nothing about Eli after that. Every time I asked she would say, 'He is fine. He is home. He is learning discipline.'

I didn't see Mrs Oko for the last few months of my time in Estcourt. A new station commander came in and began changing the way 'things worked'. Number 46 Weenen Street was Estcourt, not Wembezi jurisdiction.

Eli reminded me of my brother Bheka.

Makhosi is not quite like Eli, but they share that look in their eyes.

9

Makhosazane is the last to see her newborn sister. Her father fetches her from boarding school on a Wednesday afternoon. Thursday is a public holiday – Heritage Day – and Friday a school holiday. Makhosi runs into the maternity ward, not heeding the shouts of the nurses 'Little girl, little girl! You can't run in here!'

Her father walks in behind; not trying to stop her. Shrugging his shoulders and shaking his head in the direction of the annoyed nurses, who also shake their heads. Thulani has grown tired much faster than I have. Yet here we are, him past 40, me almost 40, about to raise another child.

Another girl child.

Makhosi has become thoughtful and caring over the years.

'No, Ma, don't buy me a new shoe. The one I used last year is still okay.'

'No, don't waste money on a new calculator. I'll use the one I have.'

Every time I try buying her new things my daughter will say, 'I will save money and get my own things.'

We send her to school with R50 every month, which is not a lot with their overpriced tuck-shop and the cheaper supermarkets being in the town, which they seldom go to. Although Makhosi does try to save, she has learned the thinner the money, the harder it is to save. She became inventive with her gift ideas, although she let go of the idea of always buying gifts.

I see she has not let go of the idea of showering gifts altogether. She gives her sister her swimming towel.

'I didn't have money, and couldn't make anything useful now. So here, sisi omncane. A towel to keep you warm,' she says, looking at the baby in my arms.

'It will be useful, sisi,' I say.

'Siyambongela. Babies need towels.' She brushes through the affirmation, something she started to do as she grew older.

'Ma, aren't you too old to have another baby?' she asks, putting out her small arms to hold the baby.

She is wearing ihiya – the red, black and white one with ihawu is her favourite – and you can see the sunburn on her skin, as ihiya wrapped around her breast-less chest. The shadow where a swimming costume has travelled her body, showing the shades of her brownness. Her arms are growing muscular, still small, but muscular from the swimming and the hockey.

MaJola, the woman who sleeps next to me in the maternity ward, laughs when she hears Makhosi's question.

'Yhuu akandwebe. Angamwisi ke umntwana,' she says.

'I'm strong,' Makhosi says, answering in a conversation about her, but not directed to her. She never has outgrown that.

'Yes, Makhosi, I am old. That's why you have to look after her. Be a good older sister,' I say, trying to hide Makhosi's response.

MaJola was at the hospital when I arrived. A complication, I presumed. Her family mostly came with people from church to pray for her. She and her husband had met at a church conference in Queenstown, she told me. He was a teacher turned evangelist turned pastor of his own church. Reviving the Children of God Ministry. MaJola's husband walks into the hospital ward holding his many cell phones and big keys in his hands. His congregants walk behind, with their heads facing the floor, Bibles in their hands.

'Is this your first child?' I asked MaJola.

She had three older boys, she told me. 'They do not come here with their father. Amaxesha amanintsi he comes from church business to here. He doesn't have time to fetch them'.

Eventually, she asked that he fetch them, but they only came once. The boys did not look their mother in the eyes. She did not look her husband in the eyes. Everyone looked down but him. MaJola wouldn't understand that Makhosi speaks back at adults, unlike her shy boys.

'Do the boys also have to take care of her?' Makhosi asks.

'Of course, sisi, you all have to take care of her,' I say.

'She's tiny,' Makhosazane says. 'Why are children so tiny, and so pink? She doesn't look like any of us.' Still swinging her arms like she is holding one of the dolls she had as a kid.

'She looks exactly like you,' I say, laughing.

'How do you know?' Makhosi swings her arms too much, like she doesn't know how to carry heavy things. She used to swing her body too much when she put those dolls on her back too. Often giving herself a headache, often dropping the 'baby'. She stopped playing with dolls after she concluded they made her sick. She was about to make this baby sick, with how she was swinging her new sister.

'A mother always knows,' I say, stretching out my arms to suggest she return the baby before she wakes her.

Thulani, who is standing next to her, sees my concern, as Makhosi moves her body further away from my arms. Moving her knees up and down too much too. Watching her is making me feel dizzy. Her father does not try to take the baby out of Makhosi's hands. He lets her bounce around, asking questions.

'Umntwana, sisi?' I remind her. She hands me her sister then sits on the bed staring down at her.

'Which school will she go to? Will she also go to boarding school? Why did you name her uNonhle?'

She doesn't seem to notice I am tired, and in pain. Or that her movements are making me dizzy. She opens and closes the blanket, trying to play with the baby.

'She'll go to whatever school you go to,' I tell her. My answer is insufficient.

'But by the time I am in Grade 7, she will still be a baby. She won't be able to come to the same school as me,' she says.

'We'll have to ask you when she needs to go to school which school you'd like her to go to then.'

'Why is her name Nonhle?' Makhosi asks, reading the

name on the hospital band. She has stopped bouncing and is now looking intensely at her sister. She removes the layer of blanket to look at her stomach. Her legs. Touches her nose. Tries to get her to hold her finger.

The task of giving names was never mine. I don't care to explain.

'Intombazane enhle,' I say.

This seems to satisfy her. She is no longer concentrating on my responses. She is fascinated by her little sister.

I am glad Makhosazane is nine years older than her sister. She will help me raise her. It's tough raising a girl child, easier when they have someone else to look up to. I hope… no, I pray… that Nonhle will ask fewer questions than Makhosazane. Perhaps be less troublesome in school.

Her father is getting more and more frustrated with the constant phone calls from the school. Outside the fact that Makhosazane demands that her father be at every activity she is involved in. School plays, the choir, hockey, swimming. There aren't enough days in the week. It doesn't help that Nombulelo has just moved to England. She has been very helpful with Makhosazane, often tiring her out during the day so that she won't ask a lot of questions later. On some days, Nombu did not mind answering all the questions, often answering questions with questions, which made Makhosi have to reflect and rethink. Keeping her quiet and in her thoughts for periods of time. But she would always return with an answer and counter question. Sometimes hours later, sometimes a day later. Whatever the activity, Makhosi needs constant presence, and Nombu, to a big extent, provided that.

'Pick your talents like you pick your struggles. Pick one,' her father tried joking with her. He regretted it soon after.

'People don't choose their struggles, Baba,' Makhosi said. 'Look at uMa. She has the struggle of cooking when she gets home, and being pregnant, and having to go chase criminals. Ma has many struggles.'

Her father didn't have a quick enough response. He was

running out of responses for his daughter the older she grew. So, he avoided her questions.

'I'm watching the news, I'm reading the newspaper, I need to go.' Those were his quick escapes. Even those soon didn't provide excuses enough for our daughter, not once Nombu moved away and me always at work.

Nkosana, the brother Makhosi is the closest to, is in his final year of school. He, too, is busy. Attending study groups elokishini. Attending extra classes at the university on weekends. Mpumelelo and Makhosi were born too close after each other as siblings. Their interactions always end in some fight, where Mpumelelo will remind Makhosi he is older; and Makhosi will point out: 'But you're not the oldest.'

'Can't you watch and listen?' Makhosi asked her father once. Thulani just walked out. He spoke to her less, and less. I think she saw it. She loves her father. They used to go shopping together during her quarterly breaks. Gradually, she started withdrawing from him as well. Asked less of him, spoke to him less.

I am grateful Makhosazane will be there with Nonhle. To assist where we fall short. Perhaps, if Nonhle does become as inquisitive as she is, Makhosi will be the one to answer her questions.

'Hospitals really smell bad,' Makhosi says.

The ward breaks out in laughter. She can be a comedian – like Thulani used to be once I got to know him. In front of strangers he was reserved and poised. With his friends and family he was the life of the party. Constantly coming up with punchlines. The drunker he became, the funnier he became. His daughter does not need a familiar crowd, or alcohol.

As soon as Thulani and Makhosi have left, the women in the ward comment on how inquisitive my daughter is. How smart she seems to be.

'It must be really tough raising ingane yentombazane ephaphile, esemaningi kangaka amantombazane aboshwayo. Kakhulukazi phela, uyiphoyisa,' MaJola says.

'Hayi kanti kubalulekile ukuthi, we separate our work spaces from our home spaces,' I lie.

Nonhle will be good for Makhosi. She will finally watch a person grow up after her.

On my last day at work, before I went on my maternity leave, I arrested a boy who looked like my colleague's husband's child, his spitting image. I was tired, and seven months pregnant, running after little boys. I was tired.

A few days later, I heard it was indeed uZondi's love child. He was nineteen. He died in the holding cells after I left. There is a pending investigation.

I spent that night praying in my room. Unable to practise 'leave your work at work', a slogan from group training and counselling. On that day, I asked God if ever a member of the people I worked for, and represented, ever laid their hands on my child, that they may be merciful to them. That they will think: What if this is a child of someone I know?

Meanwhile MaJola has continued talking.

'Ey, ngafa ukhakhathala othi ngilale,' I say.

We had just moved from Wembezi to Sobantu in Pietermaritzburg. I had received a promotion to lieutenant general. Wembezi was still healing from the wounds of udlame. Arrests were still seen as politically influenced, even though you did not belong to any political party. The difference of where you made the arrest, a demarcating street, determined whether you were IFP or ANC.

There had been little change eWembezi after the elections. What Wembezi had been before udlame, it became worse after. Many houses had been left derelict, allowing for naughty boys to smoke dagga and rape girls. We had been working with the local and regional government in trying to get families back to their houses. Many people had fled in the middle of night for their safety; others fled during attacks. At least children and women were spared from being gunned down, but the older children would be recruited, and the women often raped. It was hard to convince people to return, to tell them Wembezi was now safe. Not with the new wave of taxi violence.

'Yaze yangakwazi ukuphumula nansi indawo,' a colleague of mine who had grown up in Wembezi, and now worked there, once said.

She told stories of sleeping at the top of the mountain behind the Wagendrift dam when the violence had been at its peak.

Between herself, her mother and her sisters, they put the toddlers on their backs, telling the older children to run before them. They lay at the top of a mountain seven kilometres away and they watched houses burn. Constantly in fear that their house was next. Their house never was. Her father had been a chief and Methodist pastor eDutch, a rural area on the outskirts of Estcourt. He was known for his ability to mediate; and negotiate. When the violence broke out, the church sent him to come live in the area as a possible deterrence of violence. He was in the church trying to keep the peace between the rivalling groups when a group of men ran into the church. He was caught by a stray bullet which killed him right there, below the statue of Jesus. A scapegoat. The community had remorse and showed pity towards her and her mother.

It was during one of the rounds of clearing up the derelict houses for a family that wanted to move back to eWembezi that I found Zondi's child. He had been sniffing benzine in one of the houses, cold and alone, late at night. I arrested him, also to keep him warm and safe. It was a cold winter's night, and it had snowed in the Drakensberg.

'Leave your work at home,' I had been trained.

We moved to Sobantu to start afresh, so I could leave my work at home. A different place would do all my children good.

Nkosana was also in high school now and easily influenced.

Makhosi had already moved to a boarding school in Pietermaritzburg. St Marie's School for Girls. She was on another partial sports scholarship. The 'part' we had to pay for, the trips and the dinners, were not covered. Saving on petrol would be useful for the household.

And a new child was on the way.

PART TWO

10

Makhosazane

I am not there when my family moves from Wembezi to Sobantu. Which I do not mind, because it means I cannot help with the moving.

Ma often says ngiyivila; uBaba yena says I am tired.

'Muyeke aphumule,' he tells uMa.

'You spoil her,' Ma says. Often.

I don't think uBaba spoils me; I think he is just lazy like me. When I am home, and Ma asks us to do big things like cleaning the yard or painting something, when uBaba gets tired he says he is taking me somewhere. Somewhere means a place for him to sit, think and drink.

uBaba doesn't think long about my questions like uMa does. He seems to answer with the first thing that comes to his mind. Maybe he already knows the questions I am going to ask before I ask them. He is getting older, and wisdom does not seem to come with age for him. He ignores me more, or simply shakes or nods his head, which is not as fun as real responses. Can he feel himself get old, and lazier, and more tired? I wonder. Can he see himself trying less and less?

He takes me to his drinking places more when we move to Pietermaritzburg. He doesn't have as many friends here, and the yards eSobantu are smaller than the yards eWembezi.

Even when he sits on the veranda, he has no one to talk to. Has no news to update me on. Maybe it's not that he is not growing wiser, maybe it's because he is still trying to figure this place out. That's what wise people do. Observe and understand first. That is what my English teacher says.

'Understand and observe the text before you start answering. Read it slowly, then observe the room and feel the energy. Text inspires feeling, response. Look around the rest of the room and feel the text. It will allow you to answer better, and more in depth.'

I struggle with doing this; observing, seeing settings and being patient.

The answer always seems to be right there, not on the unnecessarily filled walls in our classrooms, or outside across the rugby field. But Mrs Radley says I would do better if I wasn't always in such a hurry. She takes my pen or pencil away for ten minutes to give me reading time before I answer her questions. It's true; I get better marks now. But not because the answers are in the setting, no. Mostly, I look down and stare at my uniform. At a stain from lunch earlier, seeing that the blue parts of the checked uniform are fading more and more. The blocks that were once white, when I first got here, are becoming less white. But so is the school. It's changed so much over the years. When I first got there, the walls looked so much whiter walking out from the school reception to the direction of the school hall, but now I can see the traces of all the children's fingers that have run up and down those walls. On some of the walls, the paint has fallen off because of prestik, and you can see the grey cement under the white walls. At the end of the corridor, just past the hall, are the stairs to my class. uAuntie Joyce cleans them every day, but still after lunch some children have touched them with their sticky hands they didn't wash after break and it gets dirty again. Mrs Radley hands me back my pen.

The ten minutes is over, and I can start writing again. I have forgotten the instructions, so the ten minutes doesn't actually help me read. But it does help me calm down before I can start my tests.

That's what uBaba is doing, feeling and observing iSobantu. He wanted to stay eWembezi. I heard him and uMa have this conversation. Ma desperately wanted to move, and uBaba kept saying we can't run away from problems.

The house had a big crack in the lounge which uMa had been telling uBaba to get someone to fix the last time I had been home. That was the only problem I saw in the house. And I did think moving was going to be good for everyone. The new house is smaller, but it has a big outside room for Nkosana. A few holidays ago, uMa asked him to stop sleeping in his room outside eWembezi. Something about his safety. Maybe she knew iSobantu would be safer for him.

And, there is a new baby. My baby sister, uNonhle. Intombi enhle, uBaba calls her. She is a lot younger than me, which I don't mind. When she gets to primary, I will be in high school and when she gets to high school, I will be in university. I will be an older sister, taking her to the mall and the library on Sundays and teaching her everything I know about being a girl. Not that I know a lot, but the girls in my dorm try to teach me.

Our hostel is a double-storey, face brick building like many buildings in our school, except on the second floor of this building there are five dorms, and three bathrooms. The Grade 7 dorm and the prefect dorm have their own entrances.

On our entrance of the hostel, the Grade 4 and 5 dorm, you find the first burglar gate, on your right. The Grade 6 dorm is further down the passage, furthest from Matron. The Junior dorm is on the opposite end of the passage, through the burglar gate on the left, past the student assistant and Matron's flat. In the Grade 4 and 5 dorm we have eighteen beds, nine beds on each side opposite each other. A curtain separates us from the beds next to us, but not the beds opposite us. Beside our beds are bedside tables, which are meant for our books and a lamp. We can only use the bedside lamp between 8 and 8:30 pm, during quiet time.

Christa's dorm, the Grade 6 dorm, unlike ours, has curtains that go all the way around like in a hospital. Whereas our lockers are still in the passage, opposite the dormitory, the Grade 6s' lockers are in their cubicles.

Christa loves asking me to visit her cubicle to dress me up in her clothes and kiss me. The other day, in the bathroom stall, she showed me a tampon and asked me to put it up her vagina. I think Christa is my girlfriend. She is twelve, in Grade 6, and she tells people we are girlfriend and girlfriend.

'Why should I put it up for you?' I asked her.

'I am showing you how to be a girl. First, you must put your finger up here,' she said, as she opened her legs. 'Go down. You won't see standing.' Her leg was on the toilet seat. She asked me what I could see. I didn't know what to say, so she took my hand and led it to where I should put the tampon. She asked me to put my finger further and further up as she giggled. It was wet.

'See? that's how you put on a tampon,' she said. Washing my hand wet from her vaginal juices in the same basin we washed our faces every morning. I decided that day I was not going to ever wear a tampon.

I will teach Nonhle about pads. Pads are what I've seen in Life Orientation class anyway.

But Christa tells me pads are for small girls not big girls. I think even when I am a big girl, though, I will not like putting things up my vagina. But I do like putting my fingers up Christa's vagina. We do it every month, and other times she asks me to put my fingers in there without a tampon, which I like more.

'Ma, if you're an adult, why don't you use tampons?' I ask.

'Ayabiza.' Ma looks at me, shaking her head.

I had wanted Ma to ask me how I know about tampons. Or to at least tell me something I can follow up her answer with. I wanted to ask her whether all people learn to put tampons on like that. When I told Christa I wanted to ask my mom because I couldn't imagine her doing that, Christa told me not to.

'You're going to get in trouble,' she said. 'Your parents are going to start thinking you're acting older than you are, and parents don't like that.'

She wasn't lying. Ma says that to Nkosana, a lot.

'If uzenza mdala mfana wami, hamba uyoba mdala mase unekwakho.' Nkosana has started coming home late, but he is older. Much older.

'Angeke ngifuye isigebengu mina la kwami,' Ma once said when Nkosana came back after a burglary had happened on our street. uMa was often very worried her sons would, could, also get arrested.

'Hambani nje ebusuku, nizoboshelwa into engekho ngoba anazi nenzani ezindaweni zabelungu. Ngingahlushwa mina,' Ma shouts.

The boys don't seem to take much notice of that anymore.

'So, I can ask her when I'm twelve?' I asked Christa.

'Only if you want to be shouted at for doing things with girls,' she said. 'Parents don't like it either, girls sleeping with girls. That's why the Grade 7 and Prefects' dorms have their own entrances, and are so far from the Matron. It's so the Matron doesn't see when girls are sleeping with each other. It must be hidden.'

I have not slept with Christa, even though she says that's what everyone does. That's how you'll get caught, she said. I haven't even had my period yet. Maybe I will ask when I am older.

11

Nonhle

Sobantu is where I was born, and raised.
   2879 Khumalo Road
   Sobantu
   Pietermaritzburg 3201
   Between Town and Northdale. It is an industrial area; that is what you call a place that has many factories. It is also home to the sewer 'for the whole of Pietermaritzburg', my sister tells me. Both those words: 'sewer' and 'industrial'. An industrial sewage township. I believe it too. Every time visitors come, they complain about the smell. So I guess it is for the whole of Pietermaritzburg, because why doesn't it smell like that where they come from?
   uMa works in the police station in Northdale. The Indian area. She is always going to neighbours' houses to report people's sons for breaking into the Indian houses. Mountain Rise. I always wanted to live there.
   Our cousin Sphesihle, she went to school in the white area, Clarendon. She told me how rich white people are. We went to fetch her on our way to kaGogo the one time. The Indian houses were a lot bigger than the white houses. The Indian schools are not very expensive, even though they are also

good schools. The schools elokishini are cheap, but they are not good schools, everyone says.

My brother Mpumelelo goes to an Indian school. He walks to school, because he is a big boy; and because uBaba says it's not far. I take itransport to school, unless I am staying at school late. Then Lelo fetches me and catches a taxi with me. It is longer to take a taxi though, because first ugibela eya eTown in Maritzburg, then you come to Sobantu, even though Sobantu is next to Mountain Rise and Northdale. There are no taxis going straight from Northdale to Sobantu.

Makhosi and Mpumelelo were already in high school when I was in Grade 1, and Nkosana was at university. The University of Durban-Westville. He had gone there to study to be a chartered accountant. So in the house it was myself and Lelo.

Nothing interesting happens in our lives, unlike in Nkosana and Makhosi's lives.

Every time Makhosi comes back from school she has a new word to teach me and many stories to tell. Nkosana didn't come back often, but when he did, uBaba told everyone he ran into that his son was going to be an accountant. 'Chartered accountant,' Nkosana corrected him.

'Kona lokho, i-accountant,' Baba said, completely ignoring that clearly to Nkosana, the 'chartered' before the 'accountant' mattered. I didn't know what an accountant was, but I knew Nkosana was at a university with many other students who were all there to learn more after they learned in high school.

Nkosana stayed at university for a long time. Never becoming an accountant. I am not sure who was disappointed more, him or uBaba. By the time I got to Grade 4, he was studying to be a teacher. Accounting is hard, I heard family members say, sounding sad and ashamed for him. I didn't understand why, and no one cared to explain. I asked Mpumelelo once, and he said something about peaking too soon. I hate when he says things he knows I don't understand, and then continues, saying, 'ngikuphendulile nje.'

Mpumelelo didn't go to university. He went to a college in town, which was great for me because I didn't want to be left alone in the house with uMa noBaba. They don't say much to each other. Lelo tells me sometimes it wasn't always like that. He says uBaba used to be uMa's personal comedian and entertainment. I can't see it. For as long as I have known both of them, they hardly say anything to each other, with the exception of the days when uBaba starts a fight. Even then uMa responds calmly, walks out from whatever room he is in.

The one time uBaba was drunk and tried following uMa, Lelo went and dragged uBaba out. uBaba screamed and shouted that Lelo was acting like the man of the house, that he was hitting him. Lelo left uBaba laying on the sofa next to me. 'Uyangishaya uMpumelelo, Nonhle, uyambona? Uyangishaya,' he slurred.

I poured uBaba a glass of water and brought him back to reality. No one had hit him. Lelo only pulled him away. He fell asleep while I was trying to calm him down. Mumbling something about failures. I went to sleep with uMa that day. Thought she would need it. Lelo didn't come back into the house until the next morning, but I was glad he was close, living in the back room at the back of the house.

Makhosi has a scholarship for sport, which sometimes means that even on the weekends she is supposed to be at home, she is away with some practice, or some tour. Or day and night games. When she got in the Natal Midlands team, we saw her less and less.

Lelo did not stay in college long. When I was in Grade 4, he started working in a factory in town. Which was great for uMa because I was almost in high school and Nkosana was about to finish his teaching degree. Nkosana would move to Johannesburg to teach when he was finished. uMa was worried he wouldn't have enough money to help in the house because

Johannesburg is expensive. Lelo is always there though. So I don't need to worry about things I can't fix, like money.

Coz you gave me a heart, and you gave me a smile.
You gave me Jesus, and you gave me a
I just want to thank you, Jesus, for making meeee...

It is a Sunday morning and the song, no, the hymn, as I had learned at Clarendon.

H Y M N pronounced like H I M.

English does that.

Bhut' Bantu is in his house, smoking insangu, as he does on Sundays. Did Jesus make him, I wondered. Did Jesus make people babheme insangu? Bhut' Bantu is my father's friend and our neighbour. Mama does not like him much, perhaps because he used to come into Mama's house and ask her for insangu sometimes. He does that less now. He is a big man elokishini. Usesebenza kaMaspala.

On Sundays I like sitting on our side of the fence listening to him and uBaba talk. Although uBaba doesn't talk much. He mostly nods. He does the same thing even with uMa.

'Hhe, Timer, abantu abakholwayo ayikho indaba yabo. Ayikho brazo uMaka Mfundo she was here last night. Asking me to help get that no-good son of hers a job. Hahaha. Me? Get her son a job. Angithi yena uyathandaza? Why engathandazi ke? Ngiyakutshela, Timer, this thing of people who say they pray. God helps those who help themselves.'

Baba, as always, just makes sounds. 'Sho ntwana,' here and there.

Bhut' Bantu is very clever. I heard elokishini that insangu makes people very clever, up until they end up behlala emakhoneni, but Bhut' Bantu never sat emakhoneni, and he was respected, unlike the other nsangwinis elokishini.

Except the one time I heard Bhut' Bantu say, 'There is no God, Timer. Into ewuNkulunkulu ayikho ngikutshele.'

My feet carried me into the house as if they, too, did not want to hear.

No God?

I couldn't ask uMa. She would shout at me for listening to izinto zabantu abadala.

You cannot unhear something you have heard. So sometimes, when I no longer want to hear things, I stop listening.

I try to remember the song I had been singing. No, the hymn. My head hurts. My head does that sometimes, when I think about too many things I cannot unhear. It just hurts.

The one time, I heard Bhut' Bantu's girlfriend shouting at uMa from across the yard, saying, 'I'phoyisa elinjani takes insangu to come sell elokishini?' My mother, selling insangu? I was very angry with that woman that day. It was Bhut' Bantu with his lies who had confused that woman. Your boyfriend comes here and asks for insangu, I wanted to say; uMa doesn't even give him. I ran to Mpumelelo. How was he closed off in his back room hearing all this and not protecting our mother?

'Loyasisi uthi uMa udayisa insangu,' I said, huffing and puffing at his open door.

'She does what she has to do,' Mpumelelo said. 'Myeke loyasisi, she will eventually get tired of screaming. Nawe uyabona, akekho lay'khaya omnakile.' He didn't even raise his head to look at me.

My head hurt a lot that day. Did Ma…?

My head also hurts a lot at school. The English language has too many r's and when Mrs Lombard, our class teacher, speaks she uses a lot of r's. Except the r's just roll off the tongue.

R-I-C-E

R-I-S-E

R-I-G-H-T

Sometimes words that start with w sound like they start with r's.

WRONG, WRITE, WREATH.

'Non-shle!' Mrs Lombard calls on me to read.

Nonshle?

I am confused by both her ability to know when and how to not pronounce w's, but also her inability to pronounce my name. That, and the r's that roll off her tongue such that by the time she is finished I have counted the r's and been thinking of silent w's and have forgotten to listen to what she is saying.

Her cold stare and the way she looks at me and shakes her head makes my head hurt more. She says a few more words. This time I focus hard. Look at her face and read the expressions, I tell myself. But she turns her back and talks while walking back to the front of the class.

She has stopped asking me to read. They only call me shy now.

Some of the learners in my class have learned to mimic the sounds and expressions that Mrs Lombard makes when they read.

I wonder how their heads do not hurt. Maybe, maybe it is because practice makes perfect and they practise at home. We do not speak isingisi ekhaya, except when Makhosi is home. Makhosi speaks like her head doesn't hurt from all the r's.

There has been a robbery at our school. Mr Gibbs announced this in assembly. Someone tried to break into the computer labs, but they were quickly seen by the security guard.

'However, it is not safe for Albert,' said Mr Gibbs. 'Albert is old now. He has worked at this school for eighteen years and anything could have happened to him. We will be moving Albert to day duty, and Thomas to night duty, but we still need to tighten the security of the school.'

Thomas and Albert are both old. Albert is even older than Mr Gibbs. I heard that Albert was the only security guard at the school for many years, until he started getting old and the doctor said the school should make his hours less. Why is he even working when he is so old? I wonder.

'Bhoooo!' The assembly went up in uproar at the news. I had stopped listening. I do that often now, stop listening. First it was because they spoke too fast; now it's because they speak too much. Prayer, announcements, class plays, more announcements, achievements, shouting... So I stopped listening.

Sometimes, like today, I miss what's being said.

Donation forms, I hear later in class when Mrs Birch tells us.

'It is for the electric fence to protect our school from criminals,' she says.

I don't mind donation forms. I just give them to uMa to get her colleagues to fill them out.

Today uMa doesn't come home at 6 pm like she normally does. I hear her come in after we have all gone to bed. Our gate makes a noise when you open it, and I am a light sleeper. I jump out of bed and go to give her the donation form. I want her to get to it tomorrow morning so that I can be the first one to return it. The first person who returns a full donation form, with more than R50, gets a merit star next to their name, and a box of chocolates. I am on the other side of the door, excited, when Ma is trying to open it. The door flies in, and Ma has blood all over her. Her eyes look sad.

I go to bed, and tell Mpumelelo in the morning. Five boys were killed trying to break into my school, we hear on the radio. Two of the boys are from eSobantu. Their parents go to church with us. When we go to church on Sunday and the deaths are announced, people look at uMa and shake their heads

Mpumelelo gives me R55 for my donation form. I do not hand the form in. I put the money in my piggy-bank. I get a demerit for not handing in the form.

Clarendon has a gymnasium and a computer lab. Even some of the classrooms, and offices, have computers. Maybe the people who tried stealing the computers wanted to put them in a school elokishini. None of the schools elokishini have computer labs or a gymnasium.

I wonder if Jesus made those boys the way they were too. Did he make them steal those computers?

The air changes when spring begins. The mood and rhythm of places too.

eSobantu, the what-were-white jerseys of the Matric students turn a subtle cream white, bordering on light brown.

The other day, a Grade 7 debater, uSibongile – she is really good at debating – she said there is no colour called cream white, like there is no such thing as a cousin brother. She spoke very loud and confident when she said these 'facts', which I knew could not be true. The teachers, and most people at school, like Sibongile. Last year it was Siphiwe, the year before that Meghan. They eventually became head girls, and continued saying facts that surely couldn't be true. During a debate about affirmative action, Siphiwe said she had never ever in her life been in a taxi. She was on the side proposing the motion 'Affirmative action assumes all black people are the same'.

'It's reverse racism,' she said.

Something about her having never been in a taxi, yet affirmative action thinking all black people were poor... The school hall erupted in chaos, a few of the students calling her 'sell-out'. I laughed so loud, on the inside though. I just laughed. It's just, yazi abazi.

The Matric jerseys do turn cream white, but it matters less and less now because they are writing their trials. Which means they are in school less and less. The September school holiday is approaching, which means December is approaching.

eMpofana, the harvest is coming. Umbila is my favourite food that grows around this time. We start eating it towards the end of November, into December. Roasting it in the oven section of the coal stove. Roasting it in the fire erondweni laMkhulu, roasting it outside as we sit around the fire with my cousins. It is warm in the evenings, and you can see the stars more clearly emakhaya. Hear the cows mooing, as they prepare to fall asleep. I think cows sleep, because eventually they start laying on the ground of isibaya. They lie in their own dung and sleep. The sound emakhaya changes more slowly than the sound elokishini. The houses are further apart. Sometimes elokishini, even when the night begins to fall and people go into their houses, if whatever is happening next door is loud enough, we can still hear it. Like Bhut' Bantu's mother shouting at him for not closing the door and letting the smell of insangu come into her house.

'Yeyi, weBantu ikwami la. Fuquza le nsangu yakho le kude!'

We did not see uGogo kaSamke often. She was old, and bedridden. She has been bedridden for as long as I have known Samke. Samke is Bhut' Bantu's daughter. She visits only during the school holidays so we only see each other for a few days, but she is my friend. Her father fetches her before schools officially close because they are no longer doing anything at school. My cousins emakhaya do that too, stop going to school a few weeks before school officially closes. My school has activities all through to the last day, which is often prize-giving. I sing in the choir, so I can't miss school because we are practising for the prize-giving. Other learners are practising for the Christmas play, which happens the evening before prize-giving.

Samke and I joke about exchanging lives in the few days we spend together. She lives very far away, which is why she only visits during the holidays, kwaNongoma. She says they drive for four hours from there to here. Samke lives with her mother's family and comes elokishini to visit. I live elokishini and go to my mother's family emakhaya to visit.

I tell Samke about the new girls on the street. I don't know a lot of the new girls because uMama tells me to never play on the street. Our gate is always closed, not really locked, but it's closed and uninviting and the children don't really invite me to play with them. Sometimes I see them standing on the other side of the gate after a ball has fallen to our side of the yard, and they are too scared to ask. I think they are scared of uMa, which I find funny. Samke doesn't know any of this. Her father drops her off with us in the morning and we stay inside the house together. Often, I make up stories about the other children's lives. Just for fun.

Samke teaches me how to not get pricked by amajingijolo, the wild berries that my cousins and I sometimes go pick. My older cousins ask us for our berries, even when they don't go. I hear they all used to go up to pick wild berries, even Nkosana, Makhosi and Mpumelelo. The older you get, the less you want to go pick the berries, even though you still want to eat them. Samke and I laugh about this. We still like berries enough to want to pick our own.

If you ask other people to bring you berries, they will pick all the big juicy dark ones for themselves; and give you the red ones that are almost still hard, but close to ready. That's what I do to my cousins, pick the best ones for myself; the not so great ones I give to them. Especially when the berries are almost finished, or when we have to go further and further up in the mountain to get them. The further and further you go, the more thorns cut and tear you. It hurts a little, but mostly it itches when you bathe. Some of the children wear amadadla, but I struggle to walk in them. Samke tells me I should wear long pants.

The thorns get stuck in my pants sometimes, after I have even forgotten that I picked berries; when they are all well settled in my stomach and my hands are a dark purple, laying in the sun watching uGogo working on imfino. She peels the leaves of imfino, which she picks in her garden. When I was younger, I thought it was spinach, like the one elokishini, but it's a different plant altogether. It grows really low and has small prickly things on its skin. It's the prickly things uGogo tries to pick out. I tried too, but I ended up tearing the whole leaf apart and getting frustrated.

'Umosha ukudla', Gogo said. So I stopped. Just laying

next to her is the best I can do. A thorn I didn't know was there pricked at me from the inside of my pants, provoked by the littlest of movements on my part. Then I had to sit there, trying to turn my track pants inside out so I could pick out the thorn. One time I tried sticking my hand down my pants, to find the thorn from the inside, but uGogo slapped my hand. She said it looked wrong.

Adults make the smallest things 'wrong' in their heads, I remember thinking.

Sometimes uGogo sits next to me cleaning out the cobs zombila. The cobs we do not cook yet; she puts erondweni lakhe to let them dry. We will pick out the corn pieces off the cob; roasting and boiling the dried corn. Izinkobe are my favourite snack in January. Just before I go back to school. We do not make fires eSobantu. So even though uGogo sends me home with a lot of corn, I cannot roast them, boil them and add a bit of salt. Make izinkobe.

When I was younger uGogo would send me away with umphako, ujeqe nenyama yenkukhu that is boiled and salted. uGogo knows we have chicken at home, in the fridge. Braai packs. Which we don't use for braaing often. Just to make chicken stews and curry. Sometimes we roast it in the oven but uMa is convinced the oven uses more electricity. I begged uGogo to stop packing boiled chicken with me; it would go off before we even got home, I would argue. uGogo stopped fighting this fight and started thinking of new things to send home with me. I preferred izinkobe the most, because there was no other place in town where you could find them. Other things we could find in the city when we needed them.

There is a part of town, East Street, and the rest of downtown where you can find most of the things you find emakhaya. Imithi, and other medicines. Others already in bottles, others still in plant form. To impepho, and even foods. Ma and I go there to buy amadumbe and ubatata when their seasons have come. Amadumbe are also only boiled and eaten with a bit of salt. Salt does so much more emakhaya than it does at home. Ma has a cupboard full of spices, herbs and other things. uGogo mostly just uses salt. Her food does not confuse the tongue. In the morning, umdoko with tartaric or a squeeze of lemon. A sour breakfast. Emini we eat an often bland meal, pap, and a vegetable. Imfino, spinach, beans, sometimes pap and a potato curry. I complement lunch with the berries I go pick after. Supper, we have a well-salted meat. Three meals a day. All tasting different. Tantalising all my tastebuds without shocking them with intense tastes.

The food Makhosi makes is the reason Ma's cupboards keep growing in things we don't know. Worcester sauce and soy sauce are the newest of our additions.

'Too salty,' I told Makhosi.

'Too cheesy,' I told her the night before, when she made a macaroni and cheese meal, which was dripping oily cheap cheese.

'I am tantalising your tastebuds,' my sister said.

I didn't know what tantalising meant, but I knew my tastebuds did not need to be tantalised.

'Does your mother like your father?' Samke asks me.

We are going through my crate of toys, looking for something, anything to play with. I know there is nothing in there, I never use the toys in this crate anymore.

'Ye?' I ask.

'I think. I thought. I...'

'uMa wakho, uyamthanda uBaba wakho?'

'I don't know. I mean, I think so. Why do you ask?'

'I don't know... I just. I have wondered. Women emakhaya stand by the tap, especially after their husbands have left; catching up on each other's horrible husbands. The women who don't go to stand by the tap and gossip, I think they like their husbands. So, I don't know. I wonder whether the women here all like their husbands, or they just don't have taps to stand next to and chat about their husbands. So, I wonder if they love them. Like the women on TV, they all love their husbands. I wish Ma lived elokishini or on TV,' Samke says, defeated that all the toys are broken.

'Nobody lives on TV,' I say, happy there is something I know.

'I know, Nonhle. It's just what I imagine. Like when you imagine all the girls on the street are your friends and you pretend to know about them.'

Samke had been invited to play uBha with the other girls the day before. She came to invite me too, but I said I was reading. I knew uBaba would not let me play outside. And he didn't like the girl in particular who asked uSamke to play with them.

'Ugcwala umgwaqo, nabafana', uBaba said.

I didn't need to ask. They must've told Samke that I never left the house. She must have found out I was making it all up.

Makhosi sometimes says uMa wanted her to go far because they do not love her. She tried saying that to uMa once. Ma laughed and said, 'Mxm, don't come here with your funny ideas of love. Love is sending your child to a good school because she is clever and that is what she deserves.'

We are leaving for Mpofana in three days. I get sick and don't need to see Samke again.

Makhosi comes back home with lots of stories about her friends in boarding school.

'Sisi…'

'Hmmm?'

Like always, Makhosi has buried herself in a book.

'Do you think Ma loves uBaba?'

She stares at me from the side of her eye. 'Yini lona uthando?'

I don't know.

'Your school, it has an electric fence angithi?'

'Yes,' she says, this time not moving her head.

'Would they shoot people for breaking past that electric fence?'

'For what, school supplies? There is nothing in our schools worth killing people over.'

The sewer burst eSobantu. The sewerage travels all along the roads, turning and curving, not bothered by the children who are trying to play around it.

'Also lala,' Makhosi commands. 'We're travelling!'

12

Makhosazane

Dear Mrs Zungu

We request a meeting with you to discuss the conduct of your daughter on Friday the 17th of May 2004. 10:30 am, in the principal's office.

GStLedger
ST Ledger
Principal – St Marie's School for Girls

'Arghh, uMa won't come wethu. Also, wena vele uzomnikelani?'
 'What if they have called her?'
 'We will know then. Cross that bridge when we get to it. Also, though, what did we do wrong, really? We held hands.'
 'And we kissed!'
 'We pecked on the cheek, Za. It wasn't that serious.'
 She does that, Zama. I've known her since junior primary school. We went to the same school in Mooi River, then both got partial scholarships to St Marie's. Most of us, the black girls who live in hostels, are on scholarships. It is easy to see

that we were on scholarship, too, because on weekends the white girls go home, no matter how far home is; those of us on scholarship only go home on the weekends scheduled for home, no matter how close home is. Mpofana is close to Mooi River. All my aunts and cousins are close, but they never fetch me. Zama's mother also lives close to Mooi River, eMthulini, and she doesn't visit often either.

We are children; we like kissing each other. Everywhere, especially at the hostel. Our Matron lives downstairs, and the boarder mistresses are girls who are older and go to a college in town somewhere, and they don't care what we do so long as our rooms are clean. Zama doesn't mind us kissing at hostel, like she minds us kissing at school.

She's started getting serious about God. It's that pastor man who comes to the school for SCO on Fridays. St Marie's is an Anglican school, but they allow for SCO, Muslim holidays as well. Provided we go to chapel. Most of the girls from the hostel find chapel boring, so they started going to SCO. A lot of them are changing too.

Zama is suddenly finding it very tough kissing me. She tells me homosexuality is a sin. Whatever the hell that means. I used to be able to say fuck around her too, the only person I could say fuck around. I say hell instead now. WHAT THE HELL? Although it doesn't sound the same as WHAT THE FUCK? I say what the hell though, to make her happy. She isn't as happy as she used to be in primary school. Now everything is a sin and Jesus doesn't like it, and and and…

I pretended I didn't want to get caught that day. But maybe I did. Everyone is a damn fucken lesbian; I mean, I think so.

Lesbian. A woman who is attracted to women. We learned that in LO the other day. Everyone giggled, I think because most girl have kissed girls here. The older ones may be having sex. Except, we've had a few people get suspended for that.

Our LO teacher, who is also the art teacher, told us that although the school does not allow lesbians, lesbians do exist.

In the real world. We just need to get older and more aware of ourselves before we make the final decision. Like the decision to have a child. We learned about the pros and cons of being a lesbian, even though our teacher told us she was not meant to teach us this. She did not survive in the school long. Most art teachers don't.

'One pro of lesbianism is that you won't have an unplanned pregnancy,' she said.

Two older girls from our hostel were suspended for being pregnant. The whole idea somewhat freaks me out. From the—

'Stop with this thing of yours. It was funny when we were children, but we are women now!' Zama screams at me.

'The hell, Za? Calm the hell down. How are we even women, if we get shouted at for kissing? Women do whatever the fuck they want.'

I've gotten carried away. Za walks away.

'Yes.' I said fuck. 'Fuck, fuck, fuck.'

She'll come back. She always does. I need to walk her to town. Also, she needs to sit next to me in biology class.

'Why were you screaming profane language on the field, Makhu?'

The principal had been walking behind us when I was screaming at Zama. She does that, this old woman, creeps up on students with her inaudible steps. It's how she catches so many people in the act, none of us can ever hear her coming. In class, if the teacher is not there and we want to do our own thing, we often need to have a look-out person, who will warn us when she is approaching.

'My name is MA-KHO-SA-ZANE, miss.'

'I know what your name is!'

'Then please call me by my full name, miss.'

'Enough! Enough with you now! You will be getting two Saturday detentions for that!'

'Manje kazi ucabanga ukuthi kub'hlungu yini,' I mumble under my breath.

'What are you saying? Speak English! This is STILL an English school, do you hear me?' she screams.

'I am asking if you are done so I can leave, miss?'

'YOU LISTEN HERE, YOU WILL... LEAVE... WHEN....'

She is not going to stop screaming, so I decide to walk into the classroom. The door bangs behind me but I can still hear her screaming, no doubt turning vermilion, or whatever colour it is that white people turn when black people refuse to obey.

Of course she follows me into my class.

'FOUR SATURDAY DETENTIONS, YOU HEAR ME? FOUR!'

The class roars in laughter, which makes our principal look even more ridiculous. She walks out and Mrs Bailey, our biology teacher, continues as if nothing has happened.

Zama has saved me my seat at the back of the class, where Mrs Bailey can't be bothered if we talk or not. She only teaches people who want to learn, she claims, when in honesty she doesn't want to teach at all.

'I really don't have time to listen to these people. Saturday detention? In boarding school? White people really need to get serious about punishment. I hate this school, Zama. I hate everything about it. Their brown shoes, what the hell is up with brown shoes? Their big English language, them telling us to walk up straight, to not chew gum, to not eat and walk, to tie our hair, three fingers above the knee. Don't run in the corridors. Rules, rules, stupid white people rules.'

'How is don't chew gum a stupid white people rule?' Zama asks with a smirk on her face.

'Arghh, you know what I mean,' I snap.

'I do, but you're ridiculous when you are angry. You do the same when you are angry with God, you connect everything to him.'

'Dude, are you really bringing your Jesus into this?'
'He is your Jesus too, MK.'
'I don't have a Jesus, man. I am all I have got.'
'You have me, and I come with God and He loves everyone I love. So, you have Him. Also, you sound like a teenage boy every time you say dude, and man. We're girls.'
'Are you hearing yourself? Really hearing yourself? Mxm, uzosangana wena iloJesu wakho ng'yak'tshela.'

It is free weekend. I hear my uBaba's Toyota Cressida from down the road. It is an old car, but he refuses to change it. It's a sky blue-ish colour, or it used to be. The other kids run to him when they hear the car. It's like the school siren, except this sound draws you to something you like. I wait for him to finish entertaining them before I go to the car. Drop my bags in the boot and get into the empty passenger seat.

'Banjani ekhaya?' I ask.
'Bayaphila,' he replies, offering his signature one-word response.

Free weekend is the one weekend you look forward to as a boarder. uBaba makes the best breakfast on Sundays, makes the whole kitchen look like it has been hit by inkanyamba for uMa to clean up after. Maybe that's why uMa skips church so much. It tastes good though. There is no pattern. My father is very similar to me, can't survive patterns. Can hold on only for years, like he has done with his job. Or he does sometimes with us. I have seen him escape us, run away, not allow himself to be bothered by us. Just live his life. Under the same roof. Except for the Sunday breakfasts. The only routine, that and this drive home.

'Ungakuphi westhandwa sami, kuyabanda apha ekhaya. Uzobuya nini wedali wami. Oh ngiyagodola.'

I have come to understand Ringo and Tracy Chapman as my take-me-home songs. Like iculo lomncwabo, taking me to a resting place. Home, my mother's house. My bedroom turned Nonhle's room and storeroom. So maybe uBaba likes some patterns. He has changed through the years, always finding something new to complain about at the very least. Fidgety, Mrs Radley calls it.

'What the hell is weekend uniform?' Mbali asks.

'It's uniform that you wear on weekends. It's not like a skirt and shirt. It's shorts and a T-shirt. Red and blue shirts, three of each, and five pairs of shorts.'

'Ngobani though?' They laugh as Njabulo asks that.

'So that kungabonakali ukuthi ubani onganamali, ubani ongenayo when you are together. Like uniform at school. To create a common identity nje.'

They look at me, confused, all of them. They have stopped laughing.

'Uyazizwa ukuthi uthini?' Mbali asks.

'Fuck you,' Njabulo says. 'Fuck you, actually. You know what really poor children can't do? They can't buy uniform for school and uniform for "home" and casual clothes to wear when you are on your "free" fucken weekends. Coming here telling us you are on a "free weekend". Do you know who needs a "free weekend"? We do. So we can know what this nice freedom where you can afford to hide your non-poverty feels like.'

There is itende on the street just above our street eSobantu. Right next to the factories. The speakers from itende are on a tree, right there, so that we can all hear the good news.

I have been hoping that this time I will be allowed to go with Njabulo and Mbali. Their parents let them go out at night, because it is a church. A night church. I have heard them share stories of the things they do, how they creep out of itende and go do whatever they want. They know what time the service ends, and they make their way home soon after.

They can't get caught for their lies because wherever they are Sobantu is small enough, and the speakers loud enough, for them to still be able to hear what the good news is and tell their parents, if their parents ever ask.

Driving in and seeing itende this free weekend, I ask uBaba if I can go.

'If uMbali noNjabulo are going, ungahamba nabo,' uBaba say, going back to listening to his Ringo.

I jump out the car in excitement and run straight to ask my friends if I can go with them. Every other time I have gone home, I have been in my school uniform – the checked dress with the hat – and the first thing I do, before going to my friends, is go home and change.

Today I am wearing weekend uniform. uBaba had fetched me late and Zama and I had been wrestling on the school field while we waited. The boarder mistress said we were too dirty to be seen in uniform outside the school looking like that, so we changed into weekend uniform.

Before I can even ask about going to itende with them, Njabulo looks me up and down.

'Where is that fancy uniform of yours?' she asks. 'The one you are always so quick to change out of?'

I do not go to itende with them that night.

13

Dudu

I tried calling Makhosi at school today. Hmmmm hayi inkosi impela. Yazi abantwana abazi.

Thulani keeps telling me that I spoil abantwana.

'You call her too much, you give that one too much money, you don't let me hit that one,' he preaches at me.

I wonder whether he knows I spoil him too. Doing all the parenting for him to sit and criticise. A spectator in his own children's lives.

I would argue if I thought it would take me anywhere, but you learn that it takes you nowhere with men. Especially men in positions of authority. It's like standing on quicksand. A useless task, like blowing into a horn with holes. You can blow and blow but it will not create melody. Just spits and spatters of noise. And men don't need to know they are right to continue to argue; even when they know they are wrong, they argue. Which requires a lot of energy from a generally lazy people.

And, I guess, of course when you spend your day dormant eventually you erupt. Not that Thulani erupts. He just, he sulks. No solutions. No alternatives. Just the complaining and generally looking like a wet dog trying to get attention.

The other day he came into the station drunk. Not arrested

drunk. He got drunk, then drove to the station where I work demanding to be arrested. It hadn't even been the type of day when I would expect such a tantrum from him, no. But there he was. My colleagues spotted him waddling over the rail by the stairs at the entrance of the station. They had tried to stop him while shouting for me from the back.

We had finished our day. It had been a day of celebrations and a few colleagues were gathered in the staff room. Thulani insisted on coming into the station foyer, demanding 'umfazi wakhe'. There was another couple, also a woman with her drunk man, who had been given sugar water to sober him up. There weren't enough officers at the station to drive her home. So, on the bench it was.

'Take him to the car,' I told Constable Maphanga.

Thulani tried to protest. Demanded that I take him to the car. I did not need to give him any more attention than he already had. I walked past him, out of the station to my car. Maphanga and Mkhize dropped him in the back, where he slurred and kicked.

Makhosi had taken over ten minutes to get to the phone and spent less than a minute talking to me. Because she was doing something. Some practice, for something.

'Hhe, yazi, uMakhosi, not even two minutes,' I said to Thulani, although I wasn't talking to him really; he was still laying like a blob under the sheets. 'Not even two minutes to just tell me ukuthi yena unjani. And then she will come back here and claim that we don't give her enough attention while she is at that school of hers.'

Thulani's feet were almost dangling off the bed, from him taking himself further and further down in the bed, a habit he'd also had when we were younger. I always woke up earlier than him and switched on the lights. My day always seemed to have more things to do than his. Like a snake that ate too much, he would slide down the bed, pulling the covers up above him and exposing the bottoms of his feet.

'Why ukhanyisa ekuseni kanje?' he would sulk.

'Umfazi uyasabenza,' I would joke, then pull the blankets down to cover the lower part of his feet. I don't know why I found it adorable back then. A grown man sulking from the idea of having to wake up and face responsibilities is not adorable.

We had a side lamp now, often just to read our house mail. Which Thulani also never read. Fifteen years married, and for fifteen years this man dumps all the letters regarding the house on my side of the bed. He hides the ones he doesn't want me to know about, but of course I have seen a few. They are at the back of his side cupboard, in a file with all his insurance documents, which isn't the safest place to try hide them. How is he even too lazy to keep secrets well? Again, it used to be adorable, how little he tried to hide his 'shortcomings'. Filled with apologies, and murmurs about 'It's how I am' and 'This way you know I'll never cheat… because I can't keep a secret.'

The phone also sat on my side of the bed, because Thulani was too lazy for the phone too.

I would try and call Makhosi in the mornings, when I had a little bit more time. Like this morning.

'You spoil that child. You spoil her.' Thulani woke up grumbling. 'She doesn't know the value of imali, that's why she will keep you waiting for thirty minutes. It's that private school she goes to, she thinks she is rich.'

I didn't respond, mostly because I was in shock at how quickly he managed to get up just to critique my parenting. I stepped out of the bed, jumping over one of the socks he had been wearing yesterday. He muttered something about why I wasn't picking the sock up, but I had already grabbed my gown from one of the falling wardrobe doors he was meant to fix months ago, and I headed out the bedroom.

For whatever reason Nonhle was also in a foul mood. It was 5:55 am, and she knew she woke up at 5:30 am but was still sleeping.

'Vuka, sisi,' I said, knocking at her door, which was the

door next to ours. At least she hadn't heard her bitter father again, I thought.

Hayi kazi uvukwe yini namhlanje? I wondered, as I headed to the kitchen to switch on the kettle. Still there was no movement in Nonhle's room.

'NONHLE!' I shouted across the house.

'Nasivusa ngomsindo ekuseni kangaka!' Thulani shouted back.

I laughed, as Nonhle walked out, asking, 'And then, umuntu wakho. Z'khiphani?'

Till the storm passes over
Till the thunder sounds no more
Till the clouds roll forever in the sky…

So sings the group on the radio in the background as I drive to work. The air in Sobantu is rising over the factories. I drive past Huletts, the sugar factory, and Albany, the bread factory. The roads are filled with people, and amakhumbi, and hoots and shouting. The pavement is too small to carry the vendors and the pedestrians. Some of the vendors are moving fast, preparing amagwinya for the morning rush.

It is not something new to me, open spaces as kitchens. We cooked like that when we were children; we would set up the fire outside for everything. Boiling water for bathing and tea. There was a constant flow of tea in my house and everyone else's. The fire remained somewhat alive for majority of the day. It was the first thing you would smell and see, from whichever hill on Mpofana you'd stand. Clouds of smoke from chimneys and open fires. Constantly cooking. Tea was the cheapest thing we could offer, and the kettle was often the most constant thing on that fire. After a few drinks, perhaps replacing izinkambi; the leaves. Before tea bags and Welcome Dovers.

I was six months into working when I bought my parents their first stove. A beautiful Welcome Dover I had found in a storeroom in the station. Every few years, everything gets changed and we get a cheap sale. uMa was beyond herself at the sight of that thing, even though it was almost too big to fit into our kitchen. Our kitchens were not built for stoves. Eventually I helped build urondo as a kitchen, with a chimney for our Welcome Dover. It was one of my proudest moments.

The women on the street cook with paraffin stoves. The fumes from the paraffin mix with the fumes from the factories. Driving out of Sobantu is always like driving out of a brewing storm.

Perhaps my soul knew there was a storm brewing in Thulani that day, the day he came drunk to the station.

It was the day of my promotion to station commander.

Till the storm passes over
Till the thunder sounds no more.
Till the clouds roll forever, in the sky.
Hold me firm, let me stand in the shadow of thy hand.
Keep me [and Thulani] safe
Till this storm passes by...

14

Nonhle

'Makhosi, please come put on TLC for me. I don't know what channel it is.'

'Or read a book?' Makhosi shouts from our bedroom.

I wonder where she thinks I get these books that I must read. I am only still a child and our school has a rule about township children and books, because township children don't take good care of their books, and no one will take me to the library in town. But 'Read a book,' she says. I do not tell her that I can't get books. One time I told her I wanted to draw and she asked, 'Well, why don't you?' I told her I didn't have drawing papers or crayons. She shouted at uMa, who then shouted at me. Ma had bought me pencil crayons and a drawing book earlier on in the year. She had also told me to never take it to school, unless I needed to.

What even is need? Of course I needed to take it to school with me, to show my friends and my teachers. Someone stole my drawing book and the pencil crayons they disappeared the way that crayons do. I think there is a secret place where crayons and socks, meet to laugh about how they escape us.

If only Mpumelelo was here, he would help me. Maybe even Nkosana would be more helpful than Makhosi. But Mpumelelo is at work, and Nkosana I'm not sure. We don't ask about what Nkosana is doing or where he is anymore. Sometimes people gossip about him and laugh, saying he is not at university. That he is lying to my parents. But we know he is studying, because Ma goes to visit him. He doesn't live inside the school, though, at a residence. He says residence is expensive, so he lives with other people, other students. It's a house, a grown-up house like all other houses; it just doesn't have parents. Everyone cooks for themselves, and they do whatever they want. There is an Indian girl who smokes even when Ma is around. I think Nkosana smokes, but we all pretend to hide it from uMa because she doesn't know. They also have to pay rent, to umastende, who I guess is almost like a parent there, but a parent you pay. There is someone they also call a caretaker; he lives in the yard and takes care of the things that break. So, maybe he is more like a parent?

They also sometimes bring someone in to clean, a maid who comes in and cleans up after all of them. Or at least in the main areas, maybe not the bedrooms. The kitchen has people's names written on falling cupboard doors, a lot is falling apart. The house is mostly empty. There are a few chairs that I think the mastende brought from his house. It's like, it's like a hostela more than it is umqasho. At the hostel, eMbali, the men rent the rooms also from the mastende, but even that is growing less and less now. People are renting the whole house. Nkosana lives in a hostela with women, young women. A hostela with not quite adult, not quite teenage people who go to school every day and a maid. So, maybe like a family?

I am still flipping through the channels when Ma comes home early to find the house dirty. Normally, we start cleaning an hour before she knocks off so she can find the house clean. Ma shouts the shout she always shouts when she gets back to a dirty home, but clearly Makhosazane is also in a bad mood today because she responds 'Then get a maid.'

'Akhokhelwe ngani? Yeyi, uyivila Makhosi,' Ma says,

pausing in the kitchen to put a pot of warm water on the stove to make uphuthu before heading to her bedroom.

Makhosi moves to join me in the sitting room, sitting on the corner of the sofa instead of pretending to look busy the way Lelo and I do if Ma comes home to find a dirty house. It's a sweet pink velvety sofa; the rest of the set is kwaGogo. The sofa had been okaBaba. Ma had wanted to also take it to kaGogo but uBaba would not let go. Only he and Makhosi sit on it. It looks out of place next to the new leather sofas. Cream white leather. Ma loves these sofas, but we can't sit on them dirty.

I move into Mpumelelo's old room to throw things on his bed; that is how I cheat clean now that he sleeps outside. Makhosi is still staring at her book. Ma has started to raise her voice as she moves between her bedroom, the kitchen and the bathroom, but still Makhosi won't move.

Something is in the background – a song, a child's cry, a car on the road.

'Makhosi, awufuni ukwenza lutho. Lutho mtanami. What do I have to do for you, ukuze wanele?'

Makhosi does not respond.

'Makhosi, ngibheke uma ngikhuluma nawe,' Ma says. She walks out of the kitchen into the lounge, switches off the TV, and takes Makhosi's book out of her hand. Now there is only silence. Mpumelelo is not back yet.

'Uzongibheka, Makhosi, uma ngikhuluma nawe.' Ma sits on the arm of the sofa, a thing she always tells us not to do but does today, so she can look Makhosi straight in the eye.

'Makhosi, I do a lot for you. A LOT! The very least you can do is clean up after yourself, at least in this house. My house. In that expensive fancy school of yours, you can sit and read books all you like. That is what you are there for. Here, la isekhaya kwami. Here you are not a special student. Here you are a child. MY CHILD!' From the back her neck makes her look like an angry frog, contracting and expanding.

Makhosi looks Ma right in the eye.

I don't know what happens, but Ma slaps Makhosi with the book. 'I just paid R2 000 for a school trip even, ungibonga kanje. Sies.'

Then Ma gets up and walks away.

Makhosi has still not moved. Or reacted in any way.

Ma tries pouring mielie-meal into the now boiling water when a splatter of wet mielie-meal splashes on her arm and burns her. If only it was a coal stove, I think, the water would have taken longer to boil...

'Ncese, Ma, faka iSunlight,' I say from Lelo's old room.

Makhosi's eyes search for me across the house and find me. I pretend to be folding laundry to escape her looking at me like I have betrayed her. That is how she looks at me when I don't have feedback to tell her about one of the books she's told me to read. She looks at me like that again later that evening when I help uMa with the dishes and she is still sunken in that sofa.

uBaba comes back just before supper. He sits next to Makhosi on the sofa. Bayafana, I think to myself.

I want to read the books Makhosi leaves, but sometimes they are too thick and then sometimes I have to help uMa in the house. uMa is very busy and unlike her, I don't mind helping. And during the day after school I want to play in the street with my friends. Makhosi doesn't have a lot of friends here, and I don't have a phone yet to update her. Every time she comes back, it seems like she has forgotten more and more. Maybe it's because time moves so fast and she has to keep up with everything happening at her school. She does do a lot there. It must be hard having to keep up with two worlds so young.

She cries the whole night. It doesn't even look that painful. I mean yea, sure, but umshaye kancane. She should see her when she hits you through syllables.

Makhosi cries and writes and cries. I wonder whether she is writing a book, like the ones she is always reading.

I struggle to sleep when she is crying and writing because

the lights are on the whole night. And ebemosha ugesi, so it better be a good book. If we were kaGogo, she wouldn't be able to cry like this.

She tried once; she tried everyone. My cousins just laughed at her. There was no teddy bear to hug, or diary to write in, and I didn't feel sorry for her. It happened not long after uMkhulu came back from town, Mooi River, with a canopy full of groceries. Always after umholo kaDecember, a few days after iGoli come back, but before Christmas, uMkhulu would wake up early and dress up in a suit that looked old. He looked like he was sinking into the suit. His tie now too small from having been pulled often and not re-done enough. From the visible collection of dust and dirt that formed as a triangle at the edges of the knot, you could see that the knot was tied years ago, the tie worn and just put back without being undone or washed. The small knot made his head look big. The suit was old, but hardly ever worn. uGogo told us that before any of us were even born, uMkhulu would dress up for Christmas grocery shopping. Maybe the suit is the same one, from before we were born.

We heard isigadla saMkhulu coughing from all the way at the top of the hill, from the side that taxis from Mooi River come from. He stopped by the stop and hooted for us to come get the groceries. We took the wheelbarrow, taking turns to push it up to estopini and then back home. Those who stayed behind unpacked.

Then Makhosi told uMkhulu that stopping so far away was 'unnecessary'.

If it had been one of our cousins, uMkhulu would have let out a whip from his belt. Makhosi used a lot of big English words to make old people feel bad; sometimes he did not know what she was saying, and he would be too embarrassed to ask a little girl to explain. uMkhulu knew what unnecessary meant, though, because he explained to Makhosi that a car, it was nezezari. A broken-down car was not nezezari, so he parked at the stop because the car was too full and would find itself stuck in mud from being too heavy if he drove it in. I am not sure what made my cousins the angriest. That Makhosi tried to take away something we all loved, when our neighbours and friends would see that we had lots and lots of food; that we did not have to ask anyone. Or that Makhosi didn't get a hiding like anyone else would have.

I think she only said it because she was lazy. She wanted to disappear into something, anything; hills and mountains when she was here because she couldn't bring her books. The one time she brought magazines, they ended up in a fire.

She cried then too, but she could only cry to uMkhulu, who slept in urondo lakhe where he spent all evening ebasa umlilo. Unlike inside the house, where the fire is in the stove, in urondo kaMkhulu there is smoke everywhere. Your eyes burn as you enter and soon your eyes are fully closed as you make up the lay of the room from memory until you get to your seat. The smoke mostly gathers higher in the rondo, so the lower you are the better you can see. On the day she tried us with her unnecessary, she tried coming back to the kitchen where the rest of us all were after she'd spent hours crying because everyone was 'picking on' her, which they weren't.

'Uwena, Makhosi, kulawula wena la ye? Nale kini?' Zoleka, one of our older cousins who lived kwaGogo all the time, asked.

'Ya, everywhere isicathulo sakho mphathi, phendula?' Thobani our other cousin stared down at Makhosi.

'Bengingakhulumi nani,' Makhosi said. She ran to go find uMkhulu wakhe, who had gone for a walk.

I had been playing amagenda with ingane zakwa Shabalala. That entire fight had distracted me from my concentration; and I had to concentrate when playing with izingane from here. Unlike eSobantu, where everything is concrete, here they dig holes to play amagenda, which sometimes catches me off guard, especially when they're trying to get me out of the game. The person who loses first is out of the game, and must also steal biscuits or juice, from their house for everyone playing. When they dig the hole too deep, I am always the first one who has to go steal. Mkhulu had a pack of sweets that he hid under his blankets erondweni. I didn't like them because they smelled like smoke and stale blankets, but they were the easiest thing to steal. Eventually, if we've been playing for long enough in our yard, uGogo will give us juice and scones, which we only get at our house. So in my head, even though the sweets were smelly, I was still 'giving' them something sweet; they complained about the sweets if that was all I produced, one day after another. So, sometimes I would end up asking uGogo for scones too early. Gogo only puts iRama on our scones, which is also nice, but the red jam on scones is the best.

That day we had been playing for so long that I was able to steal sweets and have the scones with Rama by the time Makhosi and uMkhulu came back. They sat on a bench outside urondo doing mostly nothing while the rest of us were preparing for the evening, some chopping logs for the fire, others cooking, others getting water; and the boys were bringing back the cows and sheep. uMakhosi and uMkhulu just sat there. Eventually they went into erondweni. Makhosi only came out after I had taken uMkhulu his food. Zoleka had said we were not to take food to Makhosi, 'singadlala yena.' It was true. She was a child; she could come get her food.

Makhosi did – but then she tried talking to one of my cousins, asking about a spoon.

'Ohho, mase kuthanda wena uyakhuluma nathi?' Thobani said.

Makhosi took her food and walked out crying.

uGogo stopped my cousins as they were screaming, 'Wakhala ubololo ekhalela izamba…'

The damage was done and the damage was done by all of them. Makhosi included. I followed her.

'Thula phela,' I said, annoyed at how childish she could be, but mostly because she always drew attention to herself, which then became attention to me when all I wanted was a quiet, peaceful house.

15

'Do you want to go to England, Makhosi?' I ask.

We are driving to fetch uMamncane waphesheya. uMamncane is a nurse in the UK. She is not married, and is seldom at family events. She even misses weddings, but never funerals. She is always here for funerals, and most Decembers. I'd heard that Mamncane wasn't really family, that she wasn't ingane kaMkhulu.

We hire a VW Kombi to go fetch her. uBaba drives and complains about Mamncane needing to get married.

'Ngisho e-England leyo. Lutho umshado. Yonke lemali ayisebenzayo uzoyenzani,' I would often hear Ma say. Makhosi and I were never concerned that uMamncane wasn't married, or that she would run out of use for her money. There was always us to buy things for. She would come through King Shaka International Airport, walking out with suitcases full, most times half of those suitcases containing clothes for Makhosi and I. Then for our cousins.

When Mamncane comes home, we usually go on holiday for a few days to Durban. We go eat at restaurants, which Ma generally complains about: 'umosha imali kodwa Nombulelo ngokuthi uze usikhiphe,' she says as she is eating the food.

Mamncane drinks wine, which Ma also doesn't like. And she wears really tight pants. She looks different from all her siblings, wears more make-up than them, threads her eyebrows, often using more perfume than is necessary.

Makhosi and Mamncane used to be inseparable. Some days, they would leave the rest of us to go shopping at the Pavilion and Gateway. Makhosi even went to visit England once. I think I was six. She came back fat with brand new clothes, refused to take the prices off. Walked around telling us about Fools and Horses and other things. I remember her saying she wanted to study in the UK a lot around that time. It was London this, London that. Mpumelelo nicknamed her London Bridge, but our Makhosi wasn't bothered.

So today as we are driving to the airport, when I ask her if she wants to go to England, her answer comes as a surprise.

'No, I don't care for the colonisers' land,' Makhosi says, looking out the window, a road we have travelled too often for her to still care.

Huh? I looked at her, confused. Colonisers' land?

'I thought you loved England?' I say. 'Didn't you want to study there?' I search for her eyes but she is still looking outside. There isn't even anything to look at – we are before the toll-gate past Hammarsdale. All there is to look at is just hills and other cars.

'Over my dead body would I hand myself over to the colonisers like that!' she says.

I really wish she'd look at me. Sometimes she says things to be 'controversial', another word she taught me. But I know her well enough to know when she is trying to be controversial. She has a certain smile that pops up when she thinks she is outsmarting a person. But Makhosi doesn't turn her head, not once, and I can't make out from the side of her face whether the smile is there or not.

I don't know what colonisers are. I will google it when I get home.

The rest of the drive is uBaba's annoying music. Mpumelelo said when they were younger the three of them – Nkosana, him and Makhosi – stole one of uBaba's tapes and pretended not to know where it was. I was always jealous of these talks about what the three of them used to do when they were younger, especially eWembezi. Everything sounded like it was more fun there.

It even sounds like uBaba was a different person when they were younger. If any of his CDs were to disappear now, we would never hear the end of it. He would accuse Lelo of stealing things. He does this even when he has misplaced something. Says Mpumelelo has stolen something, and then blames Ma for spoiling the children, saying that is why Mpumelelo is like this. uBaba blames everyone for everything, looking for fights where there are none.

We arrive at the airport before Mamncane's flight arrives. BA 2457 from Dubai is her flight, landing in fifteen minutes. Even though she is coming from London, she has explained that going past another place is often cheaper. Although she claims she isn't in those countries, just laying over or 'connecting', she calls it, I count them all as countries she has been to. She flew via Dubai last time as well, so there is no new country for me to add this time.

My favourite thing at the airport is reading the arrivals and departures boards and trying to figure out in which countries the cities are.

Dubai	13:35	Disembarking
Budapest	13:45	Landed
Tokyo	13:50	Estimated time of arrival
Maseru	13:50	Delayed

Mamncane comes out faster than I expected. As she walks out of the area where the bags are, we all shout and wave. When we were younger, we would compete over who she saw first, or who she waved to first. 'It was a wave for a collective,' Mamncane would say when we asked her.

That was the thing about Mamncane; she always knew how to get out of hard situations. Often with short answers, as she smiled.

'Uwafundiswe ubani amabhulukwe?' uMalume asked her once.

'Bengingazi ukuthi ukugqoka ibhulukwe kuyelwa esikoleni mfowethu,' Mamncane replied with the biggest smile. Everyone laughed. Malume continued drinking. Her answers were always short. She didn't speak much. Except to Makhosi, or uMa, when they were all hidden in bedrooms.

This time Makhosi does not wave or compete with us. She sits on her phone, briefly hugs uMamncane when she finally gets to us, then starts walking right back to the kombi.

'Haw', sisi. You won't even help me push my trolley?' Mamncane asks.

'Ungenwa istage,' my mother whispers. She looks so much older, like uMama, next to Mamncane, who is slimmer, shorter and darker than uMa.

Mamncane gives a short laugh. 'Hawu, size simfice. Yini useyajola?'

I know Ma hates how Mamncane takes nothing seriously.

'Kube uyajola ngabe mhlampe ngiyazi ngenze njani, Nombu. uMakhosi uphethwe ilestage sabelungu sokungakhulumi nokuzivalela. Uhlalela yona leyaphone, nezincwadi.'

Neither Ma nor her sister is whispering now.

Makhosi and uBaba are way ahead of us, him pushing the trolley, her texting. Neither of them speaking to each other.

'She's always liked books though. Don't stress, sisi, she's a smart girl. She may just be growing,' Mamncane says, failing at consoling uMa.

Mamncane has come back for a funeral. Their brother's death. uMalume. The funeral will be this weekend. This time we are not spending a few days at home before taking Mamncane kaGogo. We drop most of her suitcases and drive straight to eMpofana.

Makhosi says nothing the entire way.

Mamncane doesn't try get her to talk. I have been hoping she will, that Mamncane is the one who will finally get through to Makhosi.

I don't think uphethwe amadimoni, although Malumekazi thinks she does. No one takes Malumekazi seriously, although she mostly speaks the truth. Maybe it's because she does this when drunk, or maybe it's because she is always drunk. I have never seen her drink though; I just know she is always drunk.

Makhosi really doesn't like her. Malumekazi makes it a point to pick on her, has her loudest laughs when she does too.

'Kazi umuphi umkhwenyana ozashada umuntu oqoba ehleli efonini,' says uMalumekazi.

'Ubani uthe ngifuna ukushadwa?' Makhosi responds, angrily. You can see the anger in her eyes, hear it in her voice. It used to scare me. It doesn't scare me as much anymore. She's angry all the time now.

I stare straight into my level 59 of Candy Crush, pretend I am not there. Malumekazi breaks out into her hypnotising laugh. She bangs the table as she laughs, wiping a few tears from her eyes. Her laugh is that funny kind of laugh, except when she is laughing at you.

Everyone is laughing, everyone but Makhosazane. She walks away and I follow her. I don't like seeing her sad and she is sad a lot. She goes to sit by the fire outside, glances at me, then continues with her phone. She is calling Lethu. She is always calling Lethu, about everything. Malumekazi is right. Makhosi is on the phone a lot.

She looks at me again. 'u-right?' she asks.

'Yea, ngiright wena?' I say.

'Arghh, man, you know.'

I don't know, but I nod. I wish she wasn't this angry all the time. It makes uMa really unhappy and she tries. She is always trying with Makhosi.

When Ma told Sis Gugu that Makhosi was always angry, Sis Gugu brought church people. They said Makhosi had idemoni. Ma shouldn't have done that; she must've known Sis Gugu was going to do that. It's just, I think she is tired of praying for her alone. God doesn't seem to answer her prayers. I hear her pray until she cries, uMa. Comes into our rooms late at night, when she thinks we are sleeping. Prays for me too, but mostly prays for Makhosi. Asks God to protect her, to return her, to heal her.

I don't know what she needs healing from. She was fine. She has been fine. She wore beautiful dresses, went to church. She had a boyfriend. She was fine. She used to ask the pastors questions. The pastors liked it, said it showed she read.

It is that school that ruined her; I swear. She came back from school using big words like 'Mxm, le PAY-TREE-YARKY yomfundisi wenu' to uMa. Asked less, started being less and less interested. It is definitely the school.

'Yho, let's go inside, it's cold,' Makhosi says. She looks calmer. Her phone makes her less angry.

I go to sleep with Mamncane, but with Makhosi crying and angry and sad, Mamncane goes to sleep with her instead.

Silindile, my best friend – she also has annoying older siblings – is a ballet dancer. She started dancing here eSobantu. A white ballet teacher came with a black older woman who was a ballet dancer. She told us the story of all the places that ballet had taken her. France, Italy, Germany, England, America. Almost everyone asked, Where is France? And Italy? What does Germany look like? What language do they speak in France? Do American black people really have the same hair as us?

Very few girls asked about ballet. I didn't like ballet. It looked boring and their costumes were pink like white people skin. Why didn't she wear a black costume, the black dancer, like a swimming costume, was what I wanted to ask, but I didn't.

I would like to go to all those countries on the map the ballet teacher was holding up – but not the ones above the equator. We learned in HSS that countries north of the equator are cold and I don't like the cold. Mamncane also confirmed that it was really cold when I asked her. So, I would to go to the other countries.

Silindile just likes dancing, all dancing. She is part of every dancing group in Sobantu. Ballroom dancing, ballet; she even does isipantsula and traditional dancing. She spends many of her weekends at competitions and shows.

Now she is about to go to England. We spend the entire time Mamncane is here gathering as much information as we can. Besides it being cold, and very few people speaking isiZulu, Mamncane shows us photos of herself – in the biggest malls and stadiums. England looks like everything is bigger. A lot bigger. Silindile and I look at Mamncane's suitcases. Silindile doesn't have a suitcase that big. She has been using her brother's soccer bag to pack for the competitions in South Africa.

Mamncane gives Silindile one of her suitcases. The biggest suitcase. Silindile is going to go to England, and she is going to tell me the truth. Makhosi just confused me with big words when she came back.

I am very excited for my friend. I go to the airport with her ballet teacher and her mother to see her off.

'This is an airport,' the ballet teacher says to us.

'We've been to airports,' Silindile and I both tell her.

'Does she explain everything to you like you're stupid?' I whisper to Silindile when we have our final hug.

'What's funny?' the teacher asks when she sees us laughing.

'No, I was just asking what those small cars are,' I joke.

She really starts explaining until Silindile says, 'I have to go, miss' and we share a final secret laugh together.

Even when Silindile has gone through, the teacher carries on explaining everything, like we are stupid.

'We're going to have to go before the plane actually takes off,' she says. 'They're on the other side now, waiting to board. We may see them head to their plane, and then we'll have to leave. Because parking is expensive. All planes take off the same way.' She points at a plane that is about to leave.

uMakaSilindile looks like she is listening. I am not. There

is no reason for this woman to speak as continually as she does. There is nothing worth hearing from her for long periods of time.

As soon as we get into the car, uMakaSilindile switches on the radio. Which is better, because the talking on radio is disrupted by music. I wonder whether the people on radio enjoy talking the way this woman seems to. I wonder whether they get tired.

16

Makhosazane

Seven hundred and forty-five kilometres. The distance between Grahamstown and Pietermaritzburg, according to my Matric diary.

'Which university are you going to?' a church friend once asked me.

'Rhodes,' I confidently replied.

'Oh, have you been accepted?' she asked.

'No. I just know,' I said.

I was in Grade 11. There was no particular reason I wanted to go to Rhodes, outside the fact that it was far away from home. It didn't take long for me to soon learn that the name of my oppressors should not find comfort on my tongue.

Zama wanted to go to UKZN Medical School. We would visit each other every month, we promised each other. Spend every day of the holidays together. She never received a response from UKZN; she went to the University of the Free State instead. She hated Bloemfontein more than I hated Grahamstown. She would complain to me over emails.

'It's worse than that KZN small town, MK.'

'Another boring day, flip science is boring.'

'Went to church today. The preacher kept speaking about

judgement without speaking about Jesus's love. Arghh Christians who don't know Christ.'

'I think I met a boy at church today, his name is Sifiso. I think he likes me.'

'Girl, uJesu akeve emuhle. I thought I had failed a physics test, but I passed.'

Zama's emails were short, but consistent. A few weeks into Grahamstown, and I could not respond; but I loved finding her emails at the end of the day.

O-week was filled with loud, drunk boys, who walked the streets at night with tremendous comfort. The girls in my residence were either 'out' or watching Grey's Anatomy. The black girls particularly met to watch Generations. I was stuck in my room. No amount of excitement in the corridors or parties on the fields would allow me to leave my bed.

Ma tried to call every second day, which I didn't understand. We had not spoken more than once a week for years. Why now?

'I'm in the library,' I would whisper from the silence of my room.

I miss my first house meeting and get a warning under my door. My warden wants to know why I missed the meeting. Days and time collide into one another. Later in the week, maybe, my warden opens my door with the master key, which they had promised us was only for emergencies, when the over-zealous girl who lives down my corridor asks her to. She is a tall white woman who looks like her shoulders are hangers. She has long curly hair that's always in her face when she is talking, which at first annoyed me. Until I realised I didn't need to have to see her often.

'How long have you been in here?' she asks, not apologising for violating my privacy or for lying about what they use master keys for.

'I don't know,' I say, burying my head in my pillow. The light coming from the corridor hurts my eyes. My room has been dark for so long I can feel my eyes adjusting to the light.

'When last did you eat?' she asks.

'I don't know, but I am fine, thank you. You can leave now.' I hold my head up to say the words but not to look at her. In my head, I think I emphasise 'fine' and 'leave' but she clearly doesn't pick up on these.

'Are you having trouble adjusting?' she asks, her voice sounding like she is moving closer to me. I move my pillow from under my head to over my head, hold it down with my arms. Still not looking at her. I don't need this from her.

I feel her slowly try to sit on my bed, like I am a cat stuck up a tree that she doesn't want to scare.

'Makhosi, this is why I am here. Myself, and your house comm. We are here to help you adjust, and figure things out. For many people, this is their first experience away from home. This is why the university has counselling groups, for people who are new here and are trying to adjust. There is a homesick group that meets at the counselling centre. At the Steve Biko building. Do you know it?' she asks.

She is speaking so fast; I wonder whether she hears herself make all those assumptions. About this being my first experience out of home. About homesickness. For someone who cares, she sure didn't read from my things that I had been in boarding school most of my life. People attach so much to homes and ideas of home. Urghh.

'Makhosi?' she disturbs.

'Yes, mam. I know the Steve Biko building. Opposite College House residence. Third floor has counselling services. Thank you.'

'Okay, I will leave this brochure for you to read. I would highly recommend that you go there if you feel homesick. But we are also always here to speak to, okay? Myself, and all the members of your house comm. Okay? I will leave you to think about it and chat to you in a few days. Okay?'

I hear the paper drop on my desk. She moves back at a faster pace than she came in. She is already at the door, whispering, 'And please eat, Makhosi. People get first-year spread, not first-year death.' She tries to laugh. The door closes behind her, and I hear her shuffle down the corridor. Back to the safety of not having to interact with 'homesick' first years.

I wonder if she has ticked all the right boxes for 'homesick student' protocol.

Is she the person to address my suicide letter to? She did, after all, just say I could get first-year death.

Dear Warden (?) my suicide letter would read.

No, what is her name? Julia, Jolie, June? What is her name again...?

My cell phone breaks out into a luminous light and loud vibration on my desk. The only person who calls me is uMa; uZama is still only sending the emails. Except Sunday evenings, after church.

What day of the week is it? I try grasp for my phone to see what name is coming up.

Nonhle.

Ma must have asked Nonhle to start calling me because she has started this habit of calling me to tell me about the neighbours.

'Weee, uphindwe washaywa uSphe' – this about our neighbour who is addicted to sniffing glue – 'They even tried to remove the glue pack from his hand as they were hitting him, but it's stuck now. That thing is permanently a part of his hand.'

'uNokwanda umithi, uzwile. Kuthiwe umithiswe by that taxi driver man she has been getting beaten for dating.'

'uMadlala beat up his wife again, uBaba went there to go talk to them and take him to the police station. I think it's just to scare him, he always brings him back.'

She follows up her stories with questions.

'What's happening with you? How's school? How's philosophy? Ngisure nje wenza kakhulu, because you like words and philosophers like words.'

'Urgh, I'm trying to survive,' I answer.

I always keep my responses short. Nonhle won't try past this, which I appreciate.

'Love you, Baaaayeeeeeeeee,' she always says as she hangs up.

There is nothing new for me to say. The last time I was in class, the same boy, Mark-I-think, said something racist in class, but so did Craig and Bertha the week before. A few black students try calling it what it is – racism. The conversation eventually derails, as the lecturer lets it. Standing in front of the auditorium firmly; a person of authority refusing to exercise it. The black boys eventually swear, the white girls look scared and flustered. Finally, the lecturer says something about opinion, a black student supports the lecturer and defends the white students. The black students argue amongst themselves. The four green and white exit signs above each door invite me, but the chairs bang loudly against the table when you try get out. Breaking the fight by drawing attention to yourself. A pointless exercise, lectures.

Nonhle's phone calls are soothing, even though I don't care for their content. They are like that tree with purple and white leaves that was outside our house eWembezi. There was one outside every third or fourth house or so, but still. I liked the one outside our house. uBaba would work on the leaves and pick up the petals which had fallen, some looking pink and brown from either being burned or from dropping too early. uBaba would throw the petals into uMa's garden at the back. I don't remember seeing Ma's garden before we left. I don't remember what happened to it.

That same kind of tree is outside my res window, a few steps away from my room. It has a nostalgic smell. It begins to be all I look at. On my way to the dining hall, on my way back from class. Some days picking a few of the fallen petals to put into my diary. On the days when I can't walk out to go to the dining hall, I smell the dry petals in my diary and remind myself that there was a day when I'd made it out. Nonhle's phone calls are a similar soothing, like far away from me people are doing okay. People I know and care about, and people with bigger problems, like husbands who beat them, unplanned children, addict children, are getting up every day. My biggest task is to get out of bed. And on days after Nonhle calls, I do. I get out of bed.

When Nonhle was born, I had thought I would give her all the life lessons I had needed. Soothe her. This is how you fight racism; give her a step-by-step guide. This is what you do when you first menstruate. When you finally decide to masturbate.

For the most part of her life, she hasn't seemed to need the kind of advice I can give her. The questions she has are about things I didn't even know were happening.

'What happens when uMa comes back home with blood?' 'What happens when you hear that uMa is being suspended?' 'What happens when...?' 'What happens when...?'

Nonhle seems to know how to deal with them.

'When did uMa get suspended?' I would end up asking.

'Oh, you don't know? Never mind then. Let me not stress you. Urghh. never mind, I'll ask Lelo.'

She called him that, Mpumelelo our brother. Lelo had more answers for my sister than I did. Lelo this, Lelo that. Lelo, ngitete, Lelo, let's go for a walk, Lelo, I want isqeda. It was worse when I was younger; she didn't even seem to need me at all. 'You're on MY bed!' she would shout on my free weekends at home when she would see me laying on what had been my bed, but what was suddenly her bed.

'Can't you sleep with oMa?' I'd ask. She was still wetting her bed – my bed – and I didn't understand how Ma could put her in my room without asking me. I tried asking Ma why she would do that, and she just laughed at me.

'Your bed, Makhosi?' she said as she laughed. 'This is not a boarding school dormitory. Everything here belongs to everyone.'

I once tried coming back with a mug, my Grade 7 souvenir mug.

'That's MY mug,' I would shout from the lounge every time I saw someone taking my mug. 'Leave MY mug.' From my favourite chair, I could see right into the kitchen. The cupboard above the kettle where all the mugs and glasses were.

One day when I told Nkosana to leave my mug, Ma said, 'We share in this house.'

'But that one is MINE,' I said, as I went back into my book.

Ma dished for me in my mug that evening, rice, and chicken stew, and coleslaw, all in a small mug.

'But Ma,' I said.

'That's the only thing that is yours in this house,' she said, 'and if my children can't drink from YOUR mug, you can't eat from MY plates.'

I didn't eat my supper that night, nor did I ever scream it's MY anything ever again. At least not when Ma was around.

17

Well of course, I want to fill the silences, I tell the psychiatrist. I keep coming back here. Telling him I need a different person. There aren't enough staff members in government hospitals. I keep returning here. Swearing at him in my head. His job is to give me my monthly prescription, but he wants to fill the silences with questions. Unnecessary questions. Laughs as I tell him why I am angry.

'Do you ever hear your brain go silent?'

'How does one hear silence?'

'The thing you want to fill with silences. Whatever it is you try to fill with the music, the books, the words. What is the sound of that thing?' is his unnecessary question this session.

'Angazi,' I say, looking around his small office. He doesn't even have a picture of his family on the desk. If he had a picture of his family, maybe I could trust him with the answers to the questions he asks, but he doesn't. The campus psychologist keeps referring me here, but I prefer her. She only asks questions here and there. The rest of the time I am saying things. Half the time, I don't care what I say. Just fill the forty-five minutes of the session is how I go into it.

My sessions are compulsory, for being homesick and antisocial. I had started 'fixing' the antisocial, but it didn't matter, because they diagnosed me with depression and put me on medication before I could fix it. But I was making friends.

It was a warm Saturday morning. The tree outside my

room looked brighter today. Philela knocked on my door. Philela was from eDutywa, a small place somewhere here in the Eastern Cape. I was on my way to the Pick n Pay in town when I saw her.

'Are you going to town?' I asked.
'Yes,' she said.
'Where? Pick n Pay?'
'Yes.' So I walked down with her.
'Igama lami uMakhosi.'
'Mna ndinguPhilela,' she said.

I think she thought that I was trying to be friends with her, but in fact I was anxious about being in the centre alone that particular day. Pepper Grove is small, but it gets full on Friday afternoons of payday weekend. There are only three supermarkets in Grahamstown, Pick n Pay being the closest one.

Philela lived down the corridor of Thomas Pringle House, number 45. My room was number 37. I could not escape her. 'Makhosazane,' she would call from down the long corridor. She called my name like she was reading my name from the sign outside my door every time. I hated that, the names put on our doors, but the house comm said we could not remove them, it made it easier to find one another. What if I didn't want to be found?

A few weeks later Philela was knocking on my door three times a day, every day, asking the same question.

'Breakfast?' 'Lunch?' 'Supper?'

The answer was me dragging my feet out the door, eating very quickly, and trying to get back.

Eventually she started making jokes about people in our dining hall. About classes. About her friends from her classes. She was studying Environmental something, something to do with fish. Second year. I didn't care what she was studying, or who her friends were, but she continued telling me about them.

One Friday night she and her friends barged into my room, telling me we were going out, and demanding that I get dressed. Lethu, Sulezi, Neo – these were Philela's friends. Lethu and she were from the same village. I had seen Lethu in one of my classes once or twice the few times I went to lectures.

'Get dressed, get dressed! Let's go!' they said.

I had not showered that day. They let me at least delay them by a few hours, allowing me to get dressed. I did not need hours to shower and get dressed, but they kept insisting that I change my outfits.

'Look more girly,' they said.

I do not own girly clothes, just clothes to go to lectures and a few formal dresses that uMa had bought me. The lecture clothes were mostly jeans and chinos. Sulezi found me something to wear from her wardrobe. Her res was next to mine. 'Sulezi's wardrobe is the only one that can salvage this situation,' Lethu said.

We needed to get in before 10 pm, whatever we did.

'Okay, okay, can I at least wear this jersey over this skimpy shirt?' I asked, scratching around in my wardrobe again. Walking back and forth between the two res's for different things was what made up the hours getting dressed.

'She really is a hipster,' Lethu said. 'I see you sometimes in class.'

'I'm not a hipster, I wear the first things I see.'

'Oversized jerseys and skinny pants. Looks hipster to me,' she smirked.

'This is one of my father's jerseys. I hate skinny jeans, and my oversized clothes – I either stole them from my father, or they belonged to my favourite aunt.'

'We don't care, let's go.' Lethu pulled me out of my room. She walked with me; Philela, Neo and Sulezi walked behind.

'Pre-drinks at the union?' asked Philela, as we approached the bottom of the hill.

'If I drink at one place, I'm staying there,' I said.

'Spoilsport,' Lethu said.

At this point, I did not care what Lethu thought; I simply

was not going to club hop. We settled on EQ. The dance floor was already full, as was the bar. It took Lethu and I over thirty minutes to just get to the bar, trying to place our order.

'A bucket of Savannahs,' Lethu ordered.

'And two Black Labels, please,' I ordered.

'No one is drinking Black Label here,' Lethu said. 'We're all getting pissed drunk, or not drunk at all.' She cancelled the order of my Black Labels and bought a second bucket of Savannah instead.

The rest of our drinking team for the night had found a table and were comfortably sitting waiting for their alcohol.

'This damn thing is too sweet,' I complained to Lethu.

'Well, the next time going out is your idea, we'll get all the Blacks you want.' She had to scream to be heard through the music.

They would do this often, not just for occasions. Go out an order buckets of alcohol at ridiculous prices. I laughed at the idea of me buying twelve beers, at a nightclub. It didn't matter to tell Lethu then that it was out of my budget. It simply meant going out was never my idea. So, Savannahs it was.

'I prefer drinking indoors,' I told Lethu. I had only been at this place for just over a month, or under two months. I still didn't trust the drinking culture. In O-week all the evening activities were filled with wine, which I did not drink.

Drinking in Grahamstown is not like drinking in Pietermaritzburg. Not that I have done that a lot, but on the days I did, the drunk men would simply walk to their fancy cars and drive home or to another drinking spot. Sure, they were also annoying. An unsolicited offer to buy you and your table alcohol. An unsolicited offer to take you home or, worse, an unsolicited offer to take you to a more 'happening' drinking spot.

Ntokozo and I had done that once. Signed ourselves out of hostel one weekend and gone to go drink. It was the weekend of umemulo kaZama. In Zama's family, Umemulo is done when intombazane turns eighteen, not twenty-one. It is meant to be a ceremony after first menstruation, Zama's mother told us. Zama was recently 'born again' thanks to SCO and did not want umemulo at all, but her family insisted, and it was not her decision to make. Ntokozo and I were glad there was a real excuse to use with our parents about our whereabouts that weekend.

I had only sipped on alcohol, at family functions and friends' parties, before that. I could not get home drunk, or get to school drunk. My scholarship was very strict about any form of substance 'abuse'; we had seen people lose their scholarships because of coming back to hostel drunk.

Manzini, Zama's brother, organised alcohol for us. We drank at the back room with him and some of their cousins. Zama was both busy and greatly annoyed by the happenings of that weekend. She needed to wash in the river very early in the morning that day. Then lick inyongo, which she was convinced was ancestral worship.

She didn't take lightly to me trying to joke with her either.

'Your ancestors need to up their game and be worshipped in other ways than ukukotha inyongo,' I said, trying to calm my dear friend down. She mumbled words and got called by someone in the house before she could get angrier. She had learned to do this at school. When she was getting angry, first she would mumble all the things she wanted to say to you, saying them under her breath, then continue with her 'cleaner' version. I was convinced that what she said under her breath were a lot of fuck you's, but she still insisted she did not swear.

She walked back into the house. Ntokozo and I kept sipping on our cranberry and vodka. It helped that it looked like juice, because we could walk out with our glasses, helping where we were needed, without the adults catching us.

That evening, after umemulo, Manzini, his cousins and his friends took us out for celebratory drinks. Zama didn't want to come.

'Base yourselves,' Manzini said. 'Gather as much alcohol

as you can in your stomachs now. By the time we get to where we are drinking, you'll only want to dance and not want waste money on alcohol.'

My knees were already feeling shaky, but I did not mind. Manzini said this was only because I had been drinking sitting down.

'When you dance your knees will come alive again', he said. This wasn't true. I had been drinking, walking and working, but I guessed that wasn't the same as dancing.

It had just turned dark, after 7 pm, when we left Zama's house and went to 0333. A drinking place eMbali, on the other side of Maritzburg next to Edendale Hospital. I knew the hospital was far; it was where the adults went to visit people when I was younger. There was no hospital eSobantu. There was one in Northdale, but generally people got transferred to Edendale. uMama had told me that it was a remnant of the old system, like how she was not liked at the police station in Northdale.

'Why don't you work eMbali?' Ma said some Indian man colleague had asked her.

'How did you respond?' I asked.

'I said it was far,' uMa said simply, shrugging.

It was a Sunday afternoon. uMa was always lightest on Sunday afternoons, floating through chores.

Imbali was far, but we went anyway. We parked outside the crowded 'club', which was next to a clinic and opposite a primary school. I wondered if it got this loud while there were children in school. Ntokozo, Manzini, his cousins, his friends and I found ourselves a table as we waited for the music to get better so we could dance. Ntokozo did not need to wait for the right beat. After getting herself a shot of tequila from a boy at the next table, she was all over the dance floor. The cousins that Manzini had come with offered me a pill to dance.

'No, thank you,' I said.

I do not like dancing anyway. After a while, I was the only one at the table looking after jackets as everyone was on the dance floor. Manzini had lied. Dancing would not make me sober. Simply sitting here and looking after jackets was sobering enough for me.

Manzini came back with a bucket of alcohol, asked if I was fine and disappeared again. The table members came back only to get their alcohol, and return to the dance floor.

Ntokozo came back and asked if I was fine.

'Someone must look after the valuables,' I said, pretending to laugh.

Some man, whom Ntokozo must have known from her few minutes on the dance floor, approached us and offered us a better drinking place. I didn't want to go, but I also did not want Ntokozo to go alone either. 'We will book you girls into a nice hotel, eGolden Horse,' he said. 'Or you can stay over at mine and leave in the morning. I live in Scottsville.'

Even though I didn't want to go, Ntokozo desperately wanted us to.

I have very little recollection of that night. We did not pass by Zama's house the next morning. I went home instead, told Zama's parents I had slept at home and my parents that I had slept at Zama's. On the way back to school, Manzini driving us, I asked Ntokozo how much of the previous night she remembered. She seemed to have forgotten too; she only remembered that it was a lot of fun. Maybe it was.

I remember that I woke up on a sofa with the large-screen TV in front of me still on, playing some music channel with girls dancing at a pool party. I looked for Ntokozo, shouting around the house. She came out of a bedroom and said, 'Yho. Ngikhona.' There were more men in that house than I had memory of us getting into cars with. They kept appearing from rooms. One had been spooning with me on the sofa. Others were passed out on the one-seater sofas

I decided that day that I preferred drinking at home. Especially now that I was here in Grahamstown with this many drunk white boys out. I didn't trust black boys, the way

I hadn't trusted those men that night, but white boys do some other types of shit that I never wanted to experience.

We started drinking in my room every second or third day, which meant my door was seldom closed. By now I left the door unlocked. Mostly for Lethu to get a USB, or a book, or lecture slides, or a plate, or a packet of noodles. Whatever it was, I had fast gotten too lazy or too tired to stand up and open my door five times a day for Lethu. She didn't knock lightly either.

'Hey, hey. Why is the door locked? Are you masturbating in there?' Lethu would shout from the other side.

So, I stopped locking.

I never know what time she gets back.

Now she simply gets into bed. Asking me to move up closer to the wall.

When I first arrived here, I tried putting my bed in the middle of the room. Something I may have seen on TV.

'What white girl BS is this?' Lethu had asked.

'What?'

'Hayi, MK, tshii. We put beds against the wall to create space. So that singazuwa,' she said as she gestured me off the bed, so she could move it against the wall.

That was the first night we 'cuddled'. My body had quickly, in a shiver, responded to her hand against my breast as I lay facing the cold wall.

'Hayi wethu, we're cuddling,' she said, her hands travelling across my belly.

It always started as cuddling. At six or seven in the morning, I would feel her body behind mine. Sometimes, a first response of fear would overcome me. Her familiarity with my body against hers would quickly remind me 'it is safe here' as I rubbed the back of her hand, our fingers entering a criss-cross across my chest. After the first time, we laughed at the fact that we had become so used to each other that we didn't mind that we hadn't brushed our teeth. It was a pet peeve of Lethu's, boys who tried to kiss her with morning breath. After that first time, when I woke up I tried to get up to go brush my teeth for her, but she just pulled me closer.

'Where are you going?' she muttered, half asleep.

'To brush my teeth,' I said.

She opened one eye slightly, squinting her face, said, 'Mxm,' and pulled me back to bed.

'So, we're going to have to say whether we're lesbian or something sometime soon,' Lethu said a few months after our drinking sessions had become a Friday regular. Our Saturday mornings had become a ritual too. She would come in, at whatever time she came in. We would wake up, in fact not even fully awake to be engaged in the sex, go straight back to bed, and wake up to figure out a Saturday 'brunch'. Which was less a brunch and more of a fuller meal than the Weet-bix and cornflakes we gobbled up during the week. Not because we were going anywhere that prevented us from making an egg in the microwave like we did on Saturdays. We just, we were 'busy' during the week. Or we were too hungover during the weekend to simply eat cereal. Whatever it was, we had started a Saturday microwave brunch ritual.

Some days we spent catching up on Omnibus on YouTube.

That Saturday we had been watching Generations, the horrific and famous Senzo and Jason first scene.

'Well, not after this shit we don't,' I said.

'Angeke, tell people I am lesbian so that nami ngibizwe ngoJason? Or uBuli?'

'Buli?'

'From Home Affairs. You know, the old show?' Lethu said.

'Why would they call me Buli?'

'Well, not you, silly. Me,' Lethu said. 'They call me Buli, you know that, right? Because kuthiwa mos, surely uBuli is a lesbian and wasting that boy's time. So, ewe ke, I am a Buli kulecampus.'

About three weeks later, on Friday night, we were at EQ, our favourite club on the High Street. It was the week before the Arts Festival. Lethu had started dating Philani. He was a student, a rugby player, studying music at Rhodes. Something easy, he'd said. He also coached rugby at the local high school. Lethu had started coming with him to my room; or he would just be at the door. Although our res door was always meant to be closed, after people saw you in the corridor more than two times, they would let you in. Rhodes was small; we all knew each other. Philani would start at Lethu's door and then proceed to mine, which was still often left unlocked. He had found us cuddling once, naked, after our morning sex ritual had turned to cuddles.

'We just sleep naked,' Lethu told Philani. 'Girls do that all the time. I only sleep with clothes on with you because you're a man, you know, but generally I do not like wearing clothes to bed.'

I knew Lethu was lying. She even hated taking off her clothes during sex ('My feet get damn cold'). She was only saying this because Philani had walked in on us naked. Philani said he didn't mind. Of course he then proceeded to tell her how she was safe with him. As if I was not there in the room. Lethu had to start sleeping naked with him too. No socks even. Her poor cold feet.

'It's okay,' Lethu said. 'At least now we're only ever worried about being caught in the act, which is fine, you know. I leave him dead tired after sex anyway.' That was how she tried to reassure me.

Then Philani started coming earlier, and earlier.

'He must want to catch us in the act so he can join,' Lethu joked.

It wasn't funny. Lethu knew it wasn't funny.

'Hayi, wethu suqumba tshii. If you get a boyfriend, he will back off a little,' she said.

Lethu started saying this more and more often after Philani. First she needed to be with one boy to prove she wasn't lesbian – and now she had her boy – but still the rumour grew. So now I had to get a boyfriend too.

Philani's friends made a joke of him when the three of us were together – 'isithembu sakwa Madikana' they would call us. Which wasn't untrue. We were both doing things with Lethu; it was just Philani who didn't know. But that wasn't my problem.

'And which boy will I date who won't want to have sex with me?' I tried reasoning with Lethu.

'A church boy, ababanitsi ngeloxesha. Uzaveske nje uthi kubrother, BROTHER! I am saving myself for the Lord!' Lethu said, her cheeks expanding like she was a cartoon. 'No, but ndi serious tshomi, these loyal church boys will even think you are holier than that and sleep with other girls behind your back. And usafe ke wena, because they won't give you anything. It's easier for you. Jonga, mna uPhilani lo is probably a tub of STDs. Worse, with his rugby travelling. I suspect him. He suspects me. We argue about condoms every single time, every single time without fail.'

'I really don't enjoy talking about your sex life with your nipple engorged between my fingers,' I said to Lethu. She did that, started going off about Philani, and how their sex was, and how he didn't use lube, just his spit, which was nowhere close to sufficient lubricant for his dry, crusty penis.

'Well, then do something about the engorged nipple,' she said.

We heard Philani's voice down the corridor. Lethu jumped to get a cigarette from her bag. She carried them to smoke when drinking. There was a half-finished joint in her cigarette box, but no cigarette. She lit the joint, running to latch the door. We ignored Philani behind our coughs and laughs for a few minutes.

'I can fucken hear you! I can hear you! Are the two of you having sex again?' He sounded angry.

Lethu ran to open. 'Dude...' she said slowly in between her coughs and laughs.

'Yhu, Lethu, why the fuck do you sound like you're an American college white boy?' I asked.

Lethu and I laughed.

'What the fuck?' Philani said.

'We are high, tshii. We thought we were hearing you, and then we thought we were imagining it.'

'Kengoku, why the fuck is the door closed?' he asked.

'You want the warden to walk into whose room while we smoke weed?' I responded.

Lethu was still laughing. Philani re-lit the joint and sat on the bed.

'I keep waiting to walk in on you,' he said. 'Siveske sijoleni the three of us. You know, isithembu manyan', not okutyana kwenu, in secret. You could both be my girlfriends,' he added, through a ganja-induced cough.

Lethu and I could not stop laughing, even when I wanted to stop, to tell Philani that what he said made me a little scared. He joined in our laughter and I quickly forgot what I had been thinking about.

I met Simphiwe a few days after that. He was a boy in my dining hall. He had offered to walk me to my res a few times. He had seen me at church once, in my second week at university. He must have been sent by the student church committee or something to check up on me, to ask me why I had not been attending church lately. Pretend to care about how I was doing. All of those questions that would eventually lead to 'So when are you coming to church again?'

Simphiwe was the church boy Lethu had described. I went to church every second or so week after I met Simphiwe. You know, to keep myself grounded. But also because Zama was always asking me about church societies, and looking for a church, and discipleship. She had found His People at UFS, but whatever His People was in Grahamstown was not for me. So I jumped around between River of Life and the student SCO church. Simphiwe was the deputy chair of SCO and a member of the Full Gospel Church in Grahamstown. A local boy who loved the Lord.

He started waiting for me to come to church with him on Fridays.

'Do it,' Lethu said to me. 'What, an SCO boy? That dude won't even suspect a thing.'

And so I did.

We had been dating for a few weeks when he said he suspected I was a lesbian, that his friends from SCO had told him I was. He was worried about me and Lethu.

'Well, you'll have to wait for this bomb pussy on our wedding night,' I joked.

'That's the thing,' Simphiwe said. 'I don't think Christian women call their vaginas "pussy". Look, MK, I can tell that part of your path with Jesus is false. Your room sometimes smells like weed. So, I don't see how virginity would appeal to you?'

'Fuck, what?' I asked, confused.

Then Simphiwe started kissing me. Surely Lethu was going to walk in anytime. His penis was erect against his pants, sliding against my thigh.

'You love God though,' I said to Simphiwe.

'And God wants to save you from lesbianism,' he said, pulling down his pants and then my pants.

I wasn't wearing underwear; I seldom did.

'Ever ready, I see,' he said, moving down to kiss my breasts and stomach.

'Simphiwe. Simphiwe, you don't need to do this,' I begged, still somewhat convinced that he really would not.

My knees were shaking against each other as he kissed me lower and lower.

'Khayeke joe,' I said.

His hands threw my thighs on opposite sides. It didn't feel the same. It felt nothing like Lethu. Soon, he was on top of me and inside me. I let out a scream. He inserted four fingers into my mouth. All I could do was bite them, but every time I did, he pushed his fingers further down my throat, forcing a gag reflex. The more I gagged, the harder he went. Eventually, the only thing I could do was wait. Wait for him to finish. He would be done – eventually.

'Fuck, you stopped too soon with that biting my fingers stuff,' he said. 'I like that kind of stuff. You're tight too. Fuuck...' He let out something between a sigh and a guilty conscience. Then he said, 'Let's pray.' He was still on top of me, kissing me in between his words. Naked from the waist down – our pants were at the bottom of my bed – he got off me, knelt over on my bed and prayed. 'I didn't know you were really a virgin,' he said, part bouncing on the bed and landing another kiss. 'You're tight.' As he went down to kiss my stomach, it grumbled and he rubbed it. 'Post-sex hunger,' he said.

I wanted to vomit, but I just lay there, praying for sleep to come. He had a dawnie lecture. He would leave early.

I met Reneilwe a few days later, in the dining hall. She made a joke about me being 'the pastor's wife'.

I swore. I swore at her from the depths of all the swear words that had found a home in my body. She seemed unmoved.

'So, pray do tell,' she pried. 'He isn't half the saint he claims to be, hey? He can't be.'

'You don't know the half of it,' I said.

She really did not, but from that day on we made sure to see each other. Run into each other.

'So, does he fuck good?' she asked a week later.

'We broke up,' I said.

'Over so soon,' she sighed.

I didn't feel the need to respond. We never spoke about Simphiwe again, except for the few times we ran into him on campus. He always looked vindicated. I always looked away.

'Mfundisi wakho,' Reneilwe would joke.

Fuck off!

18

Nonhle

There was a tap dripping from something that day. A tap that wasn't closed properly. But there is no tap outside my room. Perhaps it was dripping from the drainage pipe coming down from the roof. The pipe is half-cylinder in shape, not like the ones in school. uBaba had made ours himself; it broke often. There used to be a big brown spot in the ceiling above our sitting room, which Ma insisted had to be painted every year because uBaba refused to buy a new ceiling board, or fix the plumbing. uBaba said he would make a pipe thing himself, so it wasn't a full cylinder like the one at my school. It was a half-cylinder, which awkwardly went down the side of the house, its final destination the drain on the other side of the bathroom wall. The drain behind the toilet. The toilet drain was far from my bedroom window.

So, maybe not a pipe then. Or maybe it had a leak.

There is the sound the night makes when it is quiet. I have heard people say it's frogs but even when it is not the season for frogs you hear it. I know when it's frog season because little frogs start jumping into the space under the door in the evenings; or if you leave the door open after it has rained. Mostly in summer. It rains in summer and for some reason the water gets stuck outside the door and doesn't move.

Sometimes we sweep it away, 'for mosquitoes,' Ma says. Other times she pours a lot of salt by the door to keep the frogs away.

So, it was not frog season.

A woman's voice shouted something in the background. Perhaps neighbours saying their goodbyes to guests. It faded away to the sound of the drip and creak. A car revved from the road behind ours, or even further. I couldn't tell what car it was. Not that I am good at identifying, but Mpumelelo often entertains me.

'Listen to the sound of the exhaust, it is a distinct sound,' Mpumelelo says. 'Not the sound of the engine, which is the first sound, the sound the engine pushes all the way through the exhaust. Listen to that! How the sound travels from the engine to the exhaust? Listen to that!'

The car moved faster than I could remember what to listen to. It was too far, I think. Our street is not quiet often. The factories just behind Sobantu work through the night, as do the people ba dombo. I found out when I was older that they end very late and start very early. Later than I go to bed, and earlier than I wake up. I wonder if they all live eSobantu, with finishing work that late. When would they get to Edendale, or Imbali? The factory, though, it doesn't sleep. 'Shifts,' uBaba once told me. There are people who come in and work from 6 am to 6 pm, and others who come in at 6 pm and leave at 6 am. Twenty-four hours a day the factory must work. uMa works shifts, but the police keep communities safe. Especially at night, when the boys who steal think no one can see them. It's to protect us from the evils of night. They say it at church too. The things of darkness, they are dangerous. Against demons, we have angels. Against naughty boys, we have police.

But why do the people of the factory work all night? There is the factory that makes wood, and another that makes tea. Who needs tea at 3 am? And if we don't have one type of tea, we would all still be fine. Kellogg's, the cornflakes company, is also behind us, a bit further down. I don't know why Kellogg's must be made all night and all day. We don't even buy cornflakes often, and we are fine children. Big, and strong.

Makhosazane was back for her university holidays again, and she bought muesli. I remember I looked at the price that day – it was more expensive than Kellogg's. She must eat it with yoghurt, too, which is even more expensive. Makhosi has always had scholarship money. She buys things without looking at the price.

Makhosi answered the phone. 'ikaZungu, saw'bona,' she said, as she always did.

We had been playing Crazy 8. I was glad she still remembered how to play Crazy 8, because she's forgotten almost everything else about home. Like how to eat umdoko. Going to buy muesli instead.

I was trying to steal a Joker from the pack. I looked up at her. She wasn't looking. Kept saying soft and sad 'yebo', the way you say when speaking to an adult. Almost like the b disappears.

'Ye'o,' she said.

Phone calls are not really that interesting unless one of her friends or one of my friends is calling. Her friends call her on her cell phone now, so phone calls are boring. She walks out the room to answer her phone unless she's speaking a language we don't understand. She speaks isiXhosa and sometimes speaks in Sotho sentences or something. When she first got her cell phone, while she was still in high school, she stayed in the room so we would all know about her nice boarding school life. She'd laugh over the TV and all our conversations. Until Mpumelelo slow-clapped during her phone call once. A loud and very slow clap. Ma was in the kitchen but she pretended not to hear anything. uBaba was sitting trying to watch his third episode of the news that evening. Makhosi just sat there laughing through the most sacred four hours of her father's day. Even he said nothing; nobody said a lot to

Makhosi. So Mpumelelo slow-clapped – and Makhosi ended up crying again.

'You're so good at being a white woman,' Mpumelelo said to her, laughing at her performance. Which made her cry even more.

So now she mostly takes cell phone calls outside, and anyway no one calls me except her and Auntie Nombu. When we were younger, during her longer holidays we would get excited about phone calls because the phone calls were stolen. Ma eventually got a pin code on the phone, a pin code she didn't tell us. And the phone had airtime loaded on it, and they could check the last called numbers and how much airtime was left. Phone calls became less and less exciting for me.

This phone call seemed like one of the boring ones.

I managed to get myself a Joker, a 2 of spades, a 3 of hearts and a 5 of diamonds. Makhosi was always telling me to 'take two for bhayizaring'. I didn't play the game often – I think she must have played it in boarding school – and was constantly waiting for my errors. 'How many cards?' she would scream as I was dropping the card. 'J means Jika, not reverse. Take two for bhayizaring.'

I had more cards now than I did when we started the game; she shouldn't notice my new cards.

'Yes, I will. Thank you for letting us know,' she said and hung up the phone.

I quickly returned to how I had been sitting before the phone rang. I played the Joker and the 2 of spades in one go when she came back. She didn't trust my comeback and tickled me for cheating. The cards spread all over the tiles as I kicked and screamed.

It wasn't until I heard her tell Ma that I realised her mood had changed.

'uMamncane ushonile,' Makhosi said.

Ma's scream filled the entire street. I don't think I was even done picking up the cards and uMam'Mvelase our neighbour was there. She had iduku around her shoulders, walking in with her back bent, and her hands folded behind her back.

uMa was on the floor, screaming, crying, weeping. I had never seen Ma like this.

'Hamba uyo cima iTV, neradio,' Makhosi said.

'What happened to Mamncane?' I asked.

'Ushonile,' Makhosi said, walking past me and out of the room. When she came out of our bedroom, she was also wearing iduku and had changed into a skirt. She walked right past what felt like my frozen body, walked out the house, and started sweeping the yard.

I had never seen Makhosi clean the yard, or wear iduku without being forced. Also, how did she say those words with such ease? uMamncane, her favourite adult. Her Mamncane had died, and she just rolled it off her tongue and started cleaning the yard.

The sound of Ma's crying was no longer audible to me. I could only see my sister. Greeting more women who were coming in with amaduku across their bodies, walking with their backs bent. She curtseyed with every greeting. Said 'abadala bangaphakathi' to everyone who greeted. No one asked. I just stood there. Makhosi looked at me for a few seconds and then continued sweeping our yard, picking up little bits of paper and plastic that were on the floor. She looked at me as if I was the one who was acting out of the ordinary. Eventually, I moved to switch off the TV, and radio, covered all the mirrors and started making tea for our guests.

uGogo arrived the next day. She seemed the most recognisable adult. She put me under her skirt as she always did. Offered me tea and biscuits like she always did. Protected me from adults who asked 'wenzani la?'

uMamncane's body took two weeks to arrive.

There was commotion about who would sit ocansini, uGogo or someone else. I didn't understand who else it should be, but

I heard other aunts gossiping about dying alone, and without a family. It sounded like everyone was saying this woman, our Mamncane, had lived a sad life. Which I didn't understand because she was the happiest woman I knew. But there was no one to ask any questions. Makhosi had become a cleaning master, and uMpumelelo the family chauffeur. Nkosana stayed at home to answer to requests that would come from the men. uBaba was at the back somewhere, drinking.

I didn't see much of anyone those two weeks either. Often only seeing Makhosi when we went to bed. I went to school that week, while she was on holiday. Every day Makhosi was in long skirts and iduku. Some days I found her baking. I think Mpumelelo and Nkosana were about as drunk as uBaba halfway through that week, and uMa was sitting with uGogo ocansini. I was the person running around trying to find people I didn't even know, asking about things I didn't know.

Makhosi was in the kitchen baking when I found out that Mamncane wasn't in fact Ma's sister. That she was uMkhulu's sister's daughter, umshana kaMkhulu. Her father had refused to pay inhlawulo. She got sick and couldn't live at her maternal home. uMkhulu already had many daughters who could grow up with her; it made sense that he took her. Ma also does that, takes abazala to come live with us. If Ma doesn't have a space for someone, it will be passed on to my other aunts.

That was not what made Mamncane become their child though. Apparently, Mamncane's mother was later killed by the girlfriend of the man she accused of impregnating her. When Mamncane went to school. There was no death certificate for her mother, because washona ngengozi. She was buried immediately; and they didn't have anything that belonged to her father. So uGogo noMkhulu said she was their child.

Years later, one of Nombu's paternal uncles recognised Nombu and told her she was not Gogo's child. Mamncane Nombu left to live with her paternal family, angry at uGogo noMkhulu for lying to her. During that time she was in the process of changing her surname, which uMkhulu never forgave her for. Even after she came back and apologised. Her siblings and her father never forgave her. Only uMa and uGogo forgave her.

Makhosi and I both stood with tears flowing down from our eyes as we listened to Mamkhulu Thola drunkenly speaking about our Mamncane's secrets so publicly now that she had died. There were many people in and around the kitchen hearing this for the first time. Mamkhulu Thola was not about to move either; she had found herself a chair in the middle of the kitchen, close to the sink where she was finishing cleaning amathumbu.

Having died without a surname, she continued, as if someone had asked her to start this story in the first place, it was not necessary that Nombu be buried emakhaya.

Eventually uMa crawled out of ucansi to tell Mamkhulu Thola that it was enough now.

Mamkhulu Thola just grinned and put the jug of umqombothi back under her chair; which was pointless. It was pointless to try to hide now because she was already drunk and had forgotten she'd been 'stealing sips'.

Mamncane Nombu also had not wanted to be buried emakhaya, I heard other adults say.

'Graves shouldn't be in a yard,' I had heard Mamncane say once in a heated conversation about uMalume's funeral. 'Graves are for those who remain behind, so we remember. That's why we have tombstones, to remember. Graves eyadini do not even allow us to forget so we can remember. They remain as wounds that will not heal.'

She spoke a lot of sense, I guess. Everyone seemed to understand, but even then there were murmurs.

So, it was with her funeral – umsebenzi womngcwabo was going to be ekhaya as she had mostly lived there, as Ma and uBaba's child, early in their marriage. The story I had known was that Nombu moved in with them to be closer to nursing college, not that she had left. But it seems the story may include her giving uMkhulu space to heal from her having left, and that uMa's house became her home.

I saw Makhosi's face fuelled with fury that day. But she didn't cry. The tears came, but she didn't cry. Over and over again for those weeks, I saw her swallow her tears. While Nkosana, Mpumelelo and Baba drank theirs away.

Our precious Mamncane was stuck in a foreign country, dead with no one to even pack her house. Did she have a house? And this was also not her house, or her family. Did no one else care? None of us were fighting for her, for our Mamncane.

The day before the funeral, Makhosi took off iduku. She had started wearing a beret everywhere. She wore her black beret, put on her sunglasses, got into her car and shouted, 'Asambe!'

She didn't talk the whole way. I didn't want to go with her. I wanted to hear more gossip. The body had finally arrived. It stayed at the mortuary, and there were rumours about Mamncane having started to rot. Which was why her body had not come home for umlindelo. I wanted to know if it was true.

My job for the funeral, the first part of the funeral, was to stand at the door of Khwezi High School hall and hand out the funeral programme. When uMalume died I was still very small, but I remember his funeral being ebhayeni emakhaya; even though he no longer lived there. A tent was put up in front of the door and chairs filled both the tent and the lounge. uMamncane yena was different. She had told her friends in England that she did not want to have a funeral in a church building. It did not surprise me, nor did it seem to surprise uMa. Mamncane did not like going to church. uMa tried forcing all of us to go on Christmas, but even then Mamncane would stand outside.

'Abelungu abanaJesu.' I'd once heard uMa saying something about a boy who had been beaten by a white employer for eating a pie at his store. 'uMamncane uhlale kakhulu nabelungu, that's why she doesn't like church.'

uMa had to constantly fight the rest of the family. 'Into ebeyifunwa nguyena uNombu,' she kept calmly trying to remind everyone with every fight that happened those two weeks.

'Ufuna simoshe imali nje uNombu, kusho khona ukuthi kumele thina singadli nje ngesimanga saNombu,' one of my aunts said when uMa suggested we use a community hall. Nombu had said she did not want a church funeral, but had not said where she wanted to be buried. A school hall would be what would bring the peace.

uNombulelo wazalwa ngomhla ka 10 November 1971, wakhuliswa nguMandla noGetrude Zulu. Amabanga akhe aphansi wawaqala eMehlokazulu Primary school, amabanga aphakathi wawafunda kwaMkhize High School, kwathi izifundo zamatikuletsheni waziphothula eMtshezi High School. uNombulelo wandisa ulwazi analo ngokwezemfundo wafunda iNursing eEstcourt Educational Hospital, lapho aqala khona nokusebenza. waphinda wafunda eKings College London, lapho ebesehlala khona esebenzela eRoyal Hospital of Wimbledon ngengoSonhlalakahle.

And there it was, in two languages. Mamncane really was not Ma's sister; but she was. The obituary was translated into English on the other side. I think it was to cater for all of Mamncane's friends who would have not been able to hear isiZulu. Even the choir sang a few sad English hymns, which surprised me because they didn't sing these a lot when I was at church.

The choir stood in front of the school hall singing as the people walked inside. They were all dressed in black; the women wore silky purple scarves and the men purple ties. It was my family's theme. All of us had something purple with our clothes. A purple flower on the opposite side of the pocket stuck with a pin on all the boys' shirts. The girls had either a purple thing in their hair, or a purple belt or a purple scarf. uBaba was the only one sitting on the side of the family without anything purple on him.

'OkwoTie nje?' uMa had asked him that morning when we were all getting dressed. uBaba does not like to respond and uMa was in a hurry. uBaba got away with many things because uMa was busy. No one else said anything. But instead of looking like he didn't belong, he was the only one of the older men who looked comfortable. They all took off their ties too, when they had to carry Mamncane out of the hall to the hearse.

My job this time was to stand with the rest of the family as we watched her body leave the hall for the final time. The hall was filled with people. All types of people, white people, Indian people. I heard there were even people from the United Kingdom of London.

I had seen some of the people coming in, the white people rubbing my head and hugging Makhosi as they walked in.

'Oh.'

'Ah.'

'NON-SHLE, MAK-U. Condolences,' they said.

We were meant to stay at the door until the programmes were finished, but Makhosi soon got annoyed at all the hugs and told me to put the programmes on the chairs instead. There were a lot of chairs. I would have preferred to stand at the door, but Makhosi was determined. 'Just leave them on the chairs,' she said, not waiting for my response.

She started with the chairs at the back. I followed suit and didn't need to work as hard. All the adults sitting in the back just took the stack of programmes away from me, took one and passed them forward. The school hall was filled with people. Many of those standing in the back and the aisle had to move aside to create space for the coffin. The family was asked to walk out first, and stand by the aisle. This was the saddest day I had ever seen in a school hall. The sound of tears and sniffles and people who knew me who wouldn't look me in the eye; and the ones who did would lip something that looked like they were saying 'I'm sorry.' We stood in the aisle as I held Makhosi and uMa's hands, humming a song about udondolo lokungena ezulwini. Everyone said it was Gogo's favourite song, that she used to sing it with Mamncane in the kitchen. The women were on the right, the men on the left. uBaba was the only one of the men who cried, just cried. There was no sound, but there were tears flowing from under his glasses that he took long to wipe off. The people left inside followed the coffin as it came past us. Ma and Makhosi held my hands even tighter.

The picture that sat on top of Mamncane's coffin didn't show her as very sad. A friend of hers from the UK had sent uMa the picture; apparently it was taken a month before she died. She didn't look sad to me. I didn't mind that she was resting forever. Life was tiring, she was always busy and she lived alone; I wanted to remind everyone next to me. She didn't even have a surname, I wanted to say too. How sad it must be to live without a surname. But she is resting now, so don't cry for her. Even my aunt who had shared all the gossip during the week was crying. It was through her gossip that I had heard that Mamncane's body couldn't even be seen because she had started to rot. I heard also that uMa went to go wash uMamncane the afternoon before in preparation for the funeral. Maybe that was why uMa wasn't crying. Where were all these people when Mamncane died alone? I wondered.

'Ma, why ubungakhali wena emngcwabeni?' I asked her as we were driving back home.

'Umuntu akumele umkhalele sisi uzomvalela indlela phambili,' Ma said.

I tried looking at uBaba. He was looking forward,

concentrating on driving. Tears were still flowing from under his sunglasses. He didn't wipe them at all this time.

'*Wasishiya emhlabeni zingu 29 September 2010,*' her obituary had read.

That had been my last job, collecting back all the programmes. I had been meant to help Makhosi dish up, but some women who said they had worked with Mamncane came and took over from us. We had not complained.

A few days later, Makhosi came back with a tattoo that looked like a barcode with the numbers 101171-290910. It was on the left side of her body, next to her breast. I saw it when we were changing for bed that night.

She went back to Rhodes a few days later, having said very little to anyone for the remainder of her days at home.

19

Makhosazane

Why uMamncane uNombu? Why would a loving God do that to Ma? To my family? To her?

There are no answers for me.

'I don't understand the idea of God,' I tell Reneilwe.

Less than a week after I return to Rhodes, I am institutionalised. 'Bereavement' is what triggers this first visit to Fort England.

I never did, but still, we must share. So, during our 'bereavement' session, I have to share.

Mamncane dreamed big. She wanted to do so much.

'Oh, Khosi, I will build a school the size of the schools in England. Bigger. Bigger, in fact,' she had said to me as we walked down the streets of Tunbridge Wells outside of London. She stretched her arms out wide, taking up parts of the road beside her, like she was a superhero taking on her powers, oblivious to the people around us trying to pass. 'And not just a big school. A GOOD school, Khosi.'

Mamncane moved to England in 2000. I was angry at her for leaving me, even then. I was angrier when she came back for her last visit. Except, I didn't know it was her last visit.

When she left the first time, she said she would call me every day.

'Every day?' I asked.

'Every day, sisi,' she said.

I wanted to tell her that it didn't have to be every day. I was sure she was going to be working hard and making new friends. It wasn't just a different town; it was a different country. An eighteen-hour flight from King Shaka International Airport in Durban to Heathrow International Airport in London. She was going to stop over and take another plane in between, in France, I think. But she wasn't going to be long. Just changing planes.

Mamncane was good at travelling, especially travelling for money. She liked going to Johannesburg. She bought clothes from there to sell when I was younger and sometimes I would go with her. A taxi from home to town; and another from town to Johannesburg. We took many more taxis in Johannesburg. We did not stay long the first time. Then one of her friends moved there, to Soweto, I think; I don't remember. She always had many friends. I was young, and by the time we got to Johannesburg I was tired; and this time we hadn't left early enough to catch the shops open. Which meant I didn't need to stay up to help her gather her stock. 'Sinjani leskhwama?' she would ask me, holding up bags, perfumes and jerseys.

Her friend came to pick us up. I fell asleep as soon as I got into the car and only woke up the next day. I must have been very tired. They said they didn't want to wake me up. The friend – I don't remember her name – drove us into town very early the next morning. We bought stock and travelled by taxi back to Pietermaritzburg.

Mamncane was busy, but she promised to call every day.

She didn't for the first few days. She called to say she had arrived. She still had to buy a sim card, she said, then she would call us more often. After a week, she did. Called every day, speaking to me and Ma. It was because of Mamncane that I got my first cell phone; I was the first of my boarding school friends to have one. Mamncane hated having to wait for me to be called to the phone from somewhere – often from the field. By the time I eventually got to the phone, she would have been waiting for approximately ten minutes. So, she bought me a small phone. The school did not want us to have phones on us, or if we did, they needed to stay with our Matron and were only given to us under supervision for a few hours after we had finished our homework, before quiet time. Mamncane told me I didn't have to, but she suggested I hide the phone, which I did. It was easier for me to hide the phone at school than hand it in.

Mamncane called before sports in the afternoons. I would only answer the phone in the change rooms, or the toilet, or behind the school hall, or inside the library toilets. Wherever there were the least staff members to catch me. Eventually, I had to keep it away from some of the older girls too. They all wanted to take it from me and call their friends, and they threatened to tell on me if I didn't let them. At first, I would run out of class without saying anything at the feel of the vibration in my chest. I didn't have boobs yet, but I wore a sports bra and hid my phone on me. My uniform was a horrible big dress anyway. The only way it touched your chest was if your breasts started to grow and mine simply were not growing. Which I didn't mind either; that way, I could feel the phone when it vibrated during the day.

Runny tummy. I need to blow my nose. Once I even told my class teacher that I ran out because I needed to fart. Everyone in class laughed, which made Mr Sanders angrier because he thought I was making a fool of him. That day I told uMamncane to call ten minutes after school ended. I did not mind being late for sport, but I didn't want to get detention. Besides, I was the best in most of the school teams, and the teachers liked me because I needed the least amount of coaching.

I only did the sports I liked, which excluded sports that required too much running. Except for hockey. But eventually

I switched positions in hockey, and played goalie, which meant I wasn't as active as the rest of the players. Shot put, long jump, hockey and swimming. For the rest of my extramurals, I chose arts and culture activities. We needed to have four extramurals each term. The rule was two sports, and two arts and culture, but I had learned how to make the teachers laugh and I was willing to run around for them; you could manage to get away with more if you did that.

The older I got, the busier I got. And the busier Mamncane was getting too. The phone calls became two to three times a week.

I was in Grade 9 when I went to visit Mamncane. She had recently finished her university degree. She could not afford to bring everyone to her ceremony, she only brought me. Her school was right in the middle of the big lights, bigger than Johannesburg. *King's College London Graduation 2004* read the papers with her name and the names of many other people graduating.

Mamncane worked hard in England. During the day she worked by looking after old people she didn't care for; in the evenings she worked at the hospital as a nurse.

'How did you do this ufunda, Mamncane?' I once asked. I don't remember her answer.

After returning from England, I got less needy for Mamncane's phone calls. I wasn't even angry at first. At first, I understood. Then she came home and bought a car. Then she started fixing uGogo's house. She started buying everyone fancy phones, and giving us expensive jewellery, clothes and perfume for presents. She didn't need to work so hard, I thought. She could come back now. She had wanted to have a child when I was younger, 'ngisebenzela izingane zami,' she would say. Every time she said it I would start expecting her stomach to expand, but it never did. I figured she must have changed her mind. She called less often.

'Haibo, ntombi, aren't you happy with your gift? Chips wena,' she said after she handed me a watch one time she was home to visit. A silver watch with diamond-like things. I did not like the watch. Had she forgotten who I was? Why would I want to wear that watch? Did she not care anymore even to ask? And how was she ignoring me, ignoring her? She used to ask me after two hours of not speaking to her, 'Is it me, my Khosi?'

At first I would pretend to not want to say anything, then she would tickle and beg me until I said okay I forgive her. Then she would ask what it was that I forgave, and I would eventually tell her why I was angry at her. Had she forgotten that ritual too? How to ask me if I am angry at her? Did it not matter to her?

I didn't speak to her much when she came back that last time. She wasn't back for us anyway. She was back only to bury her brother. She didn't even stay for long. She paid for everything, gave everyone clothes and gifts, and left.

Then she died.

Had her dreams all died? Was that why God was fine taking her? Was it because she no longer wanted to work for izingane zakhe and was working for nice things? But maybe dreams change too.

When Zama and I had been caught kissing at school, I told Mamncane uNombu about the letter from the school. She laughed and said, 'Namanje nisayenza leyonto?' I don't know how she knew; I didn't want to ask her either. I didn't want to know how much she knew. She called the school the next day. The school knew she was one of my guardians; they had seen her at school before. I don't know what she said, but it never did get to uMa; and Zama's mother didn't hear of it either. Mamncane uNombu was our go-to person, for both of us. Our hope was she would talk to my parents and Zama's before we gave them the letters, but she simply told us we could throw those letters away. We didn't even have to give them to our parents. She outdid herself that time.

Zama took it as a second chance at redemption or some other shit like that. We never kissed again. But Mamncane never asked about it again either. I guess it was mostly my loss.

Mamncane's last day with us was a Saturday. She was due to catch an 8 am flight from King Shaka International, which meant she would leave our house at 4 am on Sunday. The days before she left were always reserved for me and her. I would help her do a big shopping routine of getting our house, and kaGogo, a trolley's worth of groceries. I tried going into Ma's room that evening, to remind her that we had not kept our ritual. Ma and Mamncane were busy calculating how much they had spent on the funeral. Receipts were on the bed, and Mamncane was helping Ma add up the amounts. I pretended I was looking for Vaseline. I took the Vaseline and walked out of the room. I started singing, walking up and down the house.

'Waze wasenza lomuntu owafika nemali, nguye owaletha usatana lapha emhlabeni.'

I did not join Mamncane's farewell team the next morning. She came to my room to wake me and say her goodbyes. She sat at the foot of my bed.

'Are you not coming with us to the airport, Makhosi?' she asked.

'I'm tired,' I said.

I was not completely lying. I had struggled to fall asleep the whole night waiting on her to come to our room, even if it was for a few minutes to entertain me. I wanted to tell her about Simphiwe, and Lethu, and Philani. I fell asleep waiting.

'The world will not give us everything we want on silver platters,' Mamncane said.

'I don't want things on silver platters,' I responded angrily.

'Your anger tells me that you expect platters of silver, from people who have only started getting spoons of silver. You need to place your anger at the people who cause your anger, not the people trying to respond to their anger too. I love you very much. Bye.'

She walked out, and didn't close the door. I couldn't go back to sleep, with everyone scrambling around the house.

'Isikhiye?'
'Passport?'
'Jacket?'
'Asambeni, asambeni!' she shouted finally

The last time Mamncane and I had a fight like that, I was eight years old. I had come back from school asking for curly silky hair. 'A hot iron,' Mamncane said, was what made curly silky hair. We did not have a hot iron, but she had those prickly rollers.

'You're too young for rollers in your hair,' she said.

'But I want them!' I said.

That night I woke up screaming and crying for her to take the rollers off my hair.

'Kunobuhle obusetshenzelwayo,' Mamncane said, as she took them off.

I didn't know what she meant then. A few years later, Zama and I laughed at uMamncane's wisdom. By then we were in Grade 8 and preparing for our fresher's ball. The girls in our class complained about the pain they had endured just to get hairstyles. 'Ubuhle buyasetshenzelwa,' Zama and I laughed.

Mamncane was wise and busy. Busy so that she could stay here, make more money to stay here.

I do not understand why God took her instead of me.

I have nothing here. Nothing I want to stay for, work for, save for.

I get back to res to find flowers in my room. The warden and the house comm. They have also left a letter for me, saying all their doors are open as well as the counselling centre.

Reneilwe insists that counselling is the only thing that will help.

So, I go to counselling. All I say is that I want to die, and that I think about it often.

I am in the government institution for twenty-one days. Voluntarily.

I sleep in a dormitory with three other women. So, maybe not a dorm, but close. People complete their twenty-one days and leave, while new ones come in. I learn later that a lot of the new ones, who are new to me, are new to very few other people. A woman who was in my dorm, Elizabeth, comes back on my seventeenth day. I do not remember her. My first few days in the hospital, most of those remain a blur.

Like a boarding school, we have a daily routine. We go for walks.

I finish my twenty-one days, and leave.

20

Abdullah Ibrahim is playing in the background, like the sound of my father's radio on Sundays. Jazz requires silence.

I have not spoken to uMa for over a month, maybe two. It started off as a silence in preparation for going in for my next twenty-one days. Then it had been too long since we last spoke. Everything about thinking of speaking to her made me nervous and anxious. She had tried all the means of communicating with me.

'It's not your battle to fight, not your place to respond on my behalf,' I tell Reneilwe.

Ma eventually called her – to know if her daughter was really alive. She said she just needed to hear my voice.

'My mother is dramatic. It's unnecessary,' I say.

'You cannot hold people hostages of your depression,' Reneilwe says. 'We are here to support you, but do not hurt other people.'

She keeps talking, even though I have said the problem is me. I am standing over the kitchen counter rolling another joint. My hands shake. From the coffee. From insangu. From utter fear. I cannot look her in the eyes. How silent Grahamstown is able to become, especially during the university holidays when there are no loud screams of drunk students.

Abdullah Ibrahim fills the loud silences of townships as the township mourns its short-lived carefreeness; as it mourns its return to out at 5 am, in at 7 pm. Abdullah Ibrahim reminds me of Sunday afternoons in my mother's house. I long for the loud silences of my mother's Sobantu house, not Grahamstown silence. I do not require this silence.

Reneilwe is staring at me from across the kitchen counter. I think she says something. I look up from my joint, reassuring her I am listening with my eyes; the eye contact is all she needs.

'You refuse to believe that you are capable of being loved,' she continues. 'Who did this to you? Fuck that. Why did you believe them?'

I stare.

She doesn't seem to be aware of my presence anymore, or maybe my presence no longer matters. She frowns down at the book she is holding in her hands. A vegetarian recipe book – for dummies. I have even forgotten she is cooking. She cooks, I roll a joint as our starter. It has become our routine. Her hand shakes as she lays it on the counter. She takes up the knife she uses to chop.

'The world that hurts us forgets to lick our wounds,' she says, disrupting my thoughts. 'And some wounds fast become septic, hey?' Her eyes start welling up, tears falling onto the knife.

'I am septic. I think I am septic.' I need her to know it is not me, that it is beyond my control, that I am diseased and septic.

'Septicaemia can be healed,' she says as she turns back to look at me, the knife now in front of her. She stands facing me, looking into my eyes.

'Or it can kill you,' I say.

'You seem to be choosing death,' she says. 'I think we have a choice on death. I think we decide when we are done. I think we negotiate with izinyanya. I think they tell us, and ezakokwenu izinyanya are telling you have to be here for longer. It's you who is refusing.'

'Stay here for what though?' I ask, hoping this time the answers she gives me will find a place. The knife is still in her hand. The light above her head makes the knife reflect as she moves her hand. She comes closer to hand me the joint. The knife dangles as she is caught in a cough.

'Water?' I ask. She shakes her head, as her eyes almost pop out from the cough.

'Iyangena,' I joke. She doesn't laugh.

She kisses me on the cheek as she walks out. I want to give her one final hug, but something won't let me. I can't move.

I am tired of hurting the people I love.

Suicide. Or self-destruction.

Everything hurts others in the process though.

Death.

The ultimate self-destruction?

I type another suicide letter. I need to. I am going home to uMa, and I am going to try be my healthiest. She needs me strong. Note number 17. Writing suicide letters is what gives me strength now. Or at least they remind me I am not strong enough to kill myself.

So I must be strong here. For Ma.

21

Dudu

'Aw, Ngonombulelo. uSathane unomona. Unomona uSathane mkami, uyezwa!' Feeling his way across the sofas as if akaboni. The only thing leading him to his safe, regular plummeting landing on the long sofa being ukwazi. That he knows the sofa is there, even if he cannot see it.

For the first time in a long time, all my children are home early in December for us to spend time together. I do not need a December with a sulking Thulani taking away from my loss.

Nombulelo was mine before she was anyone else's. She was mine to raise. I was forced to think fast on my feet with Nombulelo. For myself, I had the constant back and forth to my parents. Mostly uZulu, as uMaDlamini could have an opinion but never the money to finance her opinion; still I went to her. Even with my own money, I went back and forth. Took my first cheque, an actual pay-cheque then, to uZulu for him to deliver emsamo but also for him to give me my share for the rest of the month. This meant they would know how much I had for months later. MaDlamini subtly passing me responsibilities until she eventually passed me Nombulelo. Nombulelo never consulted them. She consulted me instead.

I tried going back and forth with Ma about Nombulelo, but

I had quickly become like uZulu. Nombulelo was mine, and it was my money, and so I made the final decision.

Ma still offers her opinions and they comfort me. So I decide to go home for December to my mother's house.

A few days before December gets busy with Christmas shopping, Thulani drops us off with our boot full of food and house things. Old curtains. Paint for the walls. New carpets for the floor. Cups, saucers, spoons. We stop in Mooi River to get perishable foods, and Nkosana picks up sets of plastic plates and cups; and the cooler box, which is hidden behind the nice pots and pans at the top of our long drawer. Taller than his father, Nkosana just stretches himself around the house not saying much. It was Nombulelo's task before, the cutlery and 'hidden' cooler box. Yet Nkosana does it seemingly without any thought. My first children are so similar.

Makhosazane and Mpumelelo opt to stay in the car in Mooi River, to look after it. An excuse that Thulani often uses when we go shopping. This time he comes into the shops with us to rush us into getting the last groceries so he can rush back to Pietermaritzburg. To drink, of course. He still has to get home, have some conversation with my father. Then my mother. Then eat and have conversations with my siblings. Another thirty minutes to an hour before he can try to leave, saying goodbye to all the local men coming to congratulate him about his car. Which they have seen many times. He tries to keep the conversation short by reaching into his cubby-hole filled with R5 coins.

'Ukuzama nsizwa.' 'Hayi ngiyabonga, mfwethu,' he says, half reversing, half in conversation. Finally, he leaves in a cloud of dust with children first chasing behind the car but then caught up in the dust cloud and falling back.

'Akeve shesha umyeni wakho,' MaDlamini complains.

I want to say it is because he is rushing to get drunk ematavern nezingane ezincane, but my sisters are here and Nombu is not. I do not want to become them.

'Wangikhumbuza uNombulelo,' I say to MaDlamini.

She complains about Thulani's speeding too. I wonder whether she sees now that her praises before were because wayengaboni. Now she can see, uyabona, that Thulani has turned me into my sisters. We have not been home for half a day.

Nkosana walks into the kitchen and sits down next to the Welcome Dover, on the floor. That side of the stove used to be left empty because that was where Zulu sat when we were younger. Behind the stove. Like a shadow. He does not come into the kitchen anymore. I have not seen him come into the kitchen since the children were small. He eats erondweni lakhe now.

'Uzosha,' I try saying to Nkosana, but he moves closer to the wall and away from anyone's sight.

It is almost supper time and the kitchen is about to be filled with children on the floor anyway. So I let Nkosana be. The children start to gather in the kitchen in groups, finding themselves a spot. The braver ones sit on the concrete floor with a thin layer of uMata; while the others go into the rest of the house looking for amacansi. The kitchen doesn't seem big enough for all of us, and all our children. We have gifted MaDlamini many children. More children than she ever had. A wide variety of ages. Kazi uyophumula nini yena uMaDlamini I wonder. Even with the plates we have brought with us, we are still short of three plates for the children.

It is my turn to cook. It is always the turn of the one who has arrived to cook supper if they arrive in time to cook. When Nombu was here, she would twist Thulani's arm for us to stop at the KFC by the toll-gate to get two family buckets, and then we would buy five loaves of bread with the groceries. I had not cared to beg Thuani to stop at the KFC this time, and neither did the kids. So, it is my turn to cook.

'Kanti bekudliwa kanjani kushoda amaplate?' I ask.

'Izingane lana zidlena esitsheni esisodwa. Ezincane,

ezindala. Abafana, amantombazane bese ke ezakho zidla nani emakamereni angithi?'

I can feel MaDlamini's eyes on my back. I can feel everyone's eyes on my back. I dish up for my sisters and their children first, then wait for the first group to finish so I can dish for myself and my children. The older boys finish first.

Without being asked, Makhosi stands up to wash the plates and then dishes for us. After supper, my children stay sitting next to me while the others go to watch TV. It is the first time all of us have been here for as long as I can remember. Nonhle and Makhosazane are the only ones who come for a long stay. In the previous years, the boys would either stay behind or come with us only to greet uGogo noMkhulu and then go back with Thulani. With them here, at least it means I will be going back to a clean house. Unless Thulani brings his friends over. In which case, the house will be cleaner with the boys there.

'MA! WOZA UZOBONA!' Mpumelelo suddenly shouts from outside.

I don't run because I am sure whatever it is, I probably know what it was. By the time I get outside my sisters, nieces and nephews are watching Mpumelelo stare into space. Nonhle holds onto my skirt like a child, and Makhosazane is trying to pull her away behind me. We join Mpumelelo staring into nothingness.

'Yini, boy?' I ask.

'It's light. It's so light! You basically don't need street lights here. Bheka, I can see kwaShabalala nakwaMkhabela, nakwaSkhosana from here.'

Everyone goes back into their respective houses, bored by Mpumelelo's discovery of light.

'Unyezi, my boy,' I tell him, taking back indishi which he was meant to clean and bring back. 'It's been like this here since I was a child. Perfect for the nights when I slept on that mountain because kulahleke inkomo.'

'Why would you sleep on the mountain if kulahleke inkomo?' Nonhle asks.

'Wawungabuyi layikhaya if izinkomo aziphelele,' I say. 'But nights like this were good nights. Good, for light. Which also would serve to remind you that even in the light you have lost inkomo. If you're lucky, it has disappeared with its cow friends and izobuya.'

'And if ayibuyanga?'

'Then you know that the next few days are for searching and coming in and out of the house without Zulu seeing you. When he was calmer, MaDlamini would eventually know it was safe to come back. And so we would.'

'And on nights when it wasn't like this? When it was dark – nanenzenjani?'

'Wawuguqa uthandaze mtanam' umemeze okhokho bokhokho, nomkhulu bomkhulu wakho ukuthi uphephe ubsuku bonke. But you were never alone entabeni. At least you knew that. There was always a few yezinkomo ezingabuyi. So you found comfort in knowing nibaningi enilele entabeni.'

'That's not comforting,' Makhosi says.

'To you maybe,' Nkosana says. 'There is strength in numbers. Anyway, Ma, uBaba gave me imali yamakhumbi ngicabanga ukugibela k'sasa and go back home. You're fine here, right?'

'Fine? My boy, I am at home, of course I am fine. But why visit for only one night?'

'I just wanted to know you're fine. Goodnight, Ma.' Nkosana closes the door behind him.

'And you, Lelo? Do you also have taxi fare that the rest of us don't have?' Makhosi asks.

'I'm sure you would have too, if you spoke to your parents every now and then,' Mpumelelo says. 'Yes, nginayo, kodwa angihambi. But I'll stay here with uMa.'

It is interesting, watching my children speak over me, in my presence. The way my sisters and I spoke over my mother and watched her disappear.

Everyone exited the kitchen after supper. My nieces and nephews first. Then their mothers, claiming that they were checking on husbands. But I do not remember when MaDlamini walked out, and it is her I need. Her I am here for. The children could have been with their father instead of tugging at iphinifa lami.

I pull it out of Nonhle's hand and go to put away izitsha. The handle of the yellow steel two-door cupboard in the kitchen is almost falling off. It has way too many stains, of hands, of grease.

'Makhosazane, ngicela iHandy Andy nendishi,' I say.

'Sesiwachthile amanzi,' she says.

The boys must have walked out earlier too. I don't remember seeing them go. At home, I have an ability to not be fully aware. I have not been fully aware for a very long time. Perhaps it is knowing MaDlamini is here. Somewhere, in some background.

'Ma? Water? Yes or no?' Makhosazane says, almost waving the small plastic basin at me. Even the inside of the basin for dishes is dirty.

'Yes, sisi. Ashise.'

'There is no kettle here, Ma.'

I turn around. On the top of the stove is igedlela. I reach over and hand it to her.

'Urghhhhh, but it's going to take so long to get hot. FIIINE,' Makhosi says. She drags herself from the water bucket over to the stove.

The stove is as dirty as the rest of this kitchen. I wait for the water to get lukewarm, then start scrubbing the cupboards. So many of them are falling apart. Old as they are, it isn't age that's making them fall apart. It is being used by too many people, too often. I will change my kitchen, I decide, when Makhosi graduates, and give uMa my old cupboards. Then I realise that my cupboards are built in, and wood. They would be hard to install. And they will break easily here. Maybe I will buy new ones.

When did I become the person who always fixes? I wonder.

Maybe my sisters will also see these cupboards and bring it up.

The electricity wires that go from the house to Nkosana's room are a danger to everyone. That is what I need to fix.

No. Why am I always thinking about fixing? Go into song instead. I rinse the cloth out.

I am looking at the long cupboard, the one in the corner next to the short ones, and thinking even this cupboard is dirty when MaDlamini walks in. She comes in silently, like she always moves, but the door screeches so I turn. The yard is almost quiet, except for the low laughs of the boys from a distance in their rooms.

'Nak'sasa yilanga mtanam,' MaDlamini says to me.

Makhosi is on her phone next to the stove, and Nonhle has fallen asleep on the floor.

'Makhosi, hamba uyolalisa ingane,' I say, stepping over Nonhle to go sit where she had been sitting, next to the stove. Where Ma has gone to sit. It is the peak of summer, and here we are roasting ourselves. Habit.

'FIIINE,' Makhosi says, dragging herself again. 'Vuka.' She gives her sister a light kick.

'No!' I say, frowning.

'FIIIIIIIINE,' she says again, and bends over to shake Nonhle's shoulder.

MaDlamini bursts out in laughter and I join her. I have missed hearing her laugh.

Nonhle finally stands up, hanging off Makhosi, who drags the door, not caring to close it.

'Asambe siyolala mntanam',' Ma says, struggling to get up from her chair.

'Usumdala yaz', Ma,' I say.

'Wena, njengoba unemdidiyane emide ele yezintombi. Nawe umdala,' she says, still trying to hold on to the chair and manoeuvre herself out.

'Unjani, Ma?' I ask, a question, I realise, I have not asked in a very long time. I take her hands. They are cold, regardless of how hot the kitchen is.

'Ngiyancenga mtanam', ngiyancenga,' she says, looking directly at the door still open and trying to draw her fragile hand out of mine. Her skin feels old, slippery and incredibly creased. She has very little strength left in her hands. I stand up to help lift her, bending down in front of her a little, lending her my hands to hold on to.

'Kuncengeka kangcono kulezitini, buka akhona namafan namaheater asigodoli,' she says, wincing. Pulling herself up with my help and then waddling past me. 'Ulale,' she says, not looking back at me.

You need a walking stick, I say, but only in my head.

'*Ngiphe Baba. udondolo lokungena ezulwini,*' I sing as I continue cleaning the kitchen.

22

Nonhle

Ma and I are sitting on the veranda. It isn't hot, humid and stuffy like Maritzburg summers are. The thing about humidity is you never know what to do. Earlier we had argued about whose turn it was to cook. Technically, it is Ma's turn, but she pretends to have forgotten. We finally decide on amasi. I will make uphuthu, which is quick and easy, and Ma will get to rest. In fact her cooking turns are mostly suggestions these days. She is getting older, and she has become quite frail.

I like cooking, but sometimes the only food in the house is the same for weeks on end. Especially before payday. Chicken, tomatoes, onions, potatoes and carrots. So I run out of ideas. But I don't mind cooking entirely. Especially to give uMa rest. The wrinkles around her eyes are worse now, which is scary because they weren't gradual. I remember one day looking at her face, and they just were. Maybe it's that we don't see her a lot. Even on her off days and leave days, she is busy with something.

'Uyaguga,' I tell her.

'Ukuzala ukuguga,' she responds.

We hear Makhosi's car before we see it. Ma smiles the smile which seems reserved only for my sister. I think she has a particular look for both her 'first borns'.

The car makes a rattling sound as it drives up the street leading to our house, something close to a motorbike but not quite. An unhealthy car sound, I will learn, after Ma buys her first brand-new car. The only sounds a car should make are the sound of it starting, perhaps the sound as it drives over a speed bump, or when the driver is doing something wrong with pressing at the pedals. Makhosi's car sounds like a constantly sick car.

Makhosi steps out with a clean-shaven head.

She has only been home two days when the geyser in our bathroom bursts. The sound of the water exploding from the geyser gushing onto our bathroom floor makes Ma jump from the sofa. It is then that I realise how small, and weak, she can look. Which is funny because how does she survive her job if burst geysers scare her?

Instead of running around looking for towels like Ma and I are doing, Makhosi asks annoying questions like 'Who installed it?' and 'When last was it checked?', forcing Ma to give answers in her rattled state.

'Ngizoyilungisa,' Ma says.

I give Makhosi a cold stare and hand her a towel. I know the geyser will not be fixed for months. A burst tire, a car accident, a school trip. Something always stops Ma's 'budget'. Once her car broke down as she was taking me to get on a school trip. uBaba took too long to get to us and the school bus left me because I was late. Ma did not get her refund.

It was only after Mpumelelo started working that Ma bought her first brand-new car. A Volvo SUV. With seven seats. Although she didn't have seven passengers to sit there. 'Imoto engaka?' I asked Ma. 'Who will fill all these seats?'

'You, Makhosi, Mpumelelo, Nkosana and all the grand-children you will all give me,' Ma said, clearly delusional.

It was driving from Durban to Pietermaritzburg late one Friday evening, Lelo driving, that decided it for Ma. Thinking it would be better if we took the back routes so as to not be stopped by the traffic police on one of their Friday night roadblocks, we drove through Pinetown, passing Hillcrest and the Valley of a Thousand Hills. There were houses, thatched houses, on the side of the road which looked like they belonged in a version of The Hobbit. There was an on- ramp coming up which would take us back to the freeway, but before we got there, there in front of us was a roadblock. The police pulled us over, asked for Lelo's licence, walked around the car and said we could go. Ma and Lelo laughed that they wouldn't have to run away from cops, and waste petrol taking inside routes, ever again. We could see the freeway when the car broke down – again. That was when Mpumelelo convinced Ma that she needed to buy a new car. Ma always had a long list of many things that needed fixing – the geyser was one – but she also really deserved a car. She is not going to justify the necessity of buying a new car, not to Makhosi. I don't understand why she tries so hard. Ma justifies nothing to no one.

When we finish mopping up the floor from the burst geyser, I tell Makhosi it is her turn to cook. She tries making up many excuses for why she can't. Ma tries taking her side, but I force Ma to sit down across from me and ignore Makhosi's complaints. I turn on my headphones and listen to Bongeziwe Mabandla, Silindile's favourite artist. I remember wanting to tell Makhosi about having discovered him, but I also didn't want the long conversations that would follow.

Ma tries standing up.

'Udinga ini?' I ask.

'Amanzi,' she says.

'I'll get it for you.'

I walk past Makhosi, who keeps peeking her head out of the kitchen, take a glass from the cupboard, and pour some water for Ma. Makhosi has turned the kitchen upside down to try to gather more attention. She is so much like her father, I think. Ma tries turning her head to look into the kitchen, but I stop her. I give her the glass of water.

Trying to distract her from her lazy daughter, the daughter she coddles, I say, 'Let's go sit on the veranda.'

One day. One day I will leave these two to tire each other out.

178

23

Makhosazane

'I'm fighting a losing battle, my love,' I say.

I am lying on the bed, lost in some thought or another. Johannesburg evenings are like this. Constantly moving, busy. Lost in transit, and in thoughts. Even when I am trying to rest.

'Try medication, MK. Please try medication.'

This is what Tumi says. She says it again now, from the passage of our flat where she is mopping. She mops the house every evening, only for us to mess it up again every morning. I have tried telling her she can skip some days, but she insists on doing it.

'You know that shit makes me numb,' I say. 'I can't think on that shit. Fuck it. Also, you know I do not believe in western medicines. That shit is poison. You know it is.'

Besides, fuck it, alcohol is cheaper than medication. I don't say this out loud. Instead I stand up and go into the kitchen to try to help figure out what we'll have for supper.

'There is an obsession with diagnosis here, Tum-Tum,' I add. 'Everyone is mentally ill. I mean, fuck, everyone is a mess. And how else are we not messes, here?' Show me a black who does not drink, or smoke weed, and I will show you a sell-out, I will often joke, but tonight I don't bother.

'When last did you speak to your mom?' Tumi asks, leaning on the mop.

'Why do you keep bringing up my mom every time we speak about medication?' I say, looking inside the fridge, which only has lettuce leaves, and milk.

There is something about Itu that calms me down; even her invasive questions feel less invasive. I stand drinking the milk straight out of the carton.

'Stop drinking out the carton like a poor white, please,' she says. Her only jab at me, for my constant jabs at her lifestyle.

Tumi wakes up early every morning to meditate. She has something she calls... buddha beads? Who knows?

I met her on the Wits campus. She was sitting on the library lawns, legs crossed, looking blissful.

'May I borrow a lighter, please?' I asked.

'You're gorgeous,' she said.

'Thank you,' I said.

Shocked. I hadn't looked at her. Perhaps I was preoccupied. If there was a kind of woman I was attracted to, most of them did not look this content, happy. I bent down to get the lighter and light my cigarette.

'You should wear blue lipstick, it will look gorgeous with your skin tone,' she said.

'Thanks,' I said, giving back her lighter.

I walked away. Hippies. She was gorgeous though. She had green and purple dreads, or green and purple material around her dreads. Again, who knew? She looked like a hippie. A glowing hippie. A black hippie, I thought, fast removing her from my mind. A black hippie will show you the flames of whiteness.

We ran into each other again every second day after that. She would compliment me every time. I would run out of words, feeling uncomfortable. Between the random 'You're looking great in that outfit' or 'You're glowing,' or whatever other compliments she must clearly cook up every day, I felt exposed. Why was she doing this? Why was she... nice?

Then, one day, when I was sitting reading on a bench, she asked me to lunch.

'How long have you been together?' Nkosana asks, not even minutes after I have introduced him to Tumi, the woman I currently love.

How quickly I learn to love. How many I have loved. Loved them all differently. for different purposes, for different lengths of time, but loved them the best I could. The best way I know how.

Nkosana is living in a back room in Tembisa. A back room where the furniture doesn't quite fit. He has a queen-size bed, which I can't understand given the space and the fact that he lives alone.

'How long have you been together?' he asks again.

'You really need to get a smaller bed,' I say. 'You have your fridge, TV stand and bed in here. There is no need for a big bed. Buy bright bedding. It gives the illusion of a space being bigger than it is.'

I look at Tumi. Our relationship is new. We made big commitments too soon. This, too, is not new for me. I have made commitments in relationships before, then watched them disintegrate before my eyes. How easily our mouths speak resolutions that our minds do not understand, that our bodies don't know how to commit to.

'So, you're avoiding my question then?' Nkosana pesters.

I looked at Tumi again. We are tired of discussing how long we have been together. In lesbian circles, we can quickly sweep this under the rug with a quick 'Aargh, lesbian time moves faster than heterosexual time.' An old joke. A truthful joke, perhaps. In my experience.

'Look, it doesn't matter,' I say, still looking at Tumi to ascertain how much she will allow me to reveal.

That's the thing about one room. The privacy to take two minutes with your partner to discuss stances on issues can't happen in just one room. How black people must raise families with children in these poor conditions is something that haunts me. I wonder how Nkosana lives here. He had been a hope for the family for a long time. Of our generation, he had been the first to go to university. A BCom Accounting, turned to BEd, turned to this. We grew up on little, but never these small spaces. How does he reconcile himself living in a room smaller than his room at home? Not that he comes home often anymore.

First generation Johannesburg migrants, we often joke, when it is only the two of us. uMa hates iGoli, doesn't understand why this is where we chose to go.

'Drive down with Nkosana the next time you come home,' uMa always says.

I suggested this to Nkosana a few times, but eventually I learned that no amount of suggesting will get him to come home with me. 'You go home too often, always wasting petrol,' he would say.

Nkosana tried teaching for a few years and hated it. Then he stopped. Stopped going to work, was figuring himself out. And now? Now he has turned into a Johannesburg hustler. The plan was, and still is, to go back to school. He is saving, he says. He is going to go back. Try an engineering degree.

'So, one month, two months...?' he continues nagging.

'My telling you how long we have been together is your measure of the strength of our relationship, or whatever it is,' I point out. 'Time tells nothing for me where time is excluded from experience. It's our experience that speaks to our relationship. Not time.'

'So, basically uthi vele anikajoli that long?'

Nkosana has the gift of making me rethink the words I am going to say; he is not a person of many words. Even growing up, he chose to respond to my questions with questions instead of straight answers. At first, his questions annoyed me.

'You can't answer a question with a question,' I would say. 'Says who?' he'd reply.

The older I grew, the more I liked his rebuttal questions. They were often hard for me to answer, which kept me thinking and on my feet. During my days of high school debating, and public speaking, I would ask myself: What would Nkosana ask? It helped me think through the different ways that my points could be argued, and the possible questions my statements might raise.

'No, ngithi it doesn't matter,' I say.

Although he is right, asikakajoli for that long, but my answer is valid too.

'Girl you know, I la la love you. Every word I say is true.'

Itu sings at the top of her voice, facing me, pretending to hold a microphone as she feels the words of the song move her.

'Urgh, your heteronormative R&B,' I say, trying to get her to stop disturbing me, trying to concentrate on driving. We are on our way to Nottingham Road.

'You can sing to me and make it as lesbian as you want.'

'You know that's not the point.'

But Itu is no longer listening. She is back singing at the top of her voice.

'Coz I love you and I need you,' she screams.

I hate R&B and she knows it. She is the only person I allow to play R&B anywhere near me; let alone in my car on a long-distance drive. We have both agreed on this playlist, which mostly meant her begging me to add horrible love songs to my reggae, kwaito and maskandi mix. Itu is an 'appreciator' of all music, or so she will say. She doen't have a preference of genre, which makes her playlists all over the place. The one minute I'm dancing to Missy Elliot, the next I find myself singing to Rebecca Malope, then fast reminding myself I have stopped knowing the lyrics of gospel songs.

'I don't know much, but I know I love youuuuu. And that may be, all there is to know.'

Itu drags the ending of another song that hurts my ears as

I drive into the guest house parking area and quickly switch off the car lights. Which also means switching off the music in the car.

'Why won't you let me love yooou?' she asks. She has been what she'd originally called 'sipping' on wine while I drove, and wine makes her both horny and unbearably loud. I can deal with it all better when I am drunk too.

In our first year of dating, we were both drunk and high from Thursday to Sunday. With each other, with different friends. Alone, we were drunk and high, and having lots of sex. We received eleven letters from neighbours telling us about our rowdy sex that kept the complex 'awake'. The best part was trying to remember how loud we must have been. Itu tried telling herself to remember to turn on a recorder every time we got home terribly drunk, and/or had drunk to a point of losing pitch, but she never did.

We drink less now. We're working towards being 'healthy'. Mentally, emotionally and spiritually. 'Aligning chakras,' Itu says.

It is her project more than it's mine. Most weekends, I continue to drink, alone or with friends.

We 'ethically' decided to stop having sex drunk. When Itu is drunk, however, it is a perpetual fight between keeping her from trying to seduce me and trying to keep her quiet.

It is after midnight when we arrive at the guest house. Itu has organised for her room key to be left with a friend, instead of her having to fetch it from the facilitator of the writer's workshop she's here to attend, who would catch me for gate-crashing. She made up some story about why she had to drive down, not fly, so that I could sneak into a retreat I had not applied for. Nor had money to afford.

I eventually have to carry Itu on my back, to avoid her stumbling over everything and getting us caught. Her attempts to continue singing are not helping. Lebo, a poet and friend from Cape Town, is also at the retreat. Her room number is 11, ours is 12. She cannot control her laughter when she opens the door and sees Itu passed out on my shoulder, slouching over my back.

'K'sazoba mnandi,' she says as she hands over the key.

'Thank you. See you ngezikathi,' I say. Glad that if Itu does make a lot of noise, we are the last chalet and our only neighbour is a friend.

Itu drops on the first bed-adjacent thing she sees when I walk in – the couch, which is a few steps away from the bed.

'Babyyyy, Babyyyy, I'm tired. Please move to the bed,' I beg.

'Pick me up?' she asks.

'But I'm tired, Tum-Tum.' It has been a long drive. I want to step into the shower then pass out in deep sleep.

'Wheeee, WHEN – YOU – CALL – ME…' Between each long drawn-out word there is a burp.

'Tumi, please, man.'

She is not going to wake up, and I am going to get annoyed and cranky on the first night at our cheat holiday. She finished two bottles of wine on our drive; and we only stopped once, at Montrose, to allow for blood circulation and her to free her bladder of steel. I am not going to win.

The kitchen looks like Victorian people still live here. Floral wallpaper. Crockery that reminds me of my grandmother's display unit. The mugs are non-functionally small with matching saucers; also decorated with almost matching flowers. I try making a cup of coffee for Itu, begging her again to come lay on the bed.

'COZ I LAAAA YOU' stumbles out of her mouth. I abort the mission. A hangover it will be.

Tumi and I have been together for over three years. A lifetime in my relationships' history; and what had looked like my trajectory. We met in the third semester of my LLB. I hated Wits even more than I hated Rhodes, but the campus was bigger at Wits. I would cross over from West Campus to sit on the East Campus lawns. Right at the middle, so as to run into as few of my classmates as possible. In the evening

I worked in the city, anything from waitressing to being a pretentious gallery assistant on weekends and some evenings. I would find out three months into dating Itu that the day I met her she had just de-registered from Medicine to study a BA, African Literature.

She is a great writer.

Our first year together, Itu said she was shedding. That was why she allowed herself to drink that much. Feel all of it deeply, so that she could finally let it go. She carried a lot of guilt from her mother, which she decided she was going to let go of that year too. Now she was working towards her first novel, and she needed to be in a healthier head space for that.

We started drinking less in our second year of dating; almost exactly after our anniversary, which was also the anniversary of the day she let go of Medicine. We drank till the next morning that day. Sitting on the veranda of a friend's house we were house-sitting. She started a drink-less programme soon after.

We had been on many more programmes after that first one, which somehow started off as 'my journey'.

'It's my journey and you don't have to follow it,' she said when I asked her why there was no cheese in the fridge when she brought groceries and we lived together. She had turned vegan. Cooking and groceries were her roles. Cleaning and laundry became mine. Her changes in diet soon became mine too. She started meditating. Then we started going to healing retreats. Which was a lot easier when we were still students who freelanced. Nowadays we needed to schedule our retreats more carefully. We also have less money.

I have been unemployed for over six months, 'working' on myself and taking time to heal. I had suggested the break and Itu had supported it. I started writing, mostly when I was bored out of my mind at home. I shared what I had written with Itu once and she decided I was now a writer too.

I need to work. A full-time job. We can't both be writers, Itu and I. It would be killing a child.

24

Dudu

'Hawu, siyabonga. Sezimyekile lezinto zakhe?' Gugu asks.

'uMakhosazane useyasebenza,' I tell her.

Gugu is my only friend, outside of Nombulelo. We were teachers' assistants together. She moved to work kwaNongoma to be closer to her husband, who used to beat uGugu for coming back late from her work – by then she was a nurse. She moved to Sobantu a few years after we had moved there, after her husband died. He died during a taxi war when he had tried to intervene where he was not asked. He died right there, on the side of the road. All Gugu spoke about as we helped her prepare for the funeral was her upcoming move to Sobantu, about leaving Nongoma and everything behind her. Everything was her in-laws.

I watched Makhosazane change before my eyes.

It has been a tough relationship with her these last few years. She recently got a job. A permanent job, practising accounting. She tried doing other things – a law degree after her accounting degree. Then a break or something of the sort. She hardly ever came home, and I never knew where she was. Phone calls were few and far between; sometimes all I received was an SMS, saying 'I love you', or 'I'm safe.'

I kept begging her and Nkosana to come home, take their breaks here. Stay at home for a bit.

Makhosi thinks I limit her, that I want to hide her away from the world. How does one even try to hide a grown human being from anything anymore? Let alone the world. If only she knew, understood, that it isn't her I wanted to hide, not really. Yes, I want to hide her, but from them. It is from them that I want to hide her. I beg her to stay inside, whether it is here at home or elsewhere. To try to stay safe.

Nkosana yena thinks he is a disappointment to me. With Nkosana, he thought the disappointment was with him failing, when it was about him lying. For years, he lied. When he could have said the degree was hard. I would have understood.

Makhosi says I tried to control her life, how she should feel. I remember Mrs Oko and her son, Eli. I wish Makhosi knew people who look like her stop feeling early. At their first realisation that anything and everything can be used as a weapon against them.

She will learn that there are those who will work tirelessly, daily, to protect each other. Some weapons we can have meetings with the world about, like bombings and the poor girls from Nigeria who have disappeared. Those we can talk about. But some battles we fight silently, on pillows.

How does a mother explain to her child the dreams a mother carries? From the time we carry them in our wombs, we begin to shape them. To shape their lives. As the best versions of everything our lives could not become.

I remember the first time Makhosi came home with an awards evening invitation. My daughter was second in her class. Her teachers expressed great expectations of her. Expectations that I, too, had. Perhaps not a doctor or an accountant – she hated numbers then. But she could be a lawyer, one of the country's best. A politician. She would change the world. Those were the dreams I carried for my daughter.

She was accepted into Rhodes University, Wits University and the University of Cape Town. I don't think I expressed when those acceptance letters were coming how proud and excited I was. Makhosi didn't seem exceptionally excited, almost like she expected to be accepted into all these universities. What different times we lived in, her and I.

She was coming into herself with great confidence. My job was to make sure that she was able to be comfortable wherever she went. I booked a ticket for her to fly to Port Elizabeth. I had never boarded a plane.

I would later learn even this hurt my daughter. 'Why didn't you drive me?' she once asked. 'All the other students arrived with their parents,' she said. Spent Orientation week with their parents. All my attempts seem to fall short for Makhosi.

I don't know when the anger and sadness gathered in my daughter. Perhaps I was blinded by my expectations, or by her achievements. I didn't see myself lose hold of her. Then, she came home different.

She thinks I don't understand, and maybe I don't. I don't know who is worse, us or them. They who find words and phrases to term things we are familiar with in foreign tongues. They who refuse to stop speaking about it, but we do not recognise them in their big words. She thinks I don't understand, and maybe I don't. Us, we wear our pain ngenzilo, carry it on our bodies ngezingcabo. Staring you in the face, silently. Coldly.

My dorm mates and I laughed at the squirminess of our male comrades during training. When we first arrived, the tests were physical. Waking up early to run. Running through mud, running through tyres. Running around the school, picking up logs as you ran. Running was not a strength of mine, as it wasn't for most of my dorm mates. The males would of course laugh this off as proof that 'ngempela akuyona indawo yabantu besifazane le.'

The training changed. Now we were attending psychosocial classes. There was still the physical, but we were now focusing on the psychosocial aspect of our work. Our lecturer, Miss Ngwane, was a woman who had worked in the force for over twenty years. Petite and light-skinned. The men didn't take her seriously at first. A few tried hitting on her. She started the class with discussing rape, and the procedures of handling rape. Simply grasping the notion of rape made our classmates unable to handle their own selves.

'No, but what if she says no when you are inside?'
'What if you bought her alcohol? Hayi, hayi!'

The class roared. Miss Ngwane was firm. 'I do not make the law. And you do not question it, you enforce it. That is how we survive our jobs,' she said.

In the weeks that followed, we discussed domestic violence, child abuse, the abuse of the elderly. Miss Ngwane brought case studies to our classes, but the emotional intelligence she demanded could not be found in our classmates. 'Ama-emotions nje leliyaclass,' a few would whisper during breaks.

My dorm mates and I sat through those classes silently.

On her last day, Miss Ngwane showed us the statistics of how many of the psychosocial cases she had shown us had resulted in convictions of perpetrators. It was less than ten per cent. The 'facts' in many of those case studies – and they were all gruesome cases – were clear. Less than ten per cent convictions.

That class prepared none of us for what we would learn in the practice.

The cases that are reported then stricken off because black women know how to die silent deaths.

Useyasebenza manje though.

I hope she learns, Makhosi; the lessons of the choices we no longer have when we have families to feed.

She has been 'calmer' the last few years, but I have learned to not trust those calm moments either. If anything, it means a severe storm is heading our way. Sometime. Anytime. And I expect anything at this point really. I already used my position in the SAPS to rescue Nkosana. He disappeared too, eventually.

University was nothing like he thought it would be. We

spoke about it, often. He started being challenged in his first year. Something about essays. He had been good at History but not English in high school. Amongst the highest in the district schools for History. Awarded a partial bursary from the Office of the Premier. It hung heavily over him. BCom Accounting was not for him; he knew early, but he tried. He tried the full four years, but he was still struggling with two second-year modules. So he changed and I supported his change. Then he studied Education at the old Teachers' College in Pinetown. It was a previously black college, so it was different from Howard, but it was the same university and there was less pressure. Or so I thought. He graduated. It was one of the happiest days of my life. The moment colleagues and friends spoke about; the day when your child makes you immensely proud.

He took a teaching position in Pretoria, Soshanguve. He didn't understand siPitori, and so he moved to eGoli, eZola. An isiZulu-speaking area. Then he was broken into. Then he was getting broken into every second week. Then he moved to Dube, Dlamini...

Eventually, Thulani said, 'Nkosana is lying to you. He does not want to come home.'

I resented that Thulani thought I had raised children who hated home. Although, by Nkosana's age I was married to Thulani and seldom going home myself. But uMa was always welcome to visit.

Nkosana never allowed me to come visit him. Come help him. Even financially. He would be fine, he said. He came home during December holidays to show his head akhothwe amadlozi. He said nothing emsamo, but he was fine. When Makhosi first moved to Johannesburg and was not coming home even for Christmas, he would reassure us that she, too, was 'fine'.

Then Makhosi started coming home, and Nkosana stopped. But Makhosi did always like home, at first. Or at least it was always an en route.

Now Makhosi stays for visits, sometimes long visits.

She is in one of her 'relationships'. This partner has a child – 'our child', Makhosi calls him.

It is noble, and maybe enlightened, of her to call another man's child 'her' child; but I guess it may be because the two of them... Whoever she chooses to have a child with, the child will always be another man's child. She speaks of being a parent with ease. Maybe it was the anxiety that brought her back home. Maybe this child is what has stabilised her. I have heard colleagues of mine who had children young, somewhere between adolescence and 'living life'. Children stabilised them, they said. Maybe a child will stabilise Makhosi. Maybe she will learn there are in betweens. That it is not black and white.

When her father and brother accused Makhosi of smoking insangu, there was an accusatory tone in Mpumelelo's voice, addressed at me. A morally higher ground.

The money from insangu was what carried them through the worst, and I knew a time when no herb was illegal. At least it was not real drugs. I have seen those from rich children, at rainbow nation parties. Cocaine. LSD. Makhosi wasn't smoking because of me. Not that she would have ever known.

My children do that, take a moral high ground every now and again. Like when I left Thulani on the sofa he'd rolled himself onto and Nonhle tried to make me feel bad. Me, carry an adult man to his bed, like I sent him to drink! I shrugged that off too, like I had shrugged off Mpumelelo, Nkosana, Thulani and Makhosi's moral high grounds before.

Eventually, they all would come tumbling down. That's the thing about being 'high'. The fall is greater.

Makhosi needs to learn these lessons fast, and carry them like the women before her. She needs to learn to stop adorning them as victory scars, our wounds of defeat. Your children don't need to know how you have been defeated. And you must hide, protect and hide their defeats too, against whatever morals you thought you had.

That's parenting.

PART THREE

25

Makhosazane

Dear Makhosazane
I am at this retreat where they have asked me to write a letter to myself. I don't think I have written a letter to myself, except perhaps for the suicide notes. Those seem like letters to myself now. I emailed them to myself, even though I never read them. I just added. An archive of all the times I have wanted to die.
The process of this letter, our yogi person says, is that we do not stop writing. Just keep writing. A letter to our younger self. She didn't mention the age of said younger self. She just said write a letter to your younger self. Why is suicide the first thing I think about when writing a letter to myself?
I was reading K Sello Duiker the other day. Literary people call his loss tragic. A friend of mine and I were trying to discuss Sello at a bar called the Kitchen in Braamfontein, when some Braam-looking person inserted themselves into our conversation.
'Ssss... Sello Duiker,' he said, stumbling over towards our table, almost spilling his alcohol over

Thembi. His skill for not spilling was commendable, and he knew it.

'We drink the alcohol; we don't spill it,' he said. A conversation with himself more than with us. He laughed, at himself, as I sat there staring at him. 'Do you, do you think Sello's work is... Do you think i'st his s... ss... ssuicide lettersss to the world?' he finally managed to ask.

His question bothered me, and I didn't care to entertain him.

Why do writers lead such sad lives? Am I a writer?

This is the first time I have ever called myself a writer. At this annoying retreat. Where I am writing a letter to my younger self, without stopping. We're not meant to stop and read what we've written so far. Just keep writing, she said, let the words flow. Fucken hippie bullshit. I swear so much now, dear younger self.

Sigh... My younger self would not know what to do with my older self.

I don't know what happened where, man, baby Makhosi. You did all you could, as right as you could when you were doing it. True to most of it too. You were true to Jesus when you thought that true. As you were to whatever fuck else you did after. I mean, you tried as much as you could, I guess.

We have to write this for 30 minutes. I don't know what else to say to you, except I don't know.

You did what you thought was right, when you thought it right. And now you're here, at a healing retreat, writing yourself a letter. When even did healing retreats become what you are interested in? Maybe I should tell younger me how you got here.

It happened in bits and pieces of moments.

Like the moment at church when the pastor insisted

you could be cured of homosexualty. Homosexuality was a sin, he said, but it could be cured.

Another pastor, a different one, one when you were younger, said that sin couldn't be cured. Like you can't cure thieving, which was what you were enquiring about the time. That pastor was nice. Even though you had said you were asking for a friend, he referred to said friend as you.

'Say you were your friend, and you were coming to me for advice,' he said. 'I'd say all have fallen short of the glory of God. In fact, Paul says one who thinks he is not a sinner is a liar. After Eve ate the fruit in the garden, we were all born in sin. That was why Jesus came – to save us from our sins. Only the blood of Jesus can cleanse us, with the Holy Spirit there to help us fight the temptation. The sin is not being a thief. The sin is acting out being a thief. All the men God called his followers were sinners. Sinners saved by grace, Makhosi.'

It's scary how deeply these things are imprinted in your memory still. You liked what that pastor said. Zama agreed with it too. It was not your fault, your sin. It was the fault of Eve for having eaten the fruit. You were just caught in the in between. The great controversy. Before we are made anew to never sin again.

The church said many AMENS the day the pastor said you could be cured of homosexuality, that it was a sin.

You walked out.

I guess it hurt. I mean, here you are writing a letter to yourself and remembering the words of pastors, and thinking about Eve. So it hurt, I guess.

I don't know what else hurt you. I mean, I do... but I'm not sure I thought it hurt then. A lot has hurt you over the years. University was hard for you. So much happened, and look. Hmmm. Look. 'So much has happened, so much and everything hurts.' You wrote that to yourself once in one of your suicide letters. 'You owe it to yourself to be happy,' you wrote in another, 'and you are not happy here. It's okay to let go of everything. Even life.'

Ah, back at damn suicide letters. You thought about suicide a lot growing up. It was a cute thought of escape at first. Urghh... if I killed myself... You wouldn't say it out loud, but you thought about it. Thoughts manifest in your head. You can't unthink. You can forget, but I mean it's there. Somewhere. Captured in memory, time and space. You thought about dying more, the older you got. But the letters you wrote then... those weren't suicide letters. For whatever reason, you wrote yourself letters reminding you to stay alive. When the words and voices, and images in your head became too much. Too loud, too bright, too alive.

You regretted entertaining the dreams you had at crèche. That was probably where it all started, at crèche, all those years ago. They began to come more frequently, voices in your head, and other things. You want to forgive yourself for that, for entertaining the voices in your head. Maybe this is how have you ended up here. You learned you were attracted to people with interesting stories. At church, the testimonies were what kept you going. You'd be laughing, gasping and clapping all at once in your head as the rest of the church said Amen. The Bible stories entertained and fuelled your imagination. Floods that end all of the earth, except for one family. Or however you interpreted it then. You loved stories. So, you followed them. On your way to becoming a story. Your story.

Everywhere you have gone, the stories have kept you. Kept you returning.

In Fort England, you became addicted to the stories. So what if people lived in their universes, in their heads? The people who 'lived' in their own universes captured you the most.

There was the woman who kept telling us she had been bestowed with the greatest ancestor. An ancestor that would heal the whole continent. Except her gift was stolen, and she ended up there, in Fort England. 'I am fine now,' she said, 'I am fine now. But they will not let me go because I killed him. Ewe njena, ndambulala. He stole my gift, ela gqwirha.' The story of how she came to know that her trainer was the one who stole her gift mesmerised you.

'But how, njani, kwaske kwathini?' you found yourself asking. You were the only person who entertained her.

Then there was the screaming girl at the last silent retreat. From the day she arrived there, every time you did chakra meditation, she screamed. The meditation was 90 minutes. She just, she screamed. She told us all at our last meeting, the only meeting where we were allowed to use words, that it was her releasing all the demons she brought there. She named her demons one by one. Her list of addictions seemed endless. Addictions you didn't know existed. She had travelled the world, constantly looking for healing. Her addictions in whatever form started ruining her relationship with her family, her body. She decided to go on a journey of healing which would last as long as her 'hurting herself and others' took. Focus on herself, before she returned to her family and friends. She emailed all of them telling them about this path. Most of them had already given up on her and have never bothered responding or looking for her. She sometimes sent postcards to her mother in Manzini, Swaziland. To let her know she was safe. Her partner from Germany was her saving grace. He was there with her. Held her hand through all of her screams. He was leading her to healing.

You loved stories. Followed them. Until eventually they followed you.

There are things I am still not ready to write on paper. See them in front of me. That is fine though. We are almost out of time. I will keep writing other things for the next five minutes.

You're doing okay, most days. You're trying. You're gonna raise a son soon. Ayanda, Itu's son. You're here now with Itu. You're uncertain about a lot. You've been together for four years, and now you are preparing to raise a child. You are barely raised yourself, and this scares you. You're all Itu has right now, though, and she needs to take Ayanda. For Ayanda's sake. This can't be about you right now. There is a child in the world you can't fuck around with. How you exist in his mother's life influences how he exists. Ayanda needs his mother. And people have had to parent with way less, way sooner.

You're better than you've been. You're starting a job when you get back to Joburg. It's laughable. A 9–5, but you'll do what you must. Ukuba umfazi omnyama is to be without options. It has been a hard lesson to learn. They are counting down.

Goodbye, baby MK.

'I'm struggling to remember to love him, like this. Like the son he is... he, he reminds me of—' Itu says.

'We cannot burden children with the burdens of their fathers,' I try reasoning with her.

'How will I raise a boy though?' she asks.

'If he will become a boy, that is,' I add, trying to lighten things. Itu is stressing about things I cannot help her with.

'Oh, Maku, please, he is a little boy in a township already showing all types of toxic masculinity.'

Ayanda is Itu's son. He is twelve years old and her family's reason for proving our relationship invalid. Her friends too. Ayanda is a quiet child, small in build. He doesn't like playing with other children. He sits in his corner, his knees hugged into his chest, following the adults' conversation with his light brown eyes.

'Izindaba zabantu abadala, Ayanda,' Itu's mother shouts.

'The other children bore him,' Itu tells her.

Itu, like all mothers, I assume, thinks her child an exception. She takes Ayanda's antisocial behaviour for intellectual ability. With Ayanda's 'exceptional' intelligence, as per Itu and her mother, he also enjoys the privilege of being the smart child. Ayanda is spoilt. It is only when visitors are around that his grandmother shouts at him for staring at adults.

'It's the inconsistency I don't like,' Itu says.

'It is keeping up appearances,' I say.

'Respectability politics, and other things. She is confusing my child.'

Ayanda's father also lives in Johannesburg. A man from the Eastern Cape, whose name is banned from all our vocabulary. Itu will not allow herself to say she fears his access to Ayanda The times – which were few and far between – when Itu and I had spoken about him, earlier in our relationship, I remember her repeating 'He was a cruel man' over and over again when retelling the story. Her words seemed to fail her exactly when she said those words. 'He was a cruel man…' Saying them repeatedly, she would rock on the bed.

Then Itu and her mother had a disagreement which seemed irreconcilable. It was the holidays; Itu had gone to visit. She called me very early on a Sunday morning, which was odd for her, because when she was home she spent her Sunday mornings in church with her mother. Ayanda had stopped going a few years before, except during Easter and Christmas, when even Itu forced him to go. I could not make out half of what Itu said during that phone call. Something about us. She had decided we were going to take Ayanda. It was not a new idea, and I was not opposed to it.

'We'll discuss everything when we're together, my love. One more lala muhlezi,' I said. 'One more, and you'll be back home. Go for a drive or something, love. Angikuzwa right now.'

Itu and I couldn't speak again on the phone that day; her house had been busy and she didn't get the chance.

I picked her up from Noord early on Monday morning. We both took the day off, sick leave, to try plot out what our lives would look like. Itu didn't go into detail about whatever had happened with her mother that had had her weeping and gasping for air on a Sunday morning. I knew it was pointless to ask; she'd tell me when it was ready.

First we decided we would tell my mother about Ayanda coming to live with us.

The times when uMa comes to visit me she takes the late-night taxi which travels across provinces and leaves you at the gate of where you are going. From town, in Pietermaritzburg, to Fort England the one time.

All the visits are some form of an emergency, all of them hit when she is struggling with money.

My warden has organised for her to sleep in my room, but she insisted on coming to the hospital first. The nurses let me know my mother has arrived. It is 6 am on a Friday morning.

'Are you ready to see her?' a nurse asks.

'Please tell her it's policy that she only sees me during visiting hours,' I say. 'The first visiting hour starts at 9 am.'

The nurses disappear for a while. At 8 am the ward psychologist comes to see me.

My mother has been insistent about seeing me. And getting

a little hysterical. I could hear her voice from our ward all the way down the corridor, as it rose higher and higher. I peeped my head into the corridor and saw her pacing up and down at the other end. By the reception area, just outside the nurses' office.

She called my father, whom I knew would be little help. Then she called her friend uGugu, who is a nurse at Fort Napier, which is a psychiatric hospital in Pietermaritzburg. I think sis' Gugu must have told her to ask for the head of staff, or the head psychologist, because a few minutes later she started walking in and out from the nurses' office.

'She must come now! I don't care when she gets here!' uMa demanded. 'She must come now, ingane yami le elele la.'

By the time the psychologist arrives, I know I need to choose. I agree to see uMa. I do not want to go home, but I know she will convince me to. So, I take a few minutes to prepare myself. My warden also thinks it best that I go home. Another lazy white woman.

The next time uMa comes, she sleeps over at Kwezi's and comes to drag me out of a friend's room, where I have been cooped up for weeks. I had stopped answering my phone. Told my friend to call her every few days and tell her I am fine. I wasn't getting high, or drunk, like she thought when she arrived. It was a res room, there was alcohol, but it belonged to my friend.

Now I am living with Itu.

It has taken me time to get my life back on track. It isn't even really on track yet, but I am about to raise a child. We will see both our parents and let them know we are taking Ayanda. It will be easier talking to uMa, I think; she will be glad just to see me alive. I guess. And I want to show her I am alive and living. Actively waking up every day; and living. What better inspiration – or pressure – than a child?

I am scared to raise a child. I still sometimes get too drunk to come home, pass out on a friend's sofa and drunk-dial Itu. You can't drunk-parent a child.

For this visit, Itu and I have paid for uMa to fly. While I am at work, Itu fetches her from the airport and takes her out to an early dinner. The plan is that I will meet up with them after work. Of course, my day is nothing like I planned it, which is how well-planned days often end for me. Neither Ma nor Itu are surprised when I walk into our flat at 7 pm instead of the agreed 5:30 pm at the restaurant.

I go over to uMa, dropping my bag and the collection of miscellaneous things I have in my hand on the floor as I am trying to hug her – which include a joint, cigarettes and a lighter. She doesn't try stand up, regardless of my effort.

'Haw' Ma,' I say.

'Weeh, nami ngikhathele. I would've had energy to stand if you'd met us more than an hour ago like you said.'

'Konje unjalo,' I say. Going down for the hug, and then walking over to Itu, who is in the kitchen doing something. We both awkwardly peck, peeping at whether uMa will provide a reaction.

None.

'Ncese, love. You know, you know. A white man fucked up, and I needed to clean the mess. Waetseba mos that thing yalaphaya. I fucken hate that place,' I say, grabbing a glass of water.

'Konje phela umuntu uzodla inhlamba,' my mother says sarcastically.

Itu breaks out in laughter, and adds, 'I tell her all the time, Ma, all the time.'

'Fine, gang up on me,' I say, walking back to pick up the things I dropped, then heading to the bedroom

'MA, have you seen your room?' I call out as I walk down the corridor.

'Yes, mtanam' ngiyabonga,' she replies.

'Okay, let me shower, and—'

'NO ONE CAN HEAR THROUGH WALLS,' Itu screams, disrupting me.

I want to shout back that she's just proved herself wrong,

but I go into the shower. When I come out Ma is preparing for bed.

'Haw' Ma, early kanje?' I say, disappointed not to catch up on how everything is at home. Even though I speak to her more often now, I feel like it's what mothers should do the first time they visit their child who is newly healthy. Drink tea from my small cups and talk.

'Ngikhathele,' she says.

'Fair, rest. We'll speak ek'seni, before I go to work. Goodnight, I love you,' I say, closing the door to her bedroom.

I go back to Tum-Tum to gauge how the day has gone.

It went well. Ma had said very little about our lifestyle, about anything really, things that had given us minor heart palpitations as we were preparing for her visit. Hiding all the ganja seeds, and the indoor ganja pot plants, which were all over all the rooms of the house. A few hours after Ma's arrival, we realise we didn't do anything about the big bong that sits on our table in the lounge. Tumi and I laughed that night, hoping Ma thought it was a vase. But Ma did not remark on it, one way or another.

'How did you enjoy your visit?' I ask Ma.

'I enjoyed it as much as any old woman would. It's busy there, all your lives are busy. You are doing so much,' Ma finally responds.

We are constantly doing a lot of nothing, it is true. Every day we come back tired, but still not rich. My corporate job, freelance work, activist-like work. Tumi isn't really an activist, but she supports and shows up for lesbian solidarity work. Tumi has signed a book deal, and I am now working full time at BWK, one of the big four accounting firms, and hating every minute. Forensic Accounting is the department I am assigned to, also because of the Accounting degree and the LLB. I did not come in at entry position. As underpaying as all my previous jobs were, they were the more fulfilling.

My soul dies every morning I step into the office. By the time the elevator reaches my floor, 8th floor, my heart has sunken to an unretrievable place. At least by the time I started working, I could wear chinos and casual shoes; I had survived the generation of the heels. But I still hated it.

'There are old women in Joburg who do just fine, kanti uyazi,' I say to uMa.

'Yes, and it's great for them. I'm an old woman from emakhaya. How did you enjoy my visit?' Ma asks.

'You didn't clean up as much as I thought you would,' I say, joking.

Tumi and I had both been shocked at uMa's lack of responses to our 'We will wash dishes in the morning…' and… 'Urghh… we mop every few days…' When she did offer to help us clean, and we declined her offer, she didn't insist. She just continued with whatever she was doing.

'What made you think I would want to clean your house?' Ma asks.

I hadn't thought it through, perhaps because it was what Tumi's mother had done. Perhaps even because I believed it was what mothers did when they visited daughters who weren't domesticated.

'Angazi, I mean you clean and are always busy ekhaya…' I say.

Ma interrupts me by laughing. 'Oh, Makhosi,' she says. 'Of course I clean kwami. If I don't clean, I must live with the filth. But I do not have any compelling desire to clean other adults' houses. No, thank you.' She laughs quietly again.

'I thought it's what mothers did,' I say, finally giving my mother a more honest answer.

'Ngobani, what do you think happens when we become mothers? That we grow a deep desire to take care of adults? I think most of my job here is done, with you. You're doing okay, you're doing well. You're not mine to tell what to do anymore. In fact, we both know you were never mine to tell what to do,' Ma says.

'I guess, in part. I keep hoping you'll let me know how much of my life you disapprove of,' I say.

Ma laughs the laugh she usually reserves only for uBaba, the laugh that means that whatever he is saying is too ridiculous to entertain. I used to try to laugh with her, but I quickly learned to hear it as a silencing tactic. Frozen between fear and deep insecurity.

'Oh, Makhosi, there are so many of your life choices I do not approve of,' Ma says. 'The same way there were many life choices I made which my mother did not approve of. I simply hope you think about the consequences of those decisions towards yourself and those you love. If you can reconcile yourself with your choices, then I sleep on the hope that you know what you're doing. You're an adult now. I've tried the best I could have.'

'Ayanda is moving in with us,' I say, the words escaping my mouth. I had not planned to tell her like this.

'I know,' she says. 'All the decorations in that room were proof that it was not 'my bedroom', as you called it,' she says, laughing again.

'I mean, it's also Nonhle's when she finally comes to Wits,' I say. 'She can also use it. It's still a guest room.'

I don't know when Ma started laughing so much during conversations, but I like it. We have come far, me and her. Mostly me. I was tougher on her than I needed to be; and I still haven't apologised. For the years of trying to whitewash her.

'You'll do great, sisi. Ayanda will be blessed to have you,' Ma says, disturbing my thoughts.

I still don't apologise.

It is the Easter holidays, and we are waiting for Tumi's mother to visit us with Ayanda – we are taking him at the end of the Easter break – but she sends Ayanda up alone, puts him in a bus so we can fetch him at Noord taxi rank. Itu had reiterated that she wants her mother to visit too, but Ayanda says she had a church thing to go to this weekend.

I can tell by simply looking at Tumi from the side of my eyes, as I help Ayanda pick up his bags, that she is upset. Trying to distract Ayanda from his five-to-exploding mother, I ask him about the trip. How was the journey? How many hours again? Do you still get excited to come to Johannesburg? We meander ourselves out of Noord and make our way to Park Station where we have parked. Ayanda is moving slower and slower, almost disappearing behind the stalls.

'Uzolahleka use Goli la,' I try joking.

I hate Noord. Hate anywhere with many people where it can't be safe for Tumi and I. Taxi ranks are at the top of this list. It's like they smell lesbians and then start harassing you. As we approach Park Station, the smell of umbila being roasted catches me. Itu's favourite. As I try stopping, Ayanda tells me his grandmother has already packed mielies in one of the bags we are carrying. I want to tell Ayanda that no one roasts mielies like Johannesburg women, but there is no time. The walk is calming Itu, but she hates crowded places too. She walks past me and continues straight into the station. We walk past the many people heading to the Metrorail, and then the many people heading to buses. We go up the escalator, out of Park Station and to my car. As soon as I open the boot, Ayanda a little way behind us at the parking ticket machine, it is as if Itu has been waiting to exhale.

'She could've not made me a fool,' she says. 'She could've simply said. I ask her for little. I ask Mme for very little, but she can't even visit me because of Easter. Easter. Doesn't Easter happen every year? She'll have next year, and the year after.'

Ayanda has finished paying for our ticket. He turns around, looking for us.

'Thanks, my boy, we're here!' I say, waving him to our direction, and throwing the last bag into the boot. I look Itu in the eyes. 'My love, I know. I know,' I half whisper. 'But not in front of Ayanda, okay? Not right now. Now, enjoy your son.' Her eyes fill with tears.

'Get in, Ayanda,' I say. 'No, you can throw that next to you. With Gogo not here, you have the whole back seat akere?'

'It's Nkhono,' Ayanda responds.

'Yes, yes. Sorry. Itu, here…'

I look at Itu through the rear window. She is finishing rubbing her eyes. She moves to the passenger side of the car and gets in without looking back at Ayanda.

'I was telling Mr A here that you're teaching me Sesotho,' I say. 'So I can stop translating everything into isiZulu. Right, Ayanda?' I look at him over my shoulder. He is gazing out the window. The same way Itu is gazing out the window.

Well, these silences I am used to. If Ayanda acts like Itu when he's going through things, then I've definitely got my work cut out for me, I think to myself.

'Well, we need to tell Ayanda about him staying, Itu,' I say.

Itu has still not told Ayanda he is moving here. Something we agreed would be done as soon as he got here.

'With your mother not coming, we can't break it to them together. So we should rip it off like a bandage.'

Itu is taking off her eyeshadow, and remoisturising her skin, looking down at that weird mirror that exposes all your pores.

'I'll tell him tomorrow. And we'll go fetch his clothes this weekend,' Itu says.

'You're telling him or we're telling him?' I ask.

'I think this I must do alone. And when we're home. Please stay in the car. We'll get in, pack, Ayanda will say his goodbyes, and we'll go,' she says, switching off the lights.

'Itumeleng, I mean… you're upset and that's fair, but don't let her turn you into that person.'

Tumi ignores my comments. She gets into bed, ignoring me sitting at the edge.

A few days later, on a Saturday morning, we drive to the North West to fetch Ayanda's clothes.

As Tumi had instructed, I do not go inside. I can make out some insults and swear words. Especially when Tumi's mother is closer to the window. Eventually Tumi and Ayanda walk out. Tumi's mother lets out a weep, as she holds on to Ayanda's bag. Tumi pulls Ayanda's hand. Tumi's mother will not let go of Ayanda's bag. Soon the whole street can tell what is happening. Tumi commands me to open the boot and help her put Ayanda's bags inside it. Then she goes back to wrestle the last bag out of her mother's hands.

I wish I could talk her out of things, or at least have the energy to try talk her out of things; but then she doesn't always listen to me.

No one says anything on the way back to Joburg.

It is too late to cook, and I doubt either of us is in the mood to. So, we grab a pizza and head home. Ayanda takes his slices into his room and bangs the door behind him.

'That could've been handled differently,' I try telling Tumi.

'But we're here now,' she says, picking up her slices and heading to our room.

They really are the same person.

Ayanda steals a chocolate from the store down the road from his school. He's with some friends. The store decides to call the school and the police, and they all decide to have them taken to holding cells. Thirteen-year-old boys in holding cells. They claim they are kept separate from adults but still, thirteen-year-old black boys in holding cells. For chocolate, a packet of cigarettes.

This is not Ayanda's first scandal this year. A month ago he was suspended for stealing calculators from other learners.

That night Tumi said it. 'He reminds me of his father.'

Something about police stations and begging for him to get released so he could open for her. He had beaten her and torn her clothes. She ran to one of the neighbours; they called to let her mother know she was lying on the floor bleeding. When the policemen came, they arrested him. She asked them if they could help her get into the house to get dressed and get the things. Or at least, let her get the key. Which he still had on him.

'You arrest him, and you still want his keys? Hayi, sisi, hayi la.'

They refused to help. Instead, they took them both.

She slept on the benches at the Jeppe police station, begging for his release, bleeding. Her mother was in Mafikeng while she was in Joburg. Her mother had not given her the blessing of coming to Joburg.

They had met at a poetry recital somewhere in Potch. He was a student at North West University; she was going to look for a place to study. They were young and in love. They left Potchefstroom the next year. He was about to start working in Joburg. Tumi had followed love and love had left her bleeding on a police station bench.

Her mother arrived the next day and took her back to Mafikeng. Tumi was three months pregnant.

'He isn't his father, Tumi. Ayanda is not his father. You can't do that to him. You can't do that to a child. You can't raise him like that.'

But Tumi is no longer listening to me. Instead, she is looking out the car window at the tree leaves from the fancy houses which droop onto Jan Smuts. It is a Friday night; Jan Smuts is busy. Hillbrow police station is where we are headed. We are seldom, if ever in Hillbrow, neither of us. Me because of the fears instilled in me from childhood to never ever go into Hillbrow. It didn't help that my father spent his New Year's Day watching the news, waiting to hear a headline about Hillbrow's New Year's Eve riots, or violence. Tumi doesnt like police stations full stop.

There is no parking directly outside the station and the streets are buzzing with activity. We park lower down and get out the car, to be greeted by a whiff of expensive-smelling marijuana. Tumi holds her bag to her chest. Don't look so scared, I want to tell her. You will draw attention to yourself. Instead I take the bag from her and hold her hand as we walk to the station. A collection of poor white people are sitting and lying around the police station. Inside, the strong smell of a fearsome authority in the room. Everyone at their mercy. The queue is long.

'Umyeni wami uyangishaya,' a woman whispers to the officer on the other side of the counter.

'He kicked me out of my house,' another cries.

'I'd like to open a case against my son. He came back to my house and locked me out,' an old man who shouldn't be at police stations during the evenings says.

The police respond to all these with no sense of urgency.

Then a woman walks into the station, shouting. A navy pants suit, and brown peep-toe heels. Tumi and I look at each other. Uzophola lomama, I think.

'I demand to see my son, now!' the woman says. 'He is a minor! The school and the police should have worked harder to ensure we got here before even their fingerprints are taken!'

She is shouting at the first police officer she sees, who pays her no attention. She tries moving on to the next, who says, 'Sisi, there is a queue.' She paces up and down the station, her shoes making an annoying clancking sound as they hit against the floor. She starts going through her phone, texting and calling people. 'They won't let me see my son,' she says, over and over again, to whoever she is calling.

Her pacing is making me anxious, so I step outside for a smoke. Hillbrow is alive, the lights, the people, the music, the cars. The car hooters. You cannot deny whatever it is – Hillbrow is alive differently from most places I have known.

The woman in the navy suit seems to not wish me peace. She comes outside, still texting.

'Bloody fools don't know I pay their salaries,' she says, I guess speaking to me, but I imagine she is speaking past me. 'May I bum a gwai, please?' she asks.

'Me?' I stupidly look behind me, even though I know there is no one behind me.

"Yes, you. I'll buy it, if you want,' she says, already putting her hand out to receive the cigarette.

I give her a cigarette, hoping she will offer me money so I can say no. I always wonder why it is that people in this city offer to buy a cigarette, instead of just a skuif. Then not offer the money? What etiquette is that?

'Damn good,' she says. 'Friday night too, to be stuck in this damn hell-hole.' She looks up and around her.

I find myself looking up too.

'I mean, I guess...'

'You won't see it here, you know, being the city centre and all, but if you were to go to Northcliff, and watch over the city and watch the sky, you would see how beautiful it is,' she says, lighting her cigarette.

'I guess,' I say again, puffing at mine.

'God, how are you going to survive being here with so little confidence?' she says, blowing her smoke in my face and pointing at the police officers inside with her occupied hand. 'You can't keep saying "I guess." These people are going to chew you and spit you out.' Her nails are a light orange; they compliment the lights reflecting on the glass window behind us and the flame of the cigarette in her hand. She does have a lot of confidence, I think. The way she walked into the room, and demanded attention. Ha. And aren't we at the same place? She may perhaps even be in a worse off position than I am, given the scene she caused.

Itu runs out screaming, 'MK, MK! They're releasing the boys!'

I am done with my cigarette and am about to run to her when the woman in the navy suit holds me back and says, 'Oh, you're the lesbian lover I have heard about. You should take my number, so I can pay you for that cigarette. And you can thank me for getting your stepson released. See – confidence gets things done.'

I don't know whether it is the smirk on her face or the way she blows that last bit of smoke into my face as she drops the stub and switches it off with her shoe. Her confidence is sexy, but I need to show up for Itu. Especially at a time like this. I release myself from the navy suit woman and run into the station. As Itu sees the boys walking out she tries to shout through her tears. I grab her from the back and hug her tight. 'Not now, Itu. Not here, not now.' The woman from outside follows soon after me. Comes straight at me and Itu. Hugs us both tightly.

'It's okay, they're safe now,' she says, rubbing Itu's shoulder. She takes out a business card and looks at me. 'Call me if the two of you ever need anything,' she says.

'Advocate Sebokeng' the card reads. Her office is in Cape Town. I would later hear that she had flown in to get her son released.

'God, she wanted you,' Itu says when we retell the story of that day to friends days later, and we both laugh.

'She was being a supportive fellow parent person,' I say.

I save the navy suit woman's number on my phone and throw away the business card. Itu says we don't need her help – she asked me to throw the card away – but still; I like having her number on my phone.

Tumi had to tell her mother about Ayanda's arrest, although I didn't think about it much. There were conversations where I had to be excluded, and I made peace with that. Ayanda was not mine, Tumi's family didn't forget to remind me. He was naturally conceived between Ayanda and a man, her mother had said when I had once tried to intervene.

This time, too, Tumi's mother found a way in which I would be to blame.

'The child is looking for his father,' she said. 'The child must be confused by the-girl-who-acts-like-a-man in your house. He sees there is no man, and he is trying to replace what a man looks like, so you can leave the-girl-who-acts- like-a-man.'

Tumi's mother had met me a few times, had even been in the house that Tumi and I share. She refused to ever call me by my name. Especially when she had something to blame me for. It removed fault from Tumi; perhaps that was why she did it. Tumi tried to protect me but couldn't. I had apparently changed Tumi. I didn't mind the narrative. But I did mind that it was used to blame me for a boy's actions, a boy she, Tumi's mother, had raised. A boy who was merely acting out the way that children do. I'd probably have done the same if I hadn't been stuck in boarding school. I did sneak out and steal once. My friends and I stole a bottle of alcohol. I think we escaped arrest because we were girls, and because of our school.

Ayanda was just being a kid, and no one would let him.

We didn't speak often, me and him. We didn't need to; and I understood. The transitions must have been hard. He liked staring at silent TV screens like I did. Or listening to the radio and drawing the characters he heard on the radio, build storylines. I bought him drawing books. He went through them quickly, although most of them had most pages torn.

'Why not rub out mistakes?' I asked.

'Why do you look at my art?' he asked.

'Oh,' I said, not shocked, more prepared. It was valid of him to ask why I was looking at his work without his consent. 'I like your work. I think you are very talented,' I said.

'Okay, well. I leave the bits that I am comfortable with you seeing in the drawing books.'

'That's fine too. Just so long as you're drawing,' I said.

Tumi wanted Ayanda and I to be close. She got excited at every little hope of the two of us bonding.

'Maybe if the two of you get along, maybe if he says what he thinks about all this. About you, about us,' Tumi would say.

'Stop centring me in the child's life,' I told her. 'This may have absolutely nothing to do with me, or you. It could just be about Ayanda. Whatever his personal journey is.'

'He needs a father figure, MK,' Tumi said, sounding annoyed at me.

'Tumi, how many children in this country grow up without father figures and are fine? You and your mother need to stop projecting onto this boy.'

'That's easy for you to say, MK. Your father was there every day for all of your life. Driving you to places. In your house having dinner every evening. Contributing to your everyday experience. You don't get to be the one who decides when children need fathers and when they don't. Not when yours was present. Whatever your deal with him is, you can never take away from the fact that he was present. And that is better than him not being present.' She walked away.

Tumi was right. uBaba had been present.

'The smoke is coming into the house!' Itu screams from the kitchen. Something she hadn't minded before Ayanda was here.

It is a cold winter evening. We have come back from a jazz show. Ayanda is with his father. Itu's mother talked her into giving him a second chance. Mme had continued speaking to Siyabulela through the years, even against her daughter's wishes. 'A child needs their father,' she would say, but Mme would've still loved Ayanda's father, even outside of Ayanda. Regardless of what he did. It was the last of Tumi's relationships she recognised.

I took to calling her 'Mme', Itu's mother, to disarm her, the way I had taken to 'Itu', to disarm Tumi. I couldn't handle the ways in which they fought, so I used what I knew – pet names and being a girl raised 'right'.

Parents live to know that other parents have worked as hard as they have.

I looked down when talking to other elders, and helped

around the house. It helped that I had mastered the art of cooking for imisebenzi. Mamncane's funeral was the first. She had often laughed at the food at funerals. Dripping in oil, she'd say. She had wanted simple sandwiches, but my family would not have it. I promised to cook a simple curry, standing over a big gas stove, trying to remember exactly how she would cook.

Zeal.

Braising spice. Mrs Ball's chutney.

Those green leaf things you only get at Indian shops.

Curry powder. And not just any curry powder. The masala spice curry powder from specialised Indian shops too.

Jeqe instead of rice. 'Rice spills everywhere,' she'd say. 'uJeqe is easier to clean. Coleslaw and beetroot for salads. Nothing more. A starch, a protein and two salads is enough.'

She made the exact same meal at my uncle's funeral a few months before her funeral. Although we weren't speaking, I watched her closely.

I tried using my cooking skills on Itu's mother. She would be convinced only for that hour, at best. Then a neighbour, family friend, church friend, cousin, or random child sent to ask for something would come to the house. As if a button had been switched on, she would continue to express her disdain for Itu's and my relationship. To the people who knew, the people she couldn't hide it from.

She tried hiding it with the church friends – 'Don't embarrass me in front of batho ba kereke.' Often, I would simply continue with whatever I was doing. Itu and I had spoken long and hard about meeting each other's families. It wouldn't be easy, we had told each other, but we had to be consistent. For Ayanda at least, for Ayanda. I laughed when Itu's mother asked her siblings to pray for us.

'uMa wami yena,' Itu shrugged.

My mother did not express disdain for our lifestyle. She simply wouldn't acknowledge that it was a relationship. 'Umngani kaMakhosi,' she would say to strangers as she sent us both around the house like we were teenagers. Sometimes, when talking to her friends, she would tell them that Tumi was a published writer. Ma had liked reading books. Mills & Boon and a barely touched set of the 1997 World Encyclopedia were what we had growing up. Some of the encyclopedias were still in our house, the rest spread across family and neighbours from the time people borrowed books and never returned them.

She liked saying that my friend was a writer, an author. Her friends would congratulate Tumi with questioning looks.

'Wena Makhosi, unjani?' Sis Gugu, one of my mother's oldest friends, would always find a way to sneak that in. She was the only person I saw Ma go out with outside of work events. A day at the beach with Sis Gugu in December.

'Ey, ngisahlanganisa, Ma.'

'But wenza iHonours angithi, noma iMasters?'

'Ngiyafunda, ngiyasebenza. Ngizobona ukuthi kwenzekani.' I didn't like oversharing with Sis Gugu. She overstepped her role in my family.

'Oho, hayi sisi ikona nje ukuthi your mother had told us the good news of ipiece job. Umsebenzi, umsebenzi. Besisho nje ukuthi asibonge.'

'Stability' and 'Consistency'.

These were the words Itu had written on the wall in our lounge. I walked under those words every day, returned to their shadow.

We started saving. Smoking less and saving. Drinking less and saving.

After Itu reconciled with her mother, we started travelling to the North West for all long weekends, and to Pietermaritzburg when Ayanda was on school holidays. For the sake of his stability.

For over six months we had both had full-time jobs and side jobs. We had been together for years. We were saving.

We decided that we would get married to allow the adoption process to go more smoothly. We had thought it through. It would be easier for Ayanda's schooling. For when I had to fetch him, and/or sign for things when Itu was away with work, with writing retreats. We were ready.

Except, I wasn't. Itu's mother's words cut my tongue every time she spoke.

And nothing was helping Ayanda. Not getting arrested. Not the long weekends with his grandfather. Not even the weekends with his father; who had fast got annoyed at how quiet Ayanda was.

You could catch Ayanda in the act, but still he would say nothing to you in response.

'He is always sitting quietly plotting new ways to give us headaches,' his father said.

'I mean, I don't think that's what the teenage brain does. I don't think he is actively trying to give us headaches. I think he is going through things. Maybe therapy?' I tried intervening on the night of the arrest; and the first time Ayanda's father stepped into our house. The house where I paid the bills and said goodnight to his child every night. He laughed and said, 'Can we talk about OUR child, Itumeleng? I won't discuss my child with lento ezenza indoda mna.'

Tumi didn't entirely defend me. He never came into our house again, just picked Ayanda up at the gate or at school.

Every week, the school reported Ayanda for something. Their final straw was marijuana. Ayanda was caught making and selling bongs in the school bathroom. That was all they needed to expel Ayanda from school.

'Boarding school,' Tumi suggested.

'Boarding schools fix nothing, Itu. If anything, they may make things worse.'

'You're giving me more problems, and no solutions,' Itu said.

I stopped trying to have solutions about Ayanda. He responded to no one.

It was a month or so before his November exams. No school would take him this late.

Tumi and Siyabulela agreed that they would temporarily send Ayanda to the Eastern Cape. Something about positive male role models and a sense of belonging were the reasons given. Not that I asked anymore; mostly I was overhearing conversations.

Ayanda left in the last week of September.

I had fantasised about our life going back to 'normal' after he left, even temporary 'normalcy'; but nothing did go back to normal. Ganja and alcohol were still banned from our house, even though we were both adults who knew what we were doing.

Tumi often worked late. When chasing deadlines, working through the night in the office was what worked best for her.

I left in the middle of the night. Packing very little.

26

'But, I just... I could've been so much more, Ma,' I say, leaning against the headboard in Ma's room. I didn't know this headboard. Where had the headboard they'd had when I was a child gone? When did so much change?

'You have more than one university degree. You are raising a child by your age. You've outdone yourself,' Ma says, taking the tub of Nivea and coming to sit on the edge of the bed.

You are your ancestors' wildest dream. I remembered a line I had seen in Kwezilomso's Newtown flat. Kwezi, like my mother, tries hard to remind me that I have outdone myself. That I have done more than most people my age. I don't believe it. It is untrue.

'But ngenzani manje, Ma? I... Zama is a doctor, Sne is an engineer, Phindile is an admitted attorney, and I wasted the opportunities given to me. I'm not an accountant, Ma. Year after year, I have tried writing those boards. Ma, I failed the first board twice; I have lost count of how many boards I have failed.' I don't care about the boards really, but I am grown up and I am still trying to write exams for something I hate. I am miserable.

'A degree is not a waste. No one can take that away from you. You haven't wasted your time, and our plans are not the same. Zama, Sne and Phindile were not the first generation to go to university. You and your brother were, and you've got the qualifications. You've done well. So, board exams are hard, but you're doing good. You're trying. You're doing good.'

Ma tries her best to reassure me with half truths, glancing back at me every now and again as she lotions herself. The back of her head looks way more grey than I remember. On the left side of the dresser, her work hats and church hats remind me why I have not seen my mother's head in a long time. If she is not in a hat, she wears iduku. Amaduku fill the first of her drawers. She takes out iduku and covers her head.

Even though the bedroom furniture is different, everything is still in the same places they have always been. The wardrobes have been changed too. When we first moved here, they had two small wardrobes on thin legs with keys to open them. Those have been split between our and the boys' bedroom now. Ma and uBaba's room has built-in wardrobes, but the clothes still sit the way they did when I was a child. Ma's wardrobe on the far right and uBaba's wardrobe closer to the door. Mamncane had presented the built-ins to uMa for her forty-fifth birthday.

'Mamncane went to university, we weren't the first generation. We were the generation that was going to free us,' I remind Ma.

'Oh, Khosi, the chains run deeper than the two of you could uproot. Nombu was basically your generation. She went to university because she lived here. She only went to university when you were already in school, and only because I'd made it through. Nombu was as much my child as you are.'

'What about Nonhle?' I ask. 'Where does that leave Nonhle and her trajectory?'

Ma laughs. 'There is no trajectory, sisi, there is just working as hard as you can to do the best you can. Nonhle will also do the best she can, and as a family we will all be happy for her; and with her. The same way we are happy for and proud of you.' She puts the lid on the tub of Nivea and comes and rubs my shoulder awkwardly.

'I am not happy, Ma. The problem is I am not happy with

anything. With this family, with my degree, with myself. I just, I am not happy,' I say, sliding beneath the blankets.

'I don't know how to make you happy, mtanami. If you would tell me how to, I would,' Ma says. There is nothing Ma can do. She rocks me to sleep, rubbing my belly when my body eventually comes out of its foetal position. The tears flow, without sound. I cannot control them. When my pillow becomes wet, Ma offers to change it. But I don't mind wet pillows anymore; I cry myself to sleep often. The cold wet pillow against my face calms me down. Returns me to myself.

'I'll be fine, Mama,' I say. 'Sleep. I will be fine, I promise.'

uMa has to be up early for work, as usual. She isn't as busy in the mornings as she used to be when I was younger. She has bought a new car, which means she can leave the house later, and there is only Nonhle who is still at school. And my sister no longer needs to be woken up.

At first, when I would come home and see uMama not wake up as early, I laughed at the thought that my mother, the woman who opened curtains at 6 am on a Saturday morning just because the sun was up, was getting lazy.

Today I realised that she is getting old. Getting tired. You can read the tiredness on the contours of her face. She never did wear make-up. Her face is always an open book to read from the lines that formed every day. I had stopped watching the lines take form over the years. Tonight, I saw my mother's face and all the tiredness she must have gathered in her many years of being alive. I cannot tell her that I have quit my job, again.

27

'People like me don't make it here,' I tell the love of my life and soul mate.

It has been years since I last saw Zama. University perhaps? No, graduation. After she went to Medical School, UFS, we planned to see each other often, but between never being able to afford it and never having time, those plans changed. We were also growing, expanding. Separately. Perhaps, expanding apart.

Here she was though. Her freckles seem brighter now. She is a mahogany brown, the cliché mahogany brown, with more freckles than I remember. She also glows. No, she shines. Her bathroom has enough cosmetics to fill trunks. I wondered if she remembers the time we showered with dishwashing liquid.

There was the Sunlight green bar, but we wanted shower gel, which neither of our parents were going to buy. Ever. It wasn't even Sunlight dishwashing liquid, I remember us laughing. Shoprite No Name perhaps. The water was cold. Township showers in the Bantustan of KwaZulu, the Colony of Natal, didn't have the privilege of geysers at all, let alone inside the house. The shower was at the back of the house. Crowded in a corner, at the end of the yard next to other showers. Jumping in and out screaming that the water was too cold. Screaming from the adrenalin. Daring each other to stay in the water for longer. 'WA-THUU-TREE-FO-FA-SI-SE!!!!' Screaming syllables between deep exhales.

Zama is a doctor at King Edward Hospital in Durban now. Lives in a penthouse flat in Glenwood with white furniture, almost like no one lives there. Pretentious African paintings hang out of place on her walls. Next to a Bible verse I don't care to read, painted boldly on a white wall. Painting words on a white wall, that I understand. Maybe not a Bible verse though.

When did we grow so differently, my best friend and I? My soul mate. My first love?

We have said very little to each other till now. We met up in Ballito for lunch, some fancy restaurant eMhlanga overlooking the ocean. Surely she can't actually live like this on the daily, I thought. We sat at a table close to the smoking section. Her choice.

'How are you?' I asked her.

'Blessed,' she responded.

I was going to need a smoke.

'How are you?' she asked, rubbing my hand unexpectedly.

I half laughed, pulling my hand back. 'Surviving. Breathing. Alive.'

The waiter disturbed us to take down our orders. I thought twice about ordering a Black Label.

'We'll have two vegetarian burgers, with a lot of mushroom sauce,' Zama ordered. An old ritual I had almost forgotten. It had started at Spur, the first time we could afford Spur, when we felt like we'd made it. We'd made a promised to keep eating vegetarian, to 'stay humble'.

'Do you both not eat meat?' the waiter asked.

'Yes,' we said in unison and laughed. We still had that in common. We still shared that. Whatever it meant to share not eating meat. But it always gave us this moment of laughter when service staff would joke about us being friends based on not eating meat. Or asking how we survived. We would laugh and say, 'We just do.'

I drink maybe three, four Black Labels on the way to her house, stopping by a Spar Tops. I need ingudu.

I am preparing to lay myself bare before this woman who doesn't understand. Or perhaps she does; there was a time when she did. Zama also suffered from depression once. Does depression stop? I wonder. She found a place though, in Jesus Christ her saviour. She prayed about everything. Recited Bible verses better than Biko-ists can think what they like.

I understood. We both understood. We had different escapes.

I need her to know, though, that my escape hurts.

'People like me don't survive here,' I say to Zama, as I am opening my quart.

'No one survives here, Khosi, no one survives here.' She pauses.

My heart gallops. She understands!

'We are not meant for here, Khosi, we are just passing through,' she continues. 'We are on our way to the new Jerusalem. Remember Revelations 21? "And then John saw the holy city, the new Jerusalem. And God himself shall wipe away their tears." It was your favourite verse!'

I do remember. I remember the time. This cannot be it, this cannot be the end; we are just passing through. That is what I used to think.

We are both too far gone now, I realise. I don't particularly mind Zama's way of numbing; in the moment I think I even envy her peace. Revelations 21. I wonder what she would say if she knew I had 21 suicide letters now. Poetic.

I walk outside to light a cigarette. The ocean sounds like it knows stories older than ourselves. It whistles and blows. Sand flies into my mouth as I try to whistle back, my whistle eaten by the echo, taking it further and further away to places I do not know. Does the ocean know where echoes go? Does the ocean know that there is never a new Jerusalem, just same old Gomorrahs? Like Alex, Diepsloot, Sobantu, and Jika Joe, and those aren't even the worst of the Gomorrahs we must face while chasing new Jerusalems.

I light my cigarette and Zama comes to close the sliding door behind me.

'You could've asked!' I shout at her, but mostly at the door, blowing my first pull out. It lands on the door, and the clouds of smoke scatterer. Down, up, back towards me. It's amazing what doors can do when closed. In this moment, with this closed glass door and the wind against my back, I desperately want to tell Zama why I have come here. To her. After leaving Tumi.

I lived between friends around Joburg. Then I found a new place. I needed to go home, take in all that was home; leave the things that must stay at home, at home. Many of these things had followed me, everywhere.

This particular thing doesn't deserve to be left at home.

I came to Zama because she lives close to the beach. If I can leave this thing close to the beach, at least, maybe my next relationship can survive.

I would start at home, then go to Zama's and tell her. She knew Simphiwe, after all. Or at least she had met him. They went to the same church.

'WE SURVIVED.'

That was another thing Tumi had painted on the wall. In a big thick haunting font, it hovered above my head. 'We survived' was something she said, often, when she did not want to share a story. A simple 'We survived' would have to do.

On the day she painted those words above our bed, she had said to me, 'You know, I mean, we're here. We're happy, we're doing okay. We've had our share of hurdles, but we survived.'

'But, I mean... okay,' I said.

I did not want to tell her I had not survived. Not me. I had not survived. But the words would not leave my mouth. My voice stayed stuck inside my stomach.

I had been numb until I saw that picture. I had never been the same again.

Tumi and I weren't in a great space and me suddenly having a problem with her mantra was not going to be the next argument we'd have. So I left.

And now I am here. Maybe I will tell Zama. I push the sliding door back.

Zama doesn't even wait for me to sit down. Half jumping on her sofa, she points to her massive TV. As if it is possible to ignore.

'Remember this? Remember Fear Factor?' she says as if she is the eTV commentator.

'Urghh, fuck off. Don't say it like that.'

'But do you remember? Do you? The white people were shook, SHOOOK. You really had a python around you that we weren't even allowed to get close to. You looked like you were about to summon chieftaincy, I tell you, friend.' She is still jumping around from excitement.

'You're exaggerating again,' I say, sitting down next to her on her white sofa.

'Nha, sis, nha, ithi awukhumbuli. You spent almost the entire term being the animal whisperer, and the 'dreamer' and the hearer of things. I'd have believed it, too, if I didn't know you were spying on half the conversations. Those white kids were five-to asking for you to be exorcised, if you hadn't stopped.'

'You're exaggerating. AGAIN.' I try returning her to the present moment, away from primary school bullshit. She is so beautiful. I had almost forgotten why I loved her when we were kids.

'No, but for real. For that short space of time, I believed ancestors could have been real, you know,' she says. 'I know you believe they're real now, and that things from the past haunt us and all. But, I promise you, friend, I promise: the blood of Jesus cleanses all. Renews all. Even Fear Factor doesn't scare me now, you know. I could do all these things, because I know the blood covers me.'

It doesn't matter now. Zama and I are in a different place. I am leaving tomorrow. I will go back to Johannesburg, take this burden of not surviving with me. With this shadow still travelling with me.

Perhaps I will go to the beach in the morning and drown it in the waves. Whisper to the waves and beg them to never let it come back again. Take it to foreign lands, I will beg of the ocean.

But in the morning Durban is hit by a big storm. As much as I want to go to the beach, I will get wet and I can't drive back to Johannesburg soaking wet. Zama and I leave together. She is rushing for a work emergency, and I need to leave so she can lock her fancy apartment.

'The disadvantages of being single, do you see? Now your singleness must make me wake up earlier than I wanted, because wena you don't have a person to leave the key with,' I joke.

'Ninjena konje manijola. Greet your partner for me,' she says, rushing to her car, hugging me, getting in and quickly ushering me to my car. She is in such a hurry that I can't even tell her I don't think I still have a partner.

It is not the first time I have driven high. I learned to forget I was high when driving. Except during the long drives back home from Grahamstown, when I needed to feel high just to finish the journey. Montrose was my rolling station. Roll, smoke, and drive. Sometimes, roll and drive while smoking.

I do not stop eMontrose this time. I don't need to feel high. This drive alone feels like my first high. First, it looks like the night is folding into itself, getting darker and darker. The red reflectors on the freeway blind me. Too bright against the dark night. And the lights from the trucks driving in the opposite direction are not helping.

I do not stop in Montrose. Just keep driving. A truck that looks like a Christmas tree is approaching. From far, it looked like a flood of lights were coming my way. The closer and closer it gets, I begin to see the shape of the truck. It is one of those big Code 14 trucks, with three sections. All around the sections are lights. Red, blue, green, red.

I wonder if this is what death looks like, like flashing lights. No. Too dramatic.

Okay, fine, but what if you die from flashing lights?

It's the perfect way to die. In case there are no flashing lights that welcome me to death.

No, man, Makhosi. You don't want to die anymore.

I drive past the Christmas lights truck.

I am going back to Johannesburg. I am going to finally go back, and speak to Tumi.

Perhaps that was why I first had to go home. To realise how ridiculous I sounded, out loud. To an audience.

I am approaching the De Hoek Toll Plaza.

I have done this many are times. I can bounce back from this as well, I promise myself.

I will survive.

I will.

I must.

In a world that is constantly trying to kill black izitabane, staying alive is my revolt. I will survive.

28

Nonhle

'I have fought too many struggles and have learned that we don't win. Not now. Not here. I can't survive.'

I had lost count of the number of times I had read her status update.

That day, our house smelled like freshly burned impepho. This is not usual in our house, but that day, that day Ma came back saying her spirit was not at peace.

I paid no attention. Ma had started doing things she didn't 'believe in' when I was younger, like burning impepho because of spirits.

I was halfway through my Matric exams; I really wanted to get into a BSc but I needed to get high marks. I had learned a few months ago, when we were studying chemistry, that I was bad at identifying colours – which meant I would always partially struggle with physics. So, I needed to work really hard on the other sections.

I logged onto Facebook like I always did. First thing in the morning, I slid my hand under my pillow and grabbed my phone.

Most of my school mates had already written statuses about the upcoming physics exam;

'Well, at least this is the last time I will feel the burn,' my best friend Silindile posted. She had applied to study Politics, Philosophy and Economics; but was hoping to spend some time dancing first. Physics was the least of her concerns.

'Insanity is doing the same thing over and over again and expecting different results.' Albert Einstein. Today I quit insanity. The results will always be the same, Physics knocking me out. I should be stressed, but I'm excited at the thought of being liberated from insanity,' wrote Khumo.

Khumo was one of the smartest boys in our school, and a crush of mine since Grade 10. At first, I tried competing with him, but I realised he took competition seriously; and there was no use in me trying to achieve my crush by looking stupid. So, I stopped. Just stalked him on Facebook. He had the most photogenic cheekbones I had ever seen, highlighting the way his eyes were small towards the edges. He had the thickest eyebrows, which I often fantasised about licking, but Siphokazi said that was weird. It probably was, but the fantasies didn't stop. I just kept them to myself.

According to Facebook, Khumo had three older sisters and a younger brother that he posted about every second day. Family orientated; I liked that. He also spent his weekends either at a sporting event, or having finished reading some really smart book. Recently, he had started posting about Economic Freedom; and other EFF-adjacent things. The African consciousness somewhat turned me off, but I liked that he loved to read.

There was never a picture with any girl, and his status update said he was single. Year after year, I waited for him to get a girlfriend. Anyone at all, and my crush would've died. He made it worse by taking a boy to the Matric dance; which for me meant he was just focusing on his studies and didn't want to be distracted in our Matric year. Focused. Which made me fall in love with him all the more. Most of the girls in our year were more interested in his date than him. They both wore tailored blue suits, the same polka dot Happy Socks and ties that matched one colour on their socks.

I had already spent an hour of my morning looking at his posts, which I had already seen a few times before while daydreaming about our future together, which I did often, when I scrolled past Makhosi's update.

There was nothing worth noticing about this status. Makhosi had her seasons, and I thought this was another one of her morbid seasons where she would bleed all over the internet.

A few weeks after my results, when we had all been looking for her for a few weeks, the status haunted me. Was it her suicide letter? Her goodbye? Was it a sign? Was she on drugs (again)?

By the time a month had passed since her 'disappearance' I started to think maybe it wasn't the drugs she was addicted to, maybe it was the escape. The experience. Of being away from this place. Even if it's for a moment, even if it's not a physical escape, it's still an escape. From here, from this, from all of it.

Maybe she will find peace, maybe peace will find her.

This time last year, I had passed my Grade 11, which everyone told me was the hardest grade. Makhosi took me to Johannesburg, to see where she, Tumi and their child lived. Ma had already been to visit, and uBaba was not interested in the life they had built for themselves. Not that Makhosi tried involving him.

A few hours into being in Johannesburg, I knew that her plans were mostly to take me drinking. She was determined to 'show me the world.' To be to me what I think she thought Mamncane should have been to her. A friend.

In a drunken state I was familiar with, she whispered, 'I want you to be open enough to share your first experiences with me. I don't want to just be your sister. The world is a shit place. A part of me wants to protect you. I don't want anyone to take advantage of you the first time you try alcohol…'

A song came on. 'Weekend Special', I think it was. She jumped up and started gyrating all over the room. She loved Brenda Fassie, said we didn't deserve her. Looked up to her.

Literally. She had a poster of Brenda Fassie in her flat which she bent down to every morning.

That night, she passed out on someone's bed. I called Tumi to call me an Uber.

'Drinking with Makhosi is an extreme sport, hey?' Tumi said when I walked in.

'An extreme Olympic sport,' I joked.

'She just wanted to show you a good time, you know?' Tumi said.

I did know. I did.

I loved my sister, I understood her desire to protect me and expose me. I wasn't her though.

I had seen the joy she said she had never seen. I had seen her happy. She called it mania; I called it her peace. The times were few and far between, but I had known her happy. Loving. Spending ridiculous amounts of money. She had known more joy than most women I know. She laughed the loudest when she did laugh. She also hurt the most, when she hurt; her wounds never seemed to heal. During that visit, I knew that my sister was happier than she had been in a very long time.

'Sebemubheke yonke indawo, namanje akaziwa,' Ma said, her voice almost breaking.

She couldn't look anyone in the eyes. It was as if someone had stripped her naked, like Mary Magdalene before Jesus. Except she wasn't standing before God or angels, just gossiping neighbours, and hateful in-laws. What sin she had borne in her womb.

It had been months since Makhosi had disappeared. At first Ma thought she was pulling one of her stunts, being dramatic. Having an 'episode'.

We were used to Makhu leaving. It's what she did, disappeared into cold nights. Returned on summer mornings as if she was always there. Sometimes, often, she would make her way back home on dry winter evenings ngathi uhlanzwe ulwandle.

She would lay in bed, debilitated. Some visits, she would spend months at home. She would eventually find her smile again, then on happy mornings say her goodbyes and promise to call more often. An old promise. A promise I learned was as empty as the promise of her taking care of herself.

Home was her rehab. A cheap healing retreat, she called it.

Her hospital, Ma would call it. And Ma didn't mind nursing her back to health. It may have been in those moments that the mother felt most connected to her prodigal daughter. There is something about a mother's need to be needed that I have never understood. Ma yearned for Makhosazane to need her, and the older Ma got the more she missed her. The visits became more frequent, on Makhosi's part. More frequent, and more dramatic, it would seem.

The last visit was anything but. She had arrived in the middle of the night, from Joburg. She had decided to drive her unnecessarily loud Beetle. It may have been just after twelve when I heard her try to slip into the house quietly. A futile task, given that her car wakes up the entire neighbourhood.

I think Ma enjoyed this too, that loud car. Ma loved waking up to make Makhosazane food when she got home. Whether it was 2 pm or 3:30 am. Whether she would eat the food or not. She would tell her she would leave it in the microwave on nights when she wouldn't eat. They'd sit and try to catch up; on the days when she would spare a minute to eat before disappearing into her bedroom.

On this visit, she didn't eat. Just crawled into her bed.

I thought I heard her sobbing, but she sobs a lot when she comes during her midnight drives. It was nothing new. Besides, 'tears cleanse the soul,' she would say.

We spent the next week without her mentioning her return to Joburg, or her partner, or their child, or work, or school. Makhosazane was away from her phone for the first time in a long time. She was here, with us. We laughed, we fought, we screamed at the TV screen watching men confess to cheating on Nyan Nyan'. She even took us to Gateway shopping mall, a task I knew she dreaded. We ate lunch. Nothing particularly fancy.

Nothing particularly stood out. My big sister was being a big sister. I enjoyed it. So did Ma.

Then she left.

Then Zama called to ask if Makhosi had come back home, because Tumi said they had broken up and she had not heard from her in weeks. Makhosi had said she was going back to Johannesburg, but no one could confirm that she had arrived.

Ma had the entire force looking, for weeks on end.

At first I thought Makhosi would be found when Makhosi wanted to be found. Five weeks into looking for Makhosi, Ma had to announce to the families.

29

Dudu

She came home thinner than I had seen her in a very long time, my daughter. Her eyes looked like they had seen stories no child should know. Except she wasn't a child anymore, as she reminded me often. All my attempts to remind her that she would forever be a child to me seemed to fall on closed off ears. She was colder in the way she looked at me. Somewhere between disgust and that first time that you accept that your mother is also a failure. It is okay to say; I know that now. Mothers fail. Parents fail. But it feels like betrayal the first time you must accept it. The last time I saw her, though, it was as if she had accepted my failures. Made peace with them and me.

My mother, MaDlamini, had her fair share of failures. She didn't have time for us, couldn't. She was too poor, and there were too many of us, with too many tasks to be done throughout the day. Every day. I would later learn that my mother had dreams too. Had gallons full of life experience, of shattered dreams, dreams deferred. She was human.

'Why do you stay in this marriage?' Makhosi asked me, when she was younger. 'Why do any women stay in these marriages?'

'Your father is a good man, Makhosazane,' I told her. 'He

puts food on the table, he puts clothes on your back.' Sharing only the things that children need to know. Provision. We provide.

'Why is your standard of good men so mediocre, Ma?' she said another time, huffing and puffing in anger. 'You work too. You put clothes on our backs. You put food on the table. But what are you doing now? Breaking your back washing everyone's clothes? Don't they have their own hands? Why do you stay in a marriage where you are treated like a maid?'

'Yazi, Makhosazane, sometimes I like washing the dishes, and cleaning the house,' I said. 'It calms me down. Have you ever thought this is what I want to do?'

She stormed off. Muttering that I had been brainwashed by men. How she had been brainwashed by other people too, although maybe not men. Maybe Candice's mother, and Mrs Radley, and Candice, the people she wanted me to become. I miss that daughter. Those questions. That anger.

Every time I saw her, her eyes seemed to tell a story of a soul that died.

I had thought she was getting better, but now I can see that I may have been lying to myself. Children will not save you from yourself. Had I not seen Thulani? They were similar, Makhosi and Thulani. Searching and crashing.

Thulani thought she was on drugs, and maybe she was. What do mothers know?

She had been better at one point, or so I had thought, but we did not speak often.

She was raising a son with Tumi. They had a house. They both worked.

When she arrived in the middle of the night, I was shocked.

'Makhosi, I saw you two months ago. How did you get so thin, so fast?' I asked her.

She gasped at my exaggeration and answered, 'The Beyoncé diet, of course.'

She knew I did not know what the Beyoncé diet was, and that I did not believe her. I missed Nombu – she would have known what the Beyoncé diet was.

The last time Nombu and I spoke, the visit home before she passed away, she didn't think there was anything out of the ordinary about Makhosi's behaviour.

'It's not istage,' my sister had tried to convince me. She said it had very little to do with adolescence and more to do with the influence that Makhosi was exposed to. 'Ngeke uMakhosi aphathwe istage njengengane yaselokishini, sisi, she's a Model C child. They don't smoke insangu and drink a lot. They just, they read and act out like she is acting out. She's being the child she was exposed to being.' I was not reassured.

'But what do I do with this?' I asked her. Nombu was more exposed to this than I was. She complained often about how rude exceptionally educated children were. She had studied at King's College London, and would constantly express her shock at how the students, all younger than her, would tell lecturers that they were wrong, or even swear at lecturers. 'Ah, ukufunda,' she would say.

'Give her time,' Nombu said as we said our goodbyes at the airport when she left to go back to England. 'Give her time.'

It was the last time I saw Nombu.

On Sunday, as I had done on many Sundays, I made ujeqe nobontshisi, one of Makhosi's favourite meals, but she ate very little. 'Eat. You will!' I told her. 'Ayikho into ethi ungadli, regardless of the stress.'

'Yazi wena, Ma, awulazi iGoli,' she joked.

'Ubani yena, uMawakho? Umawakho wake wabhekana neGoli ngqo emehlweni,' a slightly drunk Thulani said from the sofa next to Makhosi.

Nonhle lifted up her head.

'What? Wawenzani eGoli?' she asked.

'I had a life before you all yazi.'

'Well...?' Makhosi demanded.

I had not thought back to that day for a very long time. I was shocked Thulani even remembered it.

It was the day before our graduation from the police academy and we decided we would all go to Joburg. Many of my colleagues would go back and forth, but Zondi had atrocious stories about the things that happened there, which had kept me from going. Pretoria had as much as Johannesburg had, other colleagues would say, iGoli is just fuller. But for graduation I was willing to risk it. We took a taxi from Marabastad to Bree Street Taxi Rank and from there we would walk to Carlton Centre. It was not far, and that way we could walk to the post office to get our money.

I remember the post office being big and clean. I had not expected it to be clean. I had not been paying attention to most of what was around me. I knew that it was full and I clung onto my purse. I was amongst the last to walk out of the post office, to find my friends in conversation with two men and one woman. Something about how bebanjwe inkunzi and needed some money to catch a taxi to Hillbrow police station. The woman was distraught and crying, while the men were telling the story of how it happened. In a frenzy we looked through our purses, and in no time we were surrounded and we, too, were mugged. As fast as it happened, the two men and women who were telling us their story were nowhere to be seen. Disappeared into thin air. We looked around to see if anyone on the street had seen a street patrol walking in our direction. We all seemed to spot him at the same time and ran towards him to try to tell the story of how we had been mugged by 'a syndicate'.

'It was a SYNDICATE of them,' dramatic Nonhlanhla insisted.

Basifikisa eGoli, was all I could think. Soon there were people around to hear our story, a few stopping to be clear about the details while others walked slowly so they could eavesdrop. All the street patroller could say was 'Ey' bo', sisi, sebehambile, sebehambile, angeke nisabathola manje.'

'Kodwa ngemali, yabanta bam,' someone said.

'Ngisebenze kangaka,' said someone else.

My colleagues paced up and down the pavement, causing a scene.

'Ngicela ukubuza singayithola kuphi into yokufona?' I asked the street patroller.

'Ungangena ucele la,' he said, pointing to a small Portuguese shop that sold already made amagwinya, and sandwiches.

'Sikuphi la?' I asked someone, the owner, I think. 'The post office on Commissioner Street,' I said into the phone. I hung up and thanked him.

Back on the pavement, some of my colleagues were crying, others still pacing up and down. I don't remember how long we were there for, waiting to be fetched. I remember thinking about how tall the buildings were. About working or living that high up. How many incidents like this did they see from up there? Did they even see them anymore? Were the faces familiar to them? Had someone been looking down from those windows trying to warn us?

The commander sent senior colleagues to fetch us in a van, because they thought it was funny. That we were training to be officers and we just got mugged. As a collective.

I called Thulani only because I couldn't call my family and tell them about wasting money on a party. How do people simply disappear into iGoli, I kept asking Thulani. How do their families not know? Don't they look for them? '"You're making other people's problems your problems" is what your father said.'

Thulani had his eyes closed. Makhosi and Nonhle were staring at me.

'Mxm yazi,' I said, standing up to get away from my children's gaze.

30

uMaDlamini was proud I was going to police training. She had attended a funeral of a local policeman somewhere in Mooi River. He had been a police officer who assisted with removing people from their houses emaplazini. He was not a respected man; uMaDlamini was a little embarrassed to be associated with him.

Their children grew up well though. My mother was fascinated at the formation the officers entered into, the saluting, the marching drills. She came back and would not stop talking about how dignified it looked. That was when I should have asked to go study to be a police officer, because it was something she already romanticised.

By the time I reached JC, uZulu, my father, was fast becoming agitated at my having stayed at school as long as I did. There were many of us. Anything that wasn't going to produce an income was a waste of time to him now.

By the time I asked uMaDlamini if I could stop my job as a teacher's assistant and go to training, she had long forgotten the romantic funeral procession. People in the community hated the police. Introducing Thulani, who was in Correctional Services, to my mother did not help.

'He locks innocent people away,' uMaDlamini said, shaking her head at me.

The news was reaching as far as Mpofana, of arrests and deaths. Deaths while arrested.

The police were arresting them younger and younger, in the cities, which was where we would work eventually, maDlamini told me. 'There is no need for many police and prisons eMpofana and emakhaya, so of course you will work in the cities. Where you will arrest – and kill – young children. People's children.' And what would happen to our children, if Thulani and I ever had children? What would happen to them after our houses were torched down emalokishini?

uZulu said, 'Imali umbulali. Kepha, imali iyondla.'

My father made the final decision. I used the same argument against my mother. Imali may be a killer, but money is also what feeds; and my family needed to be fed. My mother did not approve of everything I ever did.

Ukungazi, kuyafana nokungaboni siyasho isiZulu.

Nonhle is going to university soon. The University of the Witwatersrand, Johannesburg. Makhosi had asked her to come to Wits after her Matric.

Nonhle had considered UCT, but it was too far. Too unsafe, too unfamiliar. When tragedy hits, and your children are too far, and they do not have money to come back, and when you also don't have money – the labour pains return, as memory. To remind you that you are as helpless now as you were then.

There is no way to know this. To lose a child. It hits me in waves, especially in the mornings.

When I lost Nombu, a part of me died with her. Perhaps the most sacred parts of me. A big part of me was happy she did not have a child. Losing a sibling I survived, but losing a child. Is Makhosi... Makhosi uyaphila? Lapho ukhona?

31

Nonhle

Silindile and I went out tonight. A club in Durban. The boy she liked arrived, Si… Asive, I think was his name. Tall, dark and handsome. At least, that's what Silindile said. I didn't see clearly. Club lights are loud. The one minute they are blue, then they are green, then they are yellow. It's hard to concentrate on people's faces. He was tall, that I remember. He picked Silindile up, with what seemed like an effortless move. Her legs flinging up in the air. Surely they can't be this corny, I thought. But they were. Every song after that, they were in each other's arms.

It was a club. People find people to dance with. I needed to find someone to dance with too. It didn't matter who, so long as it was not the 'drunken story of the night'. The last time we went out, the drunk of the night was a man who looked like he was a little older than the rest of us, too old to be here even. He held his beer high up as he made his way to the centre of the dance floor. Almost falling. Nightclubs and slippery floors? Nightclubs and drunk people, I guess.

Alcohol makes people lose all inhibitions. The inability to be shy, to be unaware of your surroundings, or to not care what your surroundings are. Maybe that's why nightclubs exist, so you can live outside all your inhibitions without caring about the surroundings. We had driven over 70 kilometres to get to this nightclub far from home. From familiar surroundings, knowing eyes.

'Asambe,' Silindile said to me, appearing from nowhere, without Asive.

I didn't care to ask why. I enjoy going clubbing up until I have no sober person to talk to. Silindile was drunk too. And her phone was off – or stolen, as we would learn later that morning. I didn't have airtime, a mistake I made often. I didn't particularly mind walking closer to the waterfront. The sea breeze against my thighs was refreshing. I took off my shoes; I had learned to love the texture of sea sand on my feet.

Silindile started vomiting.

'Let's call Asive,' I suggested.

'No!' she shouted at me.

I tried speaking reason into her. 'Why not? Let's call him so he can at least take us to the cabs. We still have another five plus kilometres to walk to get to the cabs.'

'No. Ungamfonela uAsive wakho loyo, but I would rather walk the five kilometres before ngimbheke emehlweni!' She sounded resolute.

We walked the remaining five kilometres and a few more before we got to the taxis. Getting home would cost more than we had. That night/morning I learned to negotiate, with the background of waters that will carry stories only a select few will tell.

Silindile and I met on the 'transport' that took us from eSobantu to school. She wore the white uniform of the Indian schools, Raisethorpe Primary. She was my best friend in the transport. We were in the same grade and liked the same things. The boys in the transport liked picking on girls, Silindile and I were both new to this transport. Some people stayed on the transport, year after year. Before the transport, uBaba would take me to school.

Silindile lived a few houses away from mine. Her parents' house was a light pink four-roomed house with a steel gate, and a dog chained onto that gate. The dog barked every time someone opened the gate, always catching itself, pulling too far and too hard and almost hurting its neck. Her parents sounded as strict as my parents, if not worse, with that dog at the gate to report every movement. We only met in the transport. When we first became friends, she liked asking me about having a sister. She only had brothers, older brothers, like me; but she wasn't friends with her brothers the way I was friends with Mpumelelo. Her one brother was addicted to glue, and often ran away from home; and went to beg on Church Street. Silindile told me he used to scream at his parents, but what about she did not know. She thought he was not her father's child and her father didn't like him much. He had lived with Silindile's grandmother before she died. He was fine at first, Silindile said. Quiet, but fine.

Her other brother drove amakhumbi, and everyone in the transport was scared of him; just for being a khumbi brother. Silindile didn't like him much.

When we were older, I once asked Silindile what she thought about her brother's addiction.

'I don't get to prescribe to people how to deal with their demons, numb their pain,' she said. It was the sort of thing Makhosi would say. I thought of Makhosi often when I was with Silindile.

I had not thought about my sister for a while. I mean, I thought about her but not about finding her, or when. She just didn't want to be found this time, it seemed. I was giving her space.

When we eventually got home, I decided to write to her.

Hey Sis, [typing an email]

I miss you [delete]

You've said something about people's entitlement to other people. 'We don't own people,' you said.

I am not sure which you I miss.

Makhosazane the cow herder? Makhosazane the public speaker? Makhosazane with depression? Makhosazane the lesbian. Although I do think Makhosazane the lesbian is the same as Makhosazane with depression. Who is the same Makhosazane in whose flat everyone seemed to smoke weed. I remember you saying you got your stash back home. Swazi, Skunk, Blue Ivy. I wondered what would ever happen to you if, for whatever reason – actually, not for whatever reason; there are many reasons the police could arrive at our house...

Back to the email, I reminded myself.

Unjani, sis?

I stared at the white screen on my computer for I don't know how long.

At first, I didn't know what to ask, or what to say.

Should I tell you about Ma? About how everyone is? That Nkosana is dying looking for you. He has been all over the whole of Gauteng. Written Facebook status upon Facebook status. He even tried Twitter to find you. At first, he was the only one who tried that hard. Him and Itumeleng. The rest of us, what could we do, Makhosi?

Of course uMa got the entire force, everyone she knows, to look for you, but if police couldn't find you, singobani thina?

Maybe you don't want to be found yet; because, gurl, we have even stopped Nkosana from writing to Khumbulekhaya because that would chase you away even more.

Unjani, sis.

The blank page continued to stare at me.

uMa tried everything she possibly could to try get me to go to UKZN, Pietermaritzburg campus.

Guilt tripping. Blackmail. Even threats to withhold money.

It had been a few months after Makhosi had left (and of

course she would return when she wanted to – and besides, I am not her).

Silindile sometimes tells me to be grateful for Makhosi, an older sister who put my parents through the most, so they can be more lenient on me. Except, they are not.

Living in the backdrop of a rebel means even the act furthest from your mind is your parents' biggest projection. uBaba projects drugs onto all of us.

But I was going to Wits, and for a little while I was going to be myself.

I was familiar with the bus ride, even though uMa insisted on flying down with me. Which was a waste of money. But I had already fought her on enough. So, we flew. I had been accepted to study Architecture and would be staying at a res named Jubilee.

The pillars by the Great Hall stairs and the main building always made me think of Delilah. From the Bible. I often wished some woman would sleep with the vice-chancellor, or whoever is at the top, steal all their secrets and somehow make them tear down the building and completely destroy university as a concept.

Different to how Makhosi hated studying, I think I hated having to study even more than she did. I wish everyone first had the opportunity to 'work' on different things and then decide what to study.

Everything felt fake at university, from the student societies, the sports and the faith-based ones, to the conversations. Orientation week was the bane of my existence. For the most part, I walked around the city alone, ignoring the big tall buildings at the corner of Braamfontein behind me. One of my favourite things to do in Braam was look at the maps of drool and crust on people's faces, especially in the mornings. People at Wits don't have drool and crusts, except the people in the library.

In lectures everyone looks like they don't know sleep – or living – outside those walls.

Silindile was off on a year to dance in Italy. Her life sounded, and looked, like all the dreams I had to travel. If only I'd found a talent that wasn't school. If only I'd tried harder at sports, and other things with nice opportunities that were not school. Like singing. If only I'd stuck with the choir, or something.

I met Habib walking over Queen Elizabeth Bridge the week lectures started. I almost punched him, he ran up behind me so fast. His reflexes were faster than I acted. He caught my fist in his hand a few inches from his stomach and held it.

'Wait!' The wait was caught in a laugh in his throat. 'I'm not trying to rob you,' he said as he saw me looking around for someone to scream to. 'I wanted to tell you to be careful.'

There was a group of men a few feet away from us.

'You can't walk here alone,' he said, dragging me by the arm, trying to make me walk faster. We were approaching the security guard on the other end of the bridge, who was walking towards us at the same time. He had on a red jersey, a white collar shirt and grey pants.

'Sisi, uright?' the man asked. Why did security uniform make grown adults look like schoolchildren, I wondered? 'Sisi, uright?' the man asked again, this time his hand firmly stopping the man who was also holding my hand and trying to get me over the bridge. The man whose eyes looked like they were begging me to say yes, yes, it was fine. He had a crust at the corner of his left eye, even though he smelled like he'd been dripping in a fake version of an expensive men's perfume. Cologne. You called men's perfume cologne, I reminded myself.

'Sisi weeh?' The security officer was getting impatient.

'Ngi-right, baba, ngi right,' I stuttered.

It was as if he had already decided I was fine by how quickly he let go of the strange man with a crust and walked past us. Maybe hesitation annoyed him. The strange man let go of my hand, which made me feel the gathering of sweat inside of my palm. Sticky. I wiped it off on my pants.

'I guess you would've been fine then,' he said. The group of men behind us had crossed the bridge to walk on the other side. 'Between the upper cut and being a Zulu. You would've been fine.' He tried to make a joke.

'Um'Zulu, thanks. A Zulu unyoko,' I said. A group of young women were walking towards us. Suddenly, he cracked up in a laughter I'd never heard before. Like an old laugh. How I imagine my grandfather's father laughed. As if he wasn't laughing alone. His voice, it sounded like he was laughing on behalf of many people. Like a wise person. I wondered whether he had always had the laugh of an old man.

His laugh drew the passing eyes, so I left him. He caught up with me again.

'I'm fine now. I'm almost in Braam. Thank you,' I said, hoping he'd leave me alone.

'Pleasure. My name is Habib, by the way,' he said.

'Habib?' I said. I had never met a black Habib, not even in KZN.

'Yes,' he replied.

'Well. Nice to meet you, and thank you, Habib,' I tried to shoo him away.

'I didn't mean to offend you by calling you a Zulu, I'm not uhmZulu,' he said. We were now walking fast, me trying to outrun him without actually running.

'Um'Zulu,' I corrected him again.

'Yes. Yes.'

'It's okay. Thank you,' I said. He was trying too hard.

As soon as I got to campus I facetimed Silindile, to tell her all about Habib.

'Habib?' Silindile said. 'Ohhhh, an Africaaan man. His name sounds Muslim? Maybe West African, do you think Nigeria? Guuurl.' She slurped up her words. 'No, a Ghanaian man. A real MAAAAAN!! Describe him to me? Did he look like he'd been dropped in a sea of moisturised melanin? Did he glow, friend? Friend. ANSWER!' she screamed at me.

'You asked so much, Sli, which do I answer?'

'ALL OF IT. ALL OF IT. ALL OF!'

'I told you everything. I wasn't sure whether I was getting mugged or helped. Then a security guard tried to help. Then I swore at Habib in isiZulu, and he heard me—'

'Gurl, why would you swear at a man who is helping you?' Silindile disturbed me before I could finish. 'Why? A Ghanaian man, at that.'

'Okay. We don't know any of these things. AND I didn't think he'd hear me nje. I already picked up that he wasn't um'Zulu. So, I was just, you know...'

'Urghhh, you waste opportunity, sis. Absolutely a waste. You don't know what gift you have of having African men around. Urghhh, the caucasians, sis. The caucasians. I can't believe I even miss my last of my days there with Xhosa men,' she said.

'You miss Xhosa men?' I was surprised. She hated Asive, and vicariously all Xhosa men after their short-lived relationship. He'd invited another girl to the same club and forgot.

'I miss black men in abundance,' she explained. 'I miss walking down streets and seeing more than one black man. A lot of the men here are with these white women; I mean siyabhekana. And I know it would get down, but ukuba ikhwapha to umlungu. Weeh.'

'But you just got there. You're not looking to be ikhwapha no? Just dancing?' I asked.

'Yes, I mean. Ehe... but also, I'd like to have someone to talk to, you know. It's just, mxm, maybe it will get better with time. I haven't seen a lot vele. Just going to the studio, and to theatre shows. I don't know. I'll find the rasta men. There are always rasta men.' She seemed to mostly be reassuring herself.

'We thank Jah,' I joked.

Silindile needed to go. I couldn't believe she missed men, of all things. If only she knew how annoying they were. Especially these boys on campus.

I ran into Habib a week or so later, outside the Orbit jazz

club in Braamfontein. I was glad he saw me too, because I would've probably walked past. He jumped into the middle of the pavement, a non-needed big gesture to try 'stop me', he said.

'A small wave would've also worked,' I said.

'A woman looking for small things in such a big city?'

'I'm not "looking" for anything,' I said.

'Here, in Johannesburg? You're in Johannesburg not looking for anything? You're one in a million for sure. A Wits student. Let me guess... English literature? A literary genius?' I stared at him.

'Okay, thanks. Nice to see you again. Bye,' I said, trying to walk past him. He wouldn't let me. We looked foolish going left and right on that small pavement with people trying to walk around us.

'Stop it, this is stupid,' I said. He was annoying me again.

'We're dancing,' he said, spreading his hands without seeing the girls behind him and hitting the one in the Wits Accounting hoodie across her chest with his tattooed arm. The one in the tank top said 'Nx!' Looking at the two of them together, you couldn't be sure whether it was hot or cold.

Habib began over-apologising to the girl, who was now walking past him. I couldn't hold my laugh. She looked at me and said, 'Mxm,' and then I was apologising to her too.

'No, no, I am laughing at him. Not you,' I said.

Habib started laughing.

'You're a clown, you,' I said.

'Happy to make you laugh, u mu Zulu girl,' he said. Trying too hard at enunciating um'Zulu.

I laughed again.

Some men came from behind me and Habib pulled me off the pavement closer to the parked cars.

'Okay. Before we annoy more people, let me go,' I said.

'Can I walk you?' he asked.

'Either that or dancing around like clowns in the street?' Habib let out a laugh way too loud for my dry joke.

'Let's go,' he said, holding my hand again.

He didn't ask if he could hold it, and I...

'You like walking on dangerous bridges and in the dark then?' he asked.

'This city doesn't know silence, you know,' I told him. 'Or darkness. In fact, in this city both darkness and silence are scary. So, it doesn't matter whether I am walking on dangerous bridges or in the dark. This city is what it is.'

'Philosophy. And what else?' he disturbed me.

'What else what?' I asked.

'What else are you studying?'

We were approaching the entrance on Jorissen, past the unnecessarily space-consuming statue of Jesus on a bench. I hated that statue. It took up more space than it needed.

'I'm almost at the gate, you can turn back here,' I said.

'Ahh, already? What if we never see each other again?' Habib pleaded.

'We've seen each other twice in less than a month. I'm sure I'll see you sometime in the next few years that I'm stuck in this city,' I said.

'The city is also not always one thing. The city changes. The darknesses and silences haven't always been scary. Nor will they always be. No two days in this city are the same. Nothing certain.'

'Migration Studies?' I joked.

'Or a migrant.' Habib smiled. 'Some of us are the people studied by people behind the tall walls you live in.'

Now I wanted to see Habib again.

'See you soon. I promise,' I said, releasing my hand from his hold.

'If you say so, Zulu girl,' he said, letting me go.

I realised I had not seen anything since Habib gripped my hand until I saw the bench I hated. I saw nothing even as I walked back to res. I'm sure it was busy, as it always is in the evenings. People living within walls move interestingly. Like they know they are free only within the walls. A limited freedom. I didn't mind not seeing anything, because all I wanted to do – needed to do – was facetime Silindile and tell her.

She was crying. A racial thing.

'You know, it's tougher here without the crowd of other black girls to have your back like at school, you know,' she sobbed through her words.

'I'm sorry, Silindile. I'm here. I'm here. I'll fight for you.'

'It's okay,' Silindile said. 'I'll be fine. Let me finish ugly crying it out. Love you, sis.'

She hung up, not waiting for me to say I loved her too.

I never did meet Habib again. So there was never a time to tell her again.

For months, I looked for him.

Like I had looked for Makhosi.

It felt too familiar and too close.

Silindile was meant to come back at the end of that year. To study at Wits as well; it had been the plan. But she got a scholarship to a dance school in France.

I did not come all the way to Johannesburg to re-learn waiting on people who did not want to be here.

I get my degree completed and get a job in Pretoria. I have been wanting to leave Johannesburg since first year. I got tired of looking for shadows there. People will find me if they want to. In a calmer, quieter Pretoria.

I think about calling Makhosazane, but with the years I have stopped hurting myself like that. I have her voice message memorised. The last time Ma called her number, it belonged to someone else. I didn't have it inside of me to hold her through that again. It helped that I was in Joburg.

'You know who it is, because you called me. EyakwaZungu intombi eyazalwa uMaZulu. Mabengibiza, bangibiza uMakhosazane. Abangaziyo bathi uM—'

She must have run out of space or something because the voice message stopped. As abruptly as she'd left.

I get my degree completed. I am not even sure whether it matters at all.

I miss her, I do. Because humans miss each other. Because people feel entitled to each other.

I'm also really glad I have the piece of paper.

'Colonial pieces of paper put prices on humans, dictate to the world your worth. And only if you know how to use it. It must be used with a certain accent. After which you cannot be the same. Suddenly you must use this piece of paper to access more pieces of paper to "own" things. Suddenly your township house is too small, suddenly taxis are not enough…'

I particularly remember this monologue, because I tried to search her eyes that day. Past the dilated pupils.

'Colonial pieces of paper as opposed to what?' I asked.

She stuttered and lit a cigarette. She was empty. Had poured out so much of her soul to the world and forgot to restore it.

Perhaps this is why I refuse to allow my eyes to open the way she allowed her eyes to open. You can't unsee. Perhaps no one ever told her that once you open your eyes, you can't unsee.

And so, she poured herself out, and eventually home stopped being a replenishing well. For too long my sister had been running on reserve tank.

>From:NonZungu@gmail.com
>To: MKZungu@gmail.com
>Subject: I'm graduating… Please come

>The world isn't changing, Makhosi. At least the world isn't changing now. Ma is tired now. She wants to retire now. I am hungry now. At

least the piece of paper allows me those simple basics. We can't escape the world. As hard as you tried. Watching you taught me we can't escape the world. I am glad you tried though.

I love and miss you. So does uMa.

I graduate on 28th April 2021. The 2 pm ceremony. I hope you come.

Your melanin and blood sister.

Nonhle

Acknowledgements

MaZondi omuhle engimthandayo. Ngiyabonga. Ngakho konke. Ngiyohlezi ngibonga.

Sabeliwe Khumalo, Zama and Suko's eternal gift to me. Loving you gifted me some of the words for this. May I continue to learn to be a better big sister.

Wairimu Gathoni, Keguro, Gorata Chengeta, Mosa Moerane and Kwezilomso Mbandazayo, thank you for reading my work and carrying me in a way that only black women and queers know how to.

Thabile Shale, Nelisiwe Makhabane, Kgomotso Kgasi, Anna Karuchus, Bongani Mthembu, Tiisetso Kale and Maduza niyathandwa. Ngiyabonga.

To my living ansisters Panashe Chigumadzi, Esinako Ndabeni, Malebo Sephodi thank you for being here. Your affirmations carry me still.

To my dearest Thabiso Mahlape. Ngiswele amazwi. They will never be enough. You saw me. You heard me. You facilitated a space for my words and I to exist. Thank you.

To Asanda, at the feet of the black women mentioned here you will sit and learn to grow and expand. Loving you made me complete this.

To Phillipa Penfold and Natasha Davies, the English language doesn't have enough words to explain my gratitude. Kwande lapho nithatha khona.